Collared for a NIGHT

SUSAN ARDEN

Author of *Tempted by Trouble*

CRIMSON
ROMANCE

F+W Media, Inc.

This edition published by
Crimson Romance
an imprint of F+W Media, Inc.
10151 Carver Road, Suite 200
Blue Ash, Ohio 45242
www.crimsonromance.com

Copyright © 2013 by Susan Arden

ISBN 10: 1-4405-6670-4
ISBN 13: 978-1-4405-6670-7
eISBN 10: 1-4405-6671-2
eISBN 13: 978-1-4405-6671-4

Dedication

Doug, for your never-ending belief that the right words would come and the music you provide to my spirit. The trails you cut during motocross rides inspire me to reach higher and take greater chances. Being with you has been a wild ride each and every day.

Barbara Gibbs, for making certain the words on the page made sense with your keen proofing ability.

Jennifer, Julie, and Jessica…for taking this journey with me. Again.

Chapter 1

The immense grounds of the Downtown Den lay just beyond the trees. A private club for shifters located in the hip *LoDo* section of Denver just east of the river. The Den catered to all sorts of shifter appetites. From gourmet meals, a jazz club, and then upstairs to the individual rooms reserved for more private, sensual affairs.

Diana arrived at the Den shortly before nine for her appointment. Rolling up to the front of the guard tower, she was surprised at the change since her last visit. During the day, when she'd met with an intake counselor, she'd been ushered into the club by a side entrance and had seen virtually no one other than a few staff moving about the interior, tidying and getting ready for the evening events. The private club was gaining popularity due to its ability to cater to the exclusive, decadent proclivities of members and a few select guests as well as provide services for first timers in need of heat cycle sex. The Den maintained a highly-regarded reputation of anonymity for clients, assisted by a guardhouse stationed on the perimeter, admitting private members and permitted guests on the nightly admit list. The counselor assured Diana that tonight her name would appear on that list. Two guards with holstered weapons stepped up to the driver's window. "Your name?" the one with a buzz cut asked, briefly flashing a pair of amber irises in her direction. "Diana Hambre." She'd opted to use her own name. Either she trusted the Den completely to keep her safe or not.

Hell, she'd better be able to trust the Den, considering she was about to let an alpha male sexually service her out-of-control needs for the evening. The thought sent a shiver rocketing up her spine. A few more hours, and this yearning to grind her hips against something hard would lessen. She prayed it would, twisting the hem of her dress between her fingers.

Neither of the guards cracked a smile tonight, nor had they when she'd visited a day ago. Their clipped tones directing the driver to hand over her admission form pulled her already taut nerves further apart, and she fumbled in touching the fingerprint identification screen the silent guard offered to her through the lowered car window.

"Invalid. One more time, Ms. Hambre. Press firmly on the red circle." The guard handed her back the electronic scanner. Her finger trembled as she watched the blinking red light.

The guard nodded curtly at the change to a green flashing light. He stepped back, saying. "Thank you. You're all set."

Her heartbeat slowed once her admission to the Den had been settled, and she sniffed the air. These two guards with their golden eyes were shifters, beta wolves, and held no interest for her even though their muscular physiques might help assuage her cravings in a pinch. But they couldn't totally abate the mind-blowing urge for sex.

The driver grunted a response before starting through the gates that slowly swung open. A wrought iron fence surrounded the immaculately-kept grounds featuring yards upon yards of well-manicured grass rivaling a golf course. The Den was housed in the three-story brick and cement building up ahead, lit with flickering gas flames in ornate lanterns on massive columns. Two doormen decked in crimson-colored overcoats, dark hats and white gloves were at the front of the line, assisting clientele from their cars into the building. The doormen's movements were reminiscent of military precision in that no one actually milled about even though the parking lot was filling up fast.

Diana sat back against the leather seat, crossing and uncrossing her legs. She tapped her long manicured fingers against her knee, refusing to rearrange the hem of her dress for the fifteenth time. She'd opted to wear a short little number, a black A-line dress and a laced up corset with garters to set the mood. Tonight required a little more motivation than signing forms and paying her bill.

A queue had formed in which shiny black cars similar to the one in which she rode were creeping toward the front entrance. She lowered the window a titch, glancing up at the overcast sky. Ribbons of clouds appeared to wrap around the sliver of a moon just visible and perilously perched overhead. Soon, the moon would fully rise and the heat within her would boil. The skin all over her body sweltered.

Diana jumped when the doorman opened her door, welcoming her into the club. After nodding, she moved past his gloved hand that held open one of the massive front doors. The heels of her strappy shoes announced her arrival within the entryway, tapping out of time to the music playing. She walked toward a woman whose inviting smile drew her across the polished floor.

Under a twinkling chandelier, the woman's copper-colored eyes mesmerized her. For a long moment, she forgot the lavish surroundings of the club and her reason for coming.

"Ms. Hambre, welcome to the Den. I'm Sherry. I'll escort you upstairs." The woman extended her hand. Sherry's tone and solid handshake calmed Diana's second thoughts.

Sherry started forward and continued speaking. "I hope our driver made the journey pleasant."

"Yes, he was more than hospitable." Diana's voice quivered. The trip pushed her buttons in all the right ways, and she arrived breathless from her journey in a privately-driven car by a tiger of a man. Sitting in the back seat, she'd nearly come undone from her level of arousal. Only her apprehension about making an unwelcome move on a club staff member had kept her sexual cravings in check. She couldn't…no, she wouldn't risk not having her needs dealt with as only the Downtown Den promised they would.

This heat cycle that leopard shifters experienced was common. Yet being without a partner, as she was, placed her in danger. Without question, she had to allow her sexual nature to be satisfied. Something she'd not done for nearly a year. So she'd silently drooled, observing the driver in his black leather pants, coupled with an inky shirt that seemed poured on, and accepted being reduced to a smoldering mess.

"Please come with me." Sherry's silky voice promised nothing but pleasure. "I'll show you to your room, unless you'd like to enjoy a cocktail in the lounge. There are several private members here this evening. Men and women who understand your predicament."

"No, I'd rather have a moment alone." Diana hugged her overnight bag to her side, unwilling to test her endurance one second longer than necessary.

"To unwind? You're smart. Fridays can be extremely stressful. Do you meditate?" Sherry asked, taking the lead.

"Not lately. My work schedule is so hectic. And now this…" Her voice trailed off. No need to mention the obvious.

Diana sniffed the air. An alpha scent lambasted her nervous system. She looked around, and there was no one else in the hallway. The scent was familiar. *Achingly familiar.*

"Christ," she swore, ever so softly. On top of everything else, her imagination was playing a mean-spirited game with her. She refused to give in to her warped olfactory ability even though she momentarily lost her concentration.

Sherry slowed her gait without warning. Diana had to swerve toward the wall in order to avoid bumping into her. She skimmed along the wooden panels for a few steps in order to avoid careening into several chuckling males who had just entered the corridor.

Diana brushed back her bangs. Each of them nodded to her with garnet-eyed flashing interest, yet their scents were not the right shifter type to lure her. Only one shifter could ease her maddening carnal urge. Male. Alpha. Leopard.

"Sherry, a new member?" A man wearing an elegant black suit asked, hardly able to contain the wolf lick to his lips.

With one glance over to her, Sherry shook her head. "Gentlemen, we'll do introductions at a later time." A cast of hungry gazes erupted as pairs of glowing eyes traveled over her body; so sharp was their perusal it felt like having her dress torn from her body. Passing by, she had felt utterly naked in their midst.

Sherry stepped back, brushing against Diana, their shoulders coming into contact, and for a few seconds Diana's sensation of being hunted dissipated. The woman's skin was icy-hot, delivering a burn while at the same time cooling Diana's skin.

"You're not a shifter. Are you?" Diana said the first thing that came to mind. Sherry's eyes flickered, becoming obsidian black, then changing back to copper. "No. One reason I hold this position. If you're interested in venturing beyond your room, we have a sensational restaurant, or room service if you get hungry. I mean later, of course."

Diana nodded and waited. Nothing more was said. Obviously her hostess was not going to fully respond to her question.

She followed Sherry through a corridor lined with several doorways. All the while her escort explained the layout of the Den. They passed the restaurant where candlelight flickered over linen tablecloths. Diana sniffed the air, seeking the undercurrent of a hidden aroma that lay embedded within the gourmet-scented creations pouring from the restaurant.

Her skin tightened, and her nose twitched. "Tempting. I might come down later on." Diana pretended to admire the interior, clinging to the doorway of the restaurant. Her glance scoured the space, noting each of the inhabitants and wondering if, by chance, she was right in what she perceived. But no, she didn't recognize anyone present. For a second, the heavy feeling of disappointment sank into her limbs. A second whiff and her senses perked. Regardless of her inability to pick out the source of this alluring scent, someone was present who made the space between her legs grow moist. Her belly clenched, releasing a spasm downward. She pushed away from the doorway, confused, wondering how it was possible for duplicate scents to exist.

Diana trailed after Sherry, turning into another hallway at the rear of the club. Farther down, Sherry paused outside the club's main hub on the other side of the corridor.

The hostess pulled open one of the frosted glass doors. "We specialize in privacy. Our club prides itself on providing services in an unparalleled setting."

Diana observed several areas that were divided into a bar with an intimate dance floor off to one corner and what looked like cozy rooms. Some doors were opened, where couples sat eating, drinking, conversing. Everyone under control. Everyone rational.

Again she inhaled, and the pungent male scent saturated her lungs. She swallowed a jolt of concern over her flagging self-control and the need to unfurl her catlike claws and fangs.

The scent had to be one of the alphas, some imagining on her part. A growl twisted and turned in her breast. Her fingertips pulsed, with curved nails ready to spring outward. She longed to shift, so strong was this unbearable urge. If she didn't obtain relief soon, what would become of her…she groaned. There were places for wild shifters. None of those establishments were elegant or civilized.

No, the intake counselor had promised this was the place to find relief in the form of a shifter who'd service her for the night.

• • •

Diana pulled at the steel collar encircling her throat. The metal band weighted the top of her shoulders. She lifted the locked ring, moving the edge away from the base of her neck. For now, the collar rotated easily enough. She was unconcerned by the steel-gauged chain linking the band to an iron post. A necessary detail. The post was secured by four large bolts to the wall of the stark room. She tugged the chain with both hands and gritted her teeth.

"Ugh. Solid," she groaned, dropping the heavy links to the floor, convinced she wasn't going anywhere in the near future.

A wrought iron grate covered the outside of the only window on the opposite wall. *Good idea.* Diana crossed the room, kicking at the pallet on the floor. She stopped alongside the stainless steel sink. A matching industrial commode was housed in the corner, behind a Japanese screen.

Her whole body prickled with pinpoints of heat. So far, this irritating state had seared her body for two days too long. And now, inside the stark room, she forced her thoughts elsewhere. She studied a rectangular bin above the sink containing a rainbow assortment of condoms. The utilitarian vibe of the room was out of sorts with the sophisticated layout of the club downstairs. She vaguely recalled the aroma of roses, leather, and aged cognac from below. Her nipples tightened, remembering the scent of a man. One she recalled all too well amid a wave of lustful aching. She'd already agreed to stop compulsively reliving the delicious odor, licking her lips one last time. She shook her head, accepting it was some sort of sensory mirage.

Inside the room she smelled nothing but the sanitized floors and walls. No hot, dirty sex. Nothing of the sort…yet. Obviously, the room was scrubbed down to a hospital spic-and-span level of cleanliness. She gasped. *Just how out of control did other heat-frazzled shifters become in moonlight?* From what she knew personally, extreme recklessness occurred.

The gravitational pull assaulted her bloodstream in the same way the tides were pulled. Regular cycles each day, getting stronger and stronger. Hormones spiked in her tissues, running rampant during the rise of the full moon, and leaving her hunger to mate nearly uncontrollable.

If she wasn't careful, she'd lose all sense of decorum and any panther within twenty miles would know by her pheromones that she was hot and ready. To humans the scent would be unnoticeable, but every alpha male would perceive the patchouli rose essence emanating from her skin and sex; figuratively a bud in bloom during the apex of the full moon. The pull was too strong to resist.

She cautioned herself: Don't judge or guess your way into a further frenzied state. Her skin had begun to burn from a heat that boiled under her flesh. Soon, she'd have company.

Her belly lurched. She needed something to relieve the burning sensation of her skin. *Water*. She could cool her parched body with water. Diana untied her flimsy robe in front of the sink. She pressed the lever, releasing a stream of cold water over her hands. She ran a wet palm up her arm, then switched and repeated on the other side. The water droplets cooled her aching skin. Wetting her hands again, she rubbed her palms across her chest and over her breasts. Her nipples puckered into erect points. She pulled each pebbling areola, unleashing jolts of excruciating pleasure. She thumbed each tender nipple, again and again. Finally, panting, she cried out when no relief came. Her skin now sizzled as if sunburned. Blistering ripples of pain assaulted her every few minutes from the inside out.

Christ Almighty. They didn't call this a *heat* for nothing. She shuddered under the billowing fire spreading across her body and clenched her jaw, immediately catching the skin of her lower lip with two curved canines. She opened her mouth, swiping her tongue over dagger-pointed teeth.

Without gazing into a mirror, she could only imagine the changes taking place as her body shifted toward *panthera*. No longer would she peer out to the world through murky hazel irises, but through eyes flecked with emerald green sparks. At least that's what Cole had murmured each time she had shifted, and he had provided the heat cycle relief she craved.

Tears flooded her eyes, blurring the sight of the speckled rosettes forming over her skin. She blinked, noting the design had darkened remarkably in just seconds. Before long, a honey-colored coat spotted with smoky black designs would follow. She paced over the bare floor, coming up to a gouged, white wall. She turned and crossed back over the wooden planks, walking a grid in a search-and-rescue pattern.

Downstairs, laughter pealed. Voices erupted, followed by the crash of glass and applause. She prayed the loud occurrence was unusual for such an elegant club.

Out of nowhere, a devil-may-care attitude arose inside her. Her body shivered. Her sex throbbed. "Mmm," she moaned, crossing the boundary into believing a raucous evening would be exciting, in a club catering to solo shifters without mates.

That's what she was, and wasn't. At this moment she was sorely tempted to pound on the door and demand that an alpha-whatever be sent to her. This was the first heat in which she'd agreed to coupling without Cole by her side.

She closed her eyes, shutting out the unexpected raw vision of Cole's torn body. He had been the man she'd loved since high school. She fought against remembering him as she'd found at the bottom of a ravine. Cole was dead and here she was alive, throwing herself at a stranger. It should have been her at the bottom of the ravine. Not Cole, when he'd leapt to help her. *Cole—her mate—forever gone.*

Diana pulled the robe across her shoulders and cinched the sash around her waist. She turned away from the door, picking up the chain. She steered clear of the center of the room where a crimson column of heated light fell. Her eyes flattened and she could feel the elongation of her pupils, a physical sign of her leopardess cunning, prompted by the colored light which aided night vision. Unfortunately, it also fried her skin.

She peered up at the infrared light bulb within the ceiling fixture. Impossible to unscrew the darn thing. The ceilings were at least fifteen feet tall. Soon enough, she'd have no problem leaping up to punch out the light bulb, putting an end to the scorching red glare. Soon enough, it would be dark and she'd not need the light. Soon enough, she'd have company in the form of an alpha male who'd give her release from the torturous craving that rocked her mind and body.

A roar rumbled deep inside her, and if left unrestrained, she'd give in and let the vociferous sound tumble from her lips. And at this point, her cravings more than twisted her soul. One more night and she'd have sold her spirit to have one shifting male properly fuck her past this heat. The space between her legs spasmed. Her edgy condition, or the fact that she'd agreed to let a stranger fuck her into submission, no longer shocked or bothered her. She'd gotten past her morals, thrown aside her inhibitions, and overcome her loner tendencies when she'd almost pounced on Shawn, her boss, followed by a near streaking incident at home.

She shook her head. "Oh God, I've almost lost it." She continued pacing and swinging the chain.

After tonight's coupling, she prayed tomorrow would arrive with a hint of normalcy. Her current design project was running out of time with the deadline looming. She should have notified her boss and requested an extension.

Her whole body constricted when she thought of him and her near lip-lock fantasy. Shawn Barclay's muscular build and rugged good looks had sent her over the edge after a year of going it alone. Last Friday, before her heat cycle actually came on, she almost licked his face while they had stood shoulder to shoulder at her desk reviewing her work. Afterward she had left her office, telling the receptionist she'd be at home. She didn't understand why she had become out of control *before* her heat. It was no mystery that he was a shifter. Albeit just her luck, an alpha leopard. But not once had she sought any form of attention that wasn't strictly professional. Business all the way. That was, until recently—precisely, until this heat.

Once the cycle began, her cravings required she remove herself from temptation. So far, remaining inside her home and avoiding male shifters—all male shifters—had seemed to do the trick.

For the past year, contained within her house, she'd been able to weather the storm of monthly heat cycles while working flextime. A tremendous perk and the reason she'd accepted the position at Matrix Design. Shawn didn't care as long as her projects were completed on time. He was too good to be true. And what a body…she inhaled, closing her eyes.

Shawn. No wonder, she thought. Her boss waltzed around in sneakers and a pair of snug jeans that clung to his tight ass. He constantly complimented her work, to the point she hungered for him. Her one insurmountable problem boiled down to, Shawn didn't return her admiration. The man was all business, twenty-four seven. Shawn had this uncanny way of making her feel appreciated for her creative ability and work product. She would have sworn on a stack of Bibles an undercurrent existed between them, but not once did he reveal an ounce of carnal interest—which would have been tolerable had he not smelled good enough to lick. She sighed, wishing he admired her for something less ethical and more physical.

A pulsating spasm shot through her abdomen, forcing a caterwaul to expand within her chest, rising up her throat. Her eyes sprang open. She pulled at the collar in frustration, eyeing the door.

She drew in a breath to steady her racing mind. Hard fucking with a stranger no longer frightened her. Quite the reverse. She welcomed the moment a hard cock would save her. She was well inside her cycle of this body-wrenching heat when she'd made the mistake of thinking she could beat the odds. She had for twelve months.

Pride before the fall kept looping around her mind for the last month or two. Apparently, somehow her leopardess premonition had known she was close to breaking. She had already lived through one close call and feared she'd do something more than foolish without professional help. Last month, she'd lost it at the edge of the city's nature sanctuary and bordering private woods. She'd shifted without warning. She didn't remember much except running all night, for several nights in a row, and then waking up naked, dirty, and scratched.

Then, a day ago she hungered to run free again. Standing at her back door, shifting between her leopard and woman forms, she had sniffed the air. Thankfully, her neighbor's German shepherd had howled at a feline ear-piercing pitch. The sound snapped her back into human form long enough to close and bolt the door in lieu of running naked down the alley. With a brewing desire for her boss—and a newfound interest in streaking—she put her pride aside.

The Downtown Den had been a last resort yesterday. She'd requested an emergency intake. The cost of this stud service no longer mattered if she obtained relief.

Diana ran her hands through her hair. The chain rattled with each movement. Her choices were to sit or pace. She lowered herself onto the pallet covered by a clean, soft sheet. The cushion resembled a thick futon and was wide enough for two bodies. She crossed and uncrossed her legs, studying the shadows on the wall, letting her gaze wander out the window, up into the midnight blue sky. Hope mounted within her. Any second the door would open. She bobbed her head to the bass rhythm vibrating across the floor, wiggling her legs hard enough to make her breasts bounce.

She pressed her legs together, warding off the need to plunge her finger into her opening and satisfy her hunger. That hadn't worked since the time she almost bumped into her boss by accident, her hip grazing across his crotch. His scent continued to wrap her in cords of frustration. Now, she couldn't orgasm on her own. It was as though her body wanted one unattainable thing. Or shifter, really. This far into her heat, her appetite for sex had become unmanageable.

Without thinking, she rubbed her thighs together. Undulations swelled within her sex. She shivered as her unbearable longing awoke yet again. Any brushes against her slit exacerbated a hunger threatening to overtake her on the next breath. Diana nervously ran her fingertips along a row of scratch marks on the floor.

"Ouch," she cried.

A thick splinter stuck out from her skin. Without thinking twice, she used her teeth to extract the piece of wood. A droplet of blood formed on the tip of her finger. The pungent scent wasn't so much inhaled as the air was tasted. She sipped a wisp over her Jacobson's organ, perceiving her surroundings acutely. The smallest of bursts lit as she captured the tail end of an essence. She released a puff of air from her nostrils. A low, sawing growl escaped from her throat.

She sucked her finger, thinking she must avoid touching the deeply furrowed lines gouged in the wooden floor. For now she sat and waited, listening to the music from the dance floor downstairs pound a rhythm into her chest instead of focusing on her own racing pulse. She rued her decision to come up early into this reserved room, giving up the chance to enjoy a flute of champagne to blunt her needling anxiety.

Her blood raced, sensing it was almost time. The waxing moon would be overhead, creating an apex in her intolerable craving. She hissed in anticipation. Finally, she'd make her own scratch marks on this well-worn floor and upon the body of the alpha who'd agreed to take her on. She rocked back and forth, recalling the long questionnaire she'd filled out for the Den's intake counselor and then the photographs of countless men she'd been given to ponder. No one seemed better than the next, and she'd left the decision to the Den's counselor.

In Denver, there were several places where unmated shifters could go, including online coupling services. Daring shifters braved the underground clubs to seek fulfillment using kink and elaborate bondage gear, making this mere collar and chain appear very simplistic.

The Downtown Den was a highly regarded establishment known for confidential penchants, proclaiming experience in handling first timers in search of stud, and she'd sought services after learning about them as one of Matrix's clients. Here, the club provided a supervised face-to-face meeting where she could veto the chosen stud.

In truth, she needed a modicum of security, not for her but against her uncontrollable nature. In a BDSM club, she feared what would happen when her lustful nature let loose. She almost laughed at the thought of her needing assistance. What she required amounted to being leashed and unable to break free, but also protection against someone who'd take advantage of her. She wasn't up for a roomful of alphas who might tag-team a female. Some shifters mounted a female in heat simultaneously. Her pussy clenched and spasmed uncontrollably at the image of her body filled to the brim.

Diana stretched, arching upward, releasing pent-up energy. She had no doubt her own primal nature would get her into trouble if left unbridled. So she willingly sat with the steel collar locked around her neck.

When she shifted, she'd be almost six feet long and weigh in at more than a couple hundred pounds. Nothing dainty or fragile about her leopard body, and she wouldn't have to worry about splinters with a set of curved claws replacing her French manicure.

Chapter 2

Shawn dropped into his chair, prepared to give his attention to the roster for the evening. Being a part owner of the Downtown Den meant he kept an eye on the solo shifters booking rooms and services. Things could get hairy in a second, in more ways than one. Hence the club's private menu of shifter services.

Not everyone had titanium control on his or her shifting urges. And the reason he continued to lose business to Howl, a BDSM club a few blocks away. Even his staff ventured over there to sample the menu of kink. Not him. He'd been doing this for so long, he'd adopted a Zen ability to fuck instead of mate when the urge arose.

That was one of the few points on which he and his partner agreed. They'd gone to school together and were hardcore bachelors on different paths.

For any alpha male, fucking and mating were two distinct activities, one being a primal act and the other being a near-spiritual ceremony. He doubted he'd ever find the right female shifter whom he'd be bound to care for and protect for a lifetime. Shawn wasn't about to abandon bachelorhood anytime soon.

As he reviewed the bottom of the Excel spreadsheet, he did a double-take, staring at the neatly-typed name. "No fucking way." Shawn ground his teeth. He double-clicked the mouse, opening the client directory. "Quinn, who booked room eleven?"

His partner glanced up from his cellphone with an arched brow. "I'll ring you back, doll. In five." Quinn tossed the phone on top of his desk.

Shawn studied the document displayed on the computer screen, searching for the intake counselor's name.

"I've not heard that tone in your voice since…Hmmm, when was it last? That's right—never. Who the hell is in eleven?"

"A straightforward question. Was it Bethany? Where's the file?" Shawn tunneled his fingers through his dark hair.

Quinn stood and came around the desk. He bent close to the computer, his red wolf eyes tracking across the screen. "Diana Hambre. I don't get it. She's not infamous. An ordinary woman's got your edge up. How'd that happen?"

"She's not just any woman. Miss Hambre works for me at my day job."

"Yes, I know she's part of your wiz design team. I'm still lost. Dude, what's the big deal?"

"She's my *employee*. I, for one, don't share what I do in my off time with those I file W-2s for while paying their health premiums. That's asking for complications. Didn't anyone remember to check her references and flag her for being a possible conflict of interest?"

"I guess not. What do you want to do?"

"For starters, I'll see if we have grounds to rescind the executed service contract." After opening Diana's digital file, Shawn clicked on the service agreement. He scrolled down to her place of employment. "Bingo. Diana entered freelance graphic artist for employment."

He skipped to the end of the contract. "And she signed the contract agreeing to terms. Clearly, she didn't read the fine print."

"Don't be a son of a bitch. I don't even read the fine print, and I'm a fucking attorney. That's bullshit, Shawn. Whoa." Quinn pointed at the computer screen below where Diana's photograph was displayed. "She's a widow. Says she's been going solo since her mate died last year. Are you going to do that to a woman in need?"

He glared at Quinn. "Now who's full of it? You're only taking up her cause because you're interested. Don't you get enough pussy already? Fuck you. Diana isn't up for grabs. And besides, what she needs isn't a scrappy wolf with too much testosterone." Shawn's chest expanded with the sensation of being filled with cement.

Why the hell did it bother him that Quinn wanted to service Diana? He drummed his fingers on the edge of his keyboard. Christ, he'd avoided thinking of her in terms being of a woman or a shifter. She was a graphic designer. Who was he joking?

For a year, he'd not let his imagination get the better of himself. He continually fought against thinking of her in terms of being a luscious shapeshifter needing a stud. Without warning, he envisioned her seductive pink mouth, invitingly open. He gritted his teeth, scrubbing his hand over his jaw.

Christ. No reason to continue this fantasy unless he wanted to sport a full-blown hard-on. Bad enough that Diana's body had given him one for the first month that she'd worked for him. *Espiritu Santo.* He gazed up at the ceiling. Room eleven was on the next floor above his office.

Diana—his little enigma. He'd never doubted her talent in graphic design. After all, it was her creativity and design sense that made him respect her more and more, thwarting his desire to bend her over his desk and fuck her at Matrix. He'd put aside what his dick had wanted because her talent wasn't worth crossing boundaries. Not when Diana had the goods for being an up-and-coming graphic artist.

Last month she had been nominated for the prestigious *American Design Package Award.* His complete confidence in her was reflected in his reserving a table for his staff to attend the ceremony in Las Vegas. Diana and he had a standing breakfast meeting this Monday in which he planned on presenting her with a promotion, moving up from an associate into a partnership slot.

She'd pack up her desk if she found out he owned the Den—a stud club. She and her prim sensibilities. A year she'd gone without sex. How the hell was that even possible?

Quinn backed away from his desk. "I'm not interested. I can tell this woman is off-limits by the careening macho reaction you've got going on." His partner chuckled in an irritating manner.

"Don't be so damn dense. Do you screw your office staff?"

"Eleanor, my assistant, worked with my grandfather, just to remind you. I think of her like an aunt. Don't go there. The day she retires, I'm toast. I understand the problem. I just believe you've got a screwed-up perspective on this one. Shit, Shawn, ever since you agreed to head the Southwest council, you've taken a holier-than-thou attitude. You've been asked to mete out justice, not act the part of a saint."

"Aren't you the one who constantly harps on my position in this community? That I'm supposed to be a role model for other shifters? Or was that all talk?"

Quinn cocked his head. "I see both sides in the justice system for shifters and what we're trying to do with the Den. So what if you have an employee who wants a night of release? Isn't that the point of this place? Isn't that the point of you heading the council? Giving shifters options."

"Sometimes I think it would have made more sense for you, as an attorney, to head the justice council," Shawn muttered.

"Naw, you're the one with family ties. This is more than knowing the law, it's having clan standing. I could never fill your father's shoes."

"The hell if I know how my old man did it all. Managing shifters is far from easy."

"It never is." Quinn rapped his knuckles against the desk before he stepped away. "So what's your game plan?"

Shawn frowned, picking up a paperclip and pulling it apart. Most tended to want fast action and quick results. Mercurial was part of the shifter charm. Shawn's life was embroiled in solving shifter passions. He'd proven that forging a southwest control center over the once-independent packs meant violent crimes—or at least shifter-on-shifter crimes—had lowered remarkably. Forget the court system or police; shifters lived a different life and were largely ignored by humans.

Shifters melded and fit into society by being invisible. When disputes occurred, they were settled in shifter form. Wolves and panthers, coyotes, and leopards didn't require attorneys or bail bondsmen. And the justice doled out was harsh, bloody, and wrenching. Whole families and clans were once targeted. That, too, had changed, now that he'd created the means to allow shifters an opportunity to articulate and seek justice on issues only shifters could appreciate and understand; well beyond the human justice system and what was permitted.

"Obviously, times are changing. And just because they are, I don't agree that Diana should be here…seeking this type of release from a club banger. Christ, this isn't the type of conversation I'd want to hear over the water cooler on Monday."

"Seriously, you sweat too much over the details."

Shawn stared at the photograph taken for the Downtown Den's file. Diana looked uneasy with her amazing eyes. In the photograph they were a bit too wide-open and her pupils were fully dilated, a sign of an impending shift. His gaze moved to her mouth. He could feel his pulse begin to race and he scrolled down the document. He rapidly reviewed the notes from the counselor's records, then almost slammed his mouse on the desk.

"I'm less than impressed given those are words coming from a man who does everything that crosses his sex-saturated brain. For a moment, can you see your way clear to understanding this issue? Intake has paired her with a regular player. The man is a running back on Denver's professional ball team. A regular Johnny Rocket of the Den's alpha males."

"Well, she'll leave a happy woman. Refresh me. What is she? *Felidae* or *Canis*?"

Shawn grunted, "What the hell do you think? Christ, you're such of lying sack of...."

"Your tone says one hundred percent feline. By chance, is she leopard?" Quinn's mockery rose.

Shawn spoke through clenched teeth. "Full-blood leopard. For five generations, at least."

"No stuff? Amazing coincidence, considering your lineage. How rare is that, do you think? And in Denver?"

At first Shawn didn't respond, preferring to rub his hand over his jaw. That same thought had twisted his gut for the last year. He looked away from his computer screen. "I'll send Sonya up to the room since the intake counselor has already gone for the day. She can talk with Diana; explain to her that the club alpha she'd been paired with didn't show. If Diana tries to place some demands on us, Sonya can show her the contract and terms. Sonya can always say we ran a background check and discovered Diana was linked to Matrix. Jesus, a simple online search of Diana links her to my company. I don't know why she chose the Den. She's more than aware that Matrix Design does the advertising, retail design, and branding for the club. I'm sure she won't stand her ground. Hell, Diana's not an attorney. I doubt she'd be one to put up an argument. She's nothing but a kitten at heart."

Shawn almost snorted at the idea of Diana naked and in the depth of heat. He halted his imaginings that were about to go on a rampage, envisioning Diana, a full-blood leopardess, naked and splayed open. His cock did more than twitch. He steadied his breathing, forcing the image of a hardworking designer back in place. His reverie was broken by Quinn's odd cellphone ringtone.

"What do you want me to do?" Quinn asked, glancing down at his cell screen. He silenced the phone.

"Go talk to the jock and find him another woman. I'm certain you've got several on call tonight for your own needs. Take him along and make a party out of it."

Quinn smirked. "Don't knock a ménage if you haven't tried it. When it comes to naked, shifting women—the more the merrier. I intend to take my fill before I settle down. It's now or never, buddy."

He wasn't going to waste his breath with Quinn. Women were best kept at a distance. And joining with a mate was a road he'd almost traveled down until he'd plummeted off a cliff at the last moment when his fiancée had run off with his ex-partner. It had taken a healer's powers to break that bond and it hadn't been easy or short, and he still had the scars. Shawn had decided long ago that a tender heart was a weak organ. He'd rather have no heart than one that could be broken, and refused to let anyone get that close again.

He pulled out his cellphone, tapping the screen to bring up his contact list, and pressed the icon for the club manager's number.

"Yes, Shawn. What's up?" Sonya answered. He bet she was in the storeroom moving boxes of liquor from the muffled sound of her voice.

"I thought I told you to get the bartenders to stock the bar?"

"Well, since I don't know how to mix drinks, it's either one of them leaves the bar shorthanded, or I get what's needed on the floor. This is an efficient way to delegate work, even if it means I pick myself to lug bottles. Don't you agree?"

"No. But that's not why I called. We have an issue in room eleven."

"Did she leave?"

"Not to my knowledge." He wondered why Sonya had suggested Diana would flee. "Do you think she wants to leave?" He squeezed the back of his neck, easing the tension brewing in the cords running from his shoulders up to his skull.

"Ms. Hambre reminds me of Bambi."

"Bambi's a boy." He retorted. And sure, he agreed, Diana didn't possess the predator cover that most female leopards evoked. She'd been through some sort of hell, leaving her a widow, so he wasn't surprised by the intake notes on that front. The stark details that she'd divulged during her interview last year ran to a summary recollection on his part. He only recalled that she had lost her husband due to a camping accident. He didn't believe it was prudent to stick his nose where it didn't belong, especially when he preferred to keep Diana and his dick on opposite sides of his desk. The less he knew, the better for both of them.

Shawn explained to Sonya that a conflict of interest existed and asked her to bring a hard copy of the contract. "I've already printed her signed agreement. Pick it up at the printer."

"I think you should accompany me and remain outside. I'd rather you hear her response with your own ears than an interpretation. Nothing against me, but I know how tense a female can get."

"I don't blame you. Good idea." He sucked in a breath.

Sonya arrived and stood in the doorway to his office. She shifted nervously from woman to coyote just around the eyes and mouth; her boundless energy and small frame never ceased to astound Shawn. "I've got the hard copy of the contract," Sonya said.

They climbed the backstairs in silence. Their feet echoed within the stairwell. The *whoosh* of the opening door and the free-flowing current of air sent a shiver up his spine. Instinctively he sniffed, and female leopardess pheromones saturated his senses.

Moses. His cock thickened. They walked down the hall, the plush carpeting padding their footsteps. Shawn knocked on the door for room eleven.

Diana called out. "Yes. Please come in."

Sonya opened the door and went in without a glance at him. He inhaled a sip of air over his tongue, nearly slurping in Diana's scent pervading his mouth. A growl formed on his lips. He could feel his pupils dilating, signaling the onset of leopard night vision. Fuck if he'd spontaneously shift. He forced an iron-willed determination to surface and take hold of him.

He listened to Sonya launch into her explanation and the rustle of papers.

Hell, he swore softly. One last taste. He opened his mouth, and let his long, rough tongue lap at the chemical-cocktail-saturated air swirling around his nostrils once more. He swallowed a mouthful of saliva, fighting the urge to run his cheek against the doorframe, marking his territory. His fully-erect cock throbbed. Shawn took a step closer to the doorway.

Diana's silky voice came out rich and low, drawing him to glance past the jamb. He nearly bit his tongue, holding back a responsive growl. She stood within mere feet of him, wearing a short robe tied at her incredibly tiny waist. Her skin gleamed, near-golden in the light. A seductive pattern of paired spots covered her skin. Her almond eyes were half-closed, her fangs just visible between blood-red lips. She was on the verge of shifting. Her body rippled, feline muscles pushing toward the surface, making her lush curves stand out against the material of her thin robe. Diana's scent intoxicated him.

"I can't leave here. You don't understand. I'll shift. The last time…" Diana's voice broke.

When Diana's tears spilled down her face, he choked on his breath. Retractable claws sprang from his fingers. He rasped them down the wall, unable to stop, even with the tearing sound of wallpaper being shredded.

"Sonya," he called, unable to contain himself another second. "Hold on."

Chapter 3

Diana's chest heaved, catching her breath. No way had she heard the woman correctly. Her shoulders shook uncontrollably as tears flooded her eyes. A dry sob filled her throat. She whispered, "No, this can't happen."

Out in the hallway, the woman's name was yelled. In unison, they turned toward the empty doorway. She wiped the remaining tears from her eyes using the back of her hand.

A dark masculine form began filling in the space of the doorway. She strained to separate the shifting shadow from the man. Her brain echoed the woman's name, replaying the familiar voice, ready to chalk up this whole idea as insane, bordering on the surreal. The shadow took human form, imperceptible at first, even with her perfected feline vision. She blinked, then stared, unmoving. *No, how is this possible?* This couldn't be another warped imagining.

Shawn's outlined face teased the darkness, confirming her suspicion. Her ribcage solidified, preventing her next inhalation.

"Good evening, Diana." His gravelly voice preceded him through the doorway.

He paused a moment, partially encased in shadows which prevented her from assimilating the vivid details of his face. Instead of moving, she stood rooted to the floor. Tongue-tied.

"Never mind, Sonya," he whispered. "I'll take care of this case. You've got the club tonight." He handed the woman jangling metal.

Diana squinted, distinguishing a key ring being passed from his hand to the woman's.

Sonya responded, "Sure thing. A walk in the park. Call me later."

Then Sonya glanced across the room. The woman's easygoing expression changed with the grim set of her mouth. Diana clutched her robe, suddenly conscious that she was less than dressed. The material fluttered. Regardless of how she adjusted the robe, the top of her thighs was exposed, or her nipples were visible points pushing outward.

They were alone, and her focus was drawn to him—his power evident in the way he leaned against the doorframe, more so in the way a ticking muscle worked the line of his jaw. He briefly regarded her with a brooding stare before his gaze journeyed down her body. Her skin heated under his contemplation.

She waited for her breath to return, swallowing a hundred questions; each one begging for the reason for his appearance. Yearning to claw him into speaking, she laced her hands around the chain draping down across her chest. The set of his lips foretold he had inauspicious news to deliver. All she kept thinking was, *why was he here?*

She couldn't help flinching when he pushed off the frame unexpectedly. Her heart skittered at the sound of the door closing. Locking. His entry into the closed room charged the atmosphere. Their gazes snapped together. A smoldering awareness unfurled between them—time slowed.

Her mouth went dry. Not knowing why, she stepped backward, the chain dragging against the floor. Her eyes darted from his muscular form toward the metal-barred window. His male leopard scent overpowered her.

"I understand you're in heat and alone." His stalking voice completely severed her last bit of confidence. "I'm here to help."

"You? You're the *stud*..." She couldn't finish speaking. Her knees weakened. If she didn't do something fast, her legs would buckle. She grabbed at the wall, clawing and digging. He moved too fast to perceive.

He encircled her with his forearms, anchoring her against the hard plane of his torso. "Diana," he whispered, "I could take you right now. But I've much better plans for you."

The voice in her head screamed in protest. *No, no. Don't do this.* She ignored it and molded her body against him. She shimmied her hips, moving from instinct, and curled fingers around his arms. A growl rumbled deep within his chest. His scent filled her head. Her pussy swelled and moistened. He bent his head over her throat, nipping the skin at her neck.

She pushed against a wall of muscle. "No. Shawn, tell me what you're doing here."

Barely able to get the words out, she fought a throbbing ache to let him fuck her. Not pretty romantic sex, but down-and-dirty rutting, with him pulling her hair and bending her to his will. She didn't care if he threw her on top of the futon or up against the wall. The smell wafting off his skin charged her hunger, urging her to unzip his pants. She'd experienced this type of hunger once in her life. This man had the power to bring her to her knees. Her eyesight sharpened, a sign the leopardess within her was ready to leap.

His voice drew her focus. "Suffice to say, Matrix is involved with more than designing the Den's logos and ads. I'm part owner of this club. I saw your name on the list of solo shifters. I couldn't turn you out or give you over to some stud willing to bang your brains out. I believe there's a third choice, if you're interested. Even so, I'm confused why you, of all people, are here." He squeezed her hips.

She stared at his angular face, taking in the way his jaw squared below a mouth that curled up at the corners. The spark from his golden eyes sent arcing shivers up her spine. He released her, barely stepping back more than an inch or two.

"I agreed to come here because of the Den's impeccable reputation. This is my first solo venture into joining." Her gaze never left his face. She was drawn to him, yearning wildly for his mouth, his hands, his body.

"Do you want to join with a stranger, or with someone who knows what he's doing with a leopardess?" His seductive voice and body pressed her back into the wall. His cocked rubbed against her belly, sending a wave of hungry spikes lancing across her skin.

Unabashed, she lifted her face. "Kiss me," she murmured.

His gaze clashed with hers, sending a jolt to her chest. He wrapped his hands around her hips. "First, answer my question. Are you interested in spending the night with me? A one-word answer will do. Yes or No?"

"This is a little bit more than deciding on scrambled or poached. I didn't expect to see you here as my…my date." She bit her lip. In the next second, she'd have no control. She was a step away from hurling herself at him. This was harder than joining with a stranger. She signed up for wham-bam-thank you. *Not see-you-on-Monday with her boss.*

A fleeting thought broke through her trepidation, past her urge to couple, prompting her to discover whom the woman was who'd asked her to leave. Was Sonya his intimate consort? Shawn's scent told her he was an unmated alpha leopard and the type of male that, if she wasn't careful, would dominate her.

But she could be wrong. There were scent masks some shifters wore. If she shifted, he'd have the power to cleave her to him. His seed spilled inside her body would forever change her DNA, bonding her in ways that were nearly unbreakable. Or he'd leave her marked with his scent. Either way, she'd yearn to return over and over to him for heat cycle sex. Hard, mind-blowing fucking where he'd have the power to dictate her every move. A bonded female in heat would submit and agree to anything her mate desired. Anything.

The city was filled with males who mated with several females simultaneously. If he were the same, she wouldn't need a cage or collar to be affixed to him. Shawn would own her. Her dazed brain screamed one last time to reconsider her options. Her hands shook when she unclasped his forearms. She brushed her hair in a swift motion, almost scratching her face with talon-like claws she retracted at the last second.

He took hold of her wrist, pulling her hand away from her face. "Sweetheart, be careful." The harsh concern in his voice tore into her sex-soaked brain.

Shawn released her wrist. Gently, he traced the edge of her mouth with his thumb. He pulled her up against him, heat pouring from his core. The leopardess in her sensed the tenuous need in him. She was not alone in wanting to feel him thrust his length deep into her.

A snarl issued from his lips. "You've got ten seconds."

She rubbed herself all over his body, molding herself to him. Slow. Deliberate movements. When she spoke, she answered breathlessly, "Without a doubt, I want to spend the night with you."

"Damn, I thought you'd never answer."

He pressed his erection against the space between her legs. The movement drew sharp breaths from both of them. The leopardess in her held back. This hungry longing overpowered her reason. Being with him reminded her too much of something she'd lost. She forced herself to pry away from him before all hell broke loose.

"What will happen? I want you to promise me…" How could she extract a vow that would insult him? She'd have to first insinuate he'd commit such a treacherous act. Plenty of males did, though. She had to prevent him from marking her. Or worse, bonding with her. *A simple yes or no.* She wanted to snort. Maybe simple for him.

She cocked her head against his face, preventing him from biting her neck at the point below her ear. "Do you promise nothing will harm my free will?"

He stopped trailing open-mouthed kisses over her throat. His warm breath shot over her skin. "So you feel it, too? Are you sure you're not the one who will have me caught? You, my kitten, aren't the only one in danger." He growled the challenge.

"No. I'd never trap a man. You're wrong if that's what you believe I want."

"Kitten, put away your claws. I believe you'd never intentionally ensnare a man. You've got a secret weapon. I bet you don't realize the spell you cast, do you? Baby, you could tempt a saint." He softly laughed.

She twisted in his arms. He pressed against her, and she felt his erection graze her mons, making her shudder as a burst of pleasure exploded.

He restrained his lust instead of overtly pushing her. He could have easily reached up under her robe and touched her. She wanted his hands on her skin, but needed to clarify the *'what-ifs'* before she let him unsheathe her.

"I've never wanted to risk my job," she panted in a hoarse voice. "I've always taken off work. Never once tried to tempt you or any other male. All I want is for a man to fuck the heat out of me. Can you do just that and nothing more?"

"Christ, darling. You have to ask? I think we both don't want any complications. Not with our work relationship. For God's sake, I'll take care of your needs if you promise me you won't quit working at Matrix. If you think us coupling will cramp our working together, then I'll leave and send up a stud banger. Your choice. If you let me, I'll fuck you past your heat and then it's back to business as usual. How far are you into your cycle?"

"Two days," she whispered, not wanting to believe she was having this conversation, like the hundreds of discussions they'd had regarding ad campaigns. This wasn't color matching or font selection. How cold was he?

How cold was she? was the better question.

She swiveled to the left, leaving his cock pressed snug against her belly. All she cared about was his ability to function like a sex machine. By using his cock, she'd abate the clawing desire that tore into her ability to function.

"How in the hell did you make it that long? I promise you, by the time you're ready to leave, I'll have taken you the way you need. That heat will clear from your head."

She pressed her forehead against his shoulder. "Thank you."

Shawn squeezed her ass with both hands. "Jesus, you're on fire."

Diana bit into her bottom lip, refusing to whimper her gratitude. They'd fuck tonight and that was all. Not a lifelong commitment, just this one time. She stretched, rubbing her hands up his arms, careful to keep her claws from ripping his skin. "Make this hunger go away. Take me like you say."

His mouth crashed down onto her lips without warning. His insistently hard kiss stilled her longing for just a second.

He broke their kiss. "Give me a moment." Luminous, flinty eyes stared down at her.

Shawn released his hold on her body and began unbuttoning his shirt. She glanced down for a moment and froze. His chest was delineated with striated muscles. His tight nipples were brown against his tawny skin. My God, finally she laid her eyes on his black, curling chest hair spreading into a diamond shape. She'd been teasing herself for a year, imagining running her fingers over his pectorals. His muscled belly was drool-deserving. Hard and ridged, yet that wasn't what kept her staring. The same black, curling hair formed a line down his stomach, swirled around his navel and disappeared beneath his pants. She inhaled, gazing at the massive erection outlined by slacks. Diana licked her lips and her whole body began to tremble. "Kitten," he said. His voice slid like a silk command. "Take that robe off."

• • •

He clamped his jaw, pressing his lips to keep from sucking in another mouthful of fragrant air. The scent of Diana, and now the taste of her, aroused him to the point of agreeing to any and everything she'd suggested. She didn't seem to know the power she wielded in the way she almost begged to retain her freedom. She knew he'd pounce upon her. He could see it in her startled expression, hardly hidden by the way her eyes had flitted around the room. Hell, he'd have loved the chase if they'd been in a forest. Him drafting her scent of female sex and flowers.

He inhaled a drought of her seductive fragrance just to torment his crazed brain. His skin tightened under a wave of goose bumps. Without a doubt, he would have chased her until he'd caught her and then he would have mounted her, biting her neck and fucking her every which way. He clenched his jaw, wondering who had chased her in the past. His gaze locked with hers again.

The skin over her face turned a shade darker. After letting go of the last button, he removed his shirt, wondering what on earth she was thinking. She actually blushed, standing in front of him at the edge of the crimson light. Feline predator eyes perceived distinct images in red glowing light unlike humans. Shawn observed the rigid set of her shoulders as she watched him remove his clothes.

"You can trust me," he said before unzipping his pants. He almost rolled his eyes. Famous last words for any guy to utter at this point.

Her chin trembled and she smiled across the space. "I do." She untied the robe and let it fall off her shoulders and down her body.

He stalled in his movement. The sight of Diana's unclothed body awakened the leopard in him. The act of taking in her whole form was like looking straight at the sun. For a second, his eyes reacted as if a brilliant light had blinded him. His cock strained inside his pants to the point of engorged pressure. Any second he'd be ready to burst.

When Diana had acted out her leopardess testing of the waters by rubbing up against him, she'd opened a door that had been locked. He was aware it had been a moment where a leopardess reveled in her alpha's strength before agreeing to couple. Well, this was the alpha moment, when he wanted to feel her writhing over him with her warm, supple flesh upon his flesh.

"Shall we both explore the degree of our compatibility?" The moment their bodies touched, he'd have to be careful not to let his will get away from him.

"I thought that didn't matter. You've got what I need. Isn't that enough?"

"The experience can be deepened if we give into the edge of our inner nature. Not all the way, just the pre-rituals that might help you understand your heat and how to control your urges. What drives you to the brink isn't human."

"I've never done anything to provoke my feline nature once I'm in heat. I don't know what you mean exactly."

"You're the first woman in heat I've agreed to service. But, I have worked with many shifters teaching them to control their nature. Tonight, it will take us working together out of instinct and getting in touch with what you need. Does that make sense?"

Big talk. Christ, he'd better control his urges. His throbbing shaft felt made of lead and he tempered the urge to come up behind her and rub himself against her ass. The leopard in him all but demanded he act and take her round breasts into his hands and sink his fangs into her skin. He nimbly removed his shoes and socks. Each breath he took awakened every cell in his body.

She moved slightly away from him, unleashing a primitive growl from his chest.

"Stand in front of me. I enjoy watching you."

He unzipped his pants and his cock sprang free. She gasped and her eyes widened.

"I hope that was in anticipation," he murmured.

She nodded with an air of innocent seduction, extracting a groan from him. How'd she hidden such a body from him for almost a year? Curve after curve, his gaze wandered to the point of being dizzy. Her body promised more than she realized by the way she kept in the shadows with her robe in her hands. For the love of everything holy, he'd better divest himself of his clothes before she dropped the thing and his brain overheated past thinking.

Desperation tore at him. "Come to me." He dropped his pants and stepped free of them. He took the robe from her hands. "Damn, you're stunning."

She had waxed the lips of her pussy smooth. His cock twitched up against his belly, more than painfully ready. "Let's remove this from your neck."

"No, I might leave." She recoiled, reaching up for the collar.

"Do you think I'd let you escape? From me? Kitten, you have no idea, then."

"I can't go through what happened the last time. Please."

He pressed his forefinger to her mouth. "You won't. Baby, you're mine for this evening. Perhaps for the next few days. I don't know how long your heat will last. I won't leave you alone until you're ready. Let me ease your cravings and then we'll go back to my house. I don't want us to stay here except to give you the ability to control your urge long enough to take a drive."

"Shawn, I'm trusting you. Please, just do whatever you can to calm this hunger. But know, I'll shift and run if given the chance."

"Not tonight." He unhinged the collar, carefully removing the band from her neck before tossing the damned loop of metal onto the floor in the corner.

He rotated her body, admiring the way she was put together with sweet curves and hollows. Her body rippled with each movement. His cock juddered. He pulled her against him, the leopard in him so close to the surface that he released a low roar.

He massaged her shoulders with his hands, then moved downward, taking a breast in each palm. He kneaded her swelling mounds, flicking his thumbs over her taut nipples. Diana ground her hips against his legs. The leopard demanded satisfaction. He moved behind her, cupping her ass cheeks in his hands. She swayed her hips, brushing her rump over the head of his cock. His pupils dilated, making him see flash points. He pivoted a hair so the space between her ass bumped against his cock. He held onto her hips, warring against an inner nature driving him to mount her and fill her with his seed.

"Do that again," she groaned.

He rubbed his cock against the cleft of her ass, moving himself up and down the valley between her plump cheeks. With every swaying movement of her hips, a jolt of pleasure shot through him, tearing apart his will to slowly join with her. Shawn resisted the urge to clamp his teeth down upon her flesh. He held off plunging his cock in one forceful thrust into her pussy. He followed a row of dark rosettes along her skin, gingerly tracing the edges with his fingers, moving his hands down her ribcage and over her abdomen, pressing her to him. His thumb found her slick opening and a rush of clear liquid dripped from his crown. He slipped his cock in between her thighs. He pumped, spreading her ass cheeks, gazing down at his cock sliding between her thighs. If she only knew the things that sprang to mind. Damn him for not taking her right then and fucking there. He opened her pussy lips, stroking and rubbing her folds with his fingers until she whimpered.

He spoke against her neck. "Only a few more minutes. Let me do this for you."

"I feel as though I want to flee."

He absorbed her jagged pulse, felt her heartbeat ramp and race. "But I won't let you." His voice chewed the words. He worked his finger around her clit. He licked her neck, scraping his teeth over her skin. "Mine, baby. You are mine to enjoy and savor."

He bent over her, pulling her tight against his groin. He pumped his cock, searching for her opening. Her slickness glided over his shaft, over his crown. His balls tightened. He swirled one finger down her slick folds, delving lower, sliding his finger against her slit. At the same instant, his cock found her wet opening. He thrust his finger inside her to prevent himself from giving into the urge to take her standing up against the wall. That type of fucking would be ruthlessly hard and near savage. She might think she wanted it down and dirty, but what she needed was to learn how to master her leopardess urges.

Diana rocked her hips, riding his finger. He kissed and sucked a line across her neck and shoulders, keeping his canines from taking hold of her. With his cock and fingers, he delivered her to the brink of full-blown trembling. Her ring of intimate muscles quivered. Her pussy melted around his finger. She whimpered, and then he felt the deep waves within her core.

He kissed her at the nape of her neck and inhaled the scent she released. She clenched and released around his finger. God, he wanted to thrust deep within her.

Even more, he wanted to possess her beyond this cycle. "Diana, you're incredible. So utterly raw and sensual. I could easily stay with you through this heat." *And the next.*

The synapses throughout his body absorbed her scent, branding him, and he accepted this imprinting, understanding the depth of his transformation.

Diana panted and stopped moving. A mist of perspiration covered her body. He ran his hands over her skin. He kissed her shoulder, tasting salt and her scent. She shuddered under his palm, and he murmured, "You're a vision when you climax."

She relaxed against him. "I never knew how good this could feel."

His brows knitted. Diana's inexperience kept cropping up. He kissed her neck, savoring this moment in being the alpha who possessed her. His kitten had no idea of her capabilities. Diana's inner nature was a mystery to her and so must be the type of leopardess she was destined to become. He should have known he'd be attracted to this type of woman. He pressed his forehead against her shoulder, riding out her orgasm.

It had been a long time since he'd freed himself to feel anything beyond physical release during sex. For years, he'd kept all his emotions on lock-down. Until now.

Diana turned in his arms. She lifted her face, pressing her mouth to his. She kissed him, moving her lips slowly over his mouth. She tasted him, absorbing his scent as her tongue snuck out to lick and outline his lips. Shawn held back for a moment, giving her the freedom to explore him. Then he raised his hand, tracing the line of her jaw, urging her mouth to open to him. She lurched a little when he wound his tongue around hers. He moaned his pleasure into her mouth until she relaxed against him with a soft echoing moan and opened her mouth fully to him.

Her pliable body and this sweet kiss kicked his arousal into overdrive. An unexpected bolt of desire rocketed through his body. Her kiss was more arousing than rubbing up against her had been. A need to possess, not just taste, took hold of him. Shawn's cock pressed against her abdomen. Her low moans gave way to soft growls rising from deep in her throat.

It was time. He kissed her, thrusting his tongue into her mouth, pushing this roused state to the next level. They twined their tongues, wrapping and caressing within each other's mouth. He drew back and nipped the corner of her lip. They were both breathing heavily.

He pulled apart just a little. "Time for us to dive into your heat."

Diana's emerald eyes were glazed. She whispered, "I've no idea what to do. This is all so new, being solo."

"Your nature is stronger than you suspect, sweetheart. Let me show you the way and then you can decide."

Her admission proved she hadn't learned her position of equal power, which meant her husband hadn't been the alpha to a clan. Perhaps they didn't belong to one and her husband had dominated her completely, which was common enough for paired leopards where only one could be the leader.

She nodded in response. He grabbed several condoms from the bin before kneeling. Shawn tugged her hand, drawing her down to the futon. She arched, exposing a slender column of her neck. His breath came out in short spurts. He knew she didn't want him to mark her, and he battled a raging hunger to bite her neck. Claim her. Possess her.

Diana pushed up on her hands and knees. "Are you ready?"

"Not for what you think." He caressed her hip.

She settled back on her heels, peering over her shoulder. "Whatever you suggest."

He lifted her chin. Green fire danced in her gaze. "During our first time, I want to face you and see every one of your expressions, kitten." He gently flipped Diana onto her side. He coaxed her knees apart and climbed in between her legs. Her pussy glistened pink. He rubbed his cock over her wet folds, making them both shudder.

"Shawn, please hurry." She bared her claws.

Diana raked her hands down his back. Her scratches pushed his alpha dominance to the edge. His fangs nipped the air, fighting the need to taste her skin. He tore open the foil packet, very much aware that Diana continued moving against his cock as he removed the condom.

Shuddering, he clamped his jaw shut. He took hold of his shaft and unrolled the condom down his length. His voice came out a hoarse whisper. "Give me a couple of rounds to wear the edge off you. We'll both feel better."

Shawn pressed his cock into her opening, then rocked back. She arched and he thrust full force into her. A sultry cry fell from her lips. She closed her amazing liquid eyes and he let loose the leopard nature inside him. Shawn struggled to keep from shifting.

He caught the skin of her neck between his canines and held onto her. He slammed himself into her lush body again and again, using his hands to lift her bottom. His balls slapped against her ass with the force of his thrusts.

It took a conscious effort to release his teeth from her neck; he settled for rubbing the side of his face against her cheek. The craving to go deeper, further into Diana's body spurred him into grinding his hips between her legs, seating himself as far as he could go. He drove his length into his kitten and then pulled out, almost disconnecting them. At the last centimeter he stopped and plunged deep into her pussy. Shawn continued hammering into her, again and again, rocking back only to thrust deeper into Diana, until his lungs burned and she whimpered.

Somehow he had let go of his complete control and link with her. This feeling burst apart in his brain. This woman-leopard captivated him into wanting her pleasure more than his own. He slowed, not giving into rushing Diana too soon toward climax.

Shawn pushed up on his arms, and without leaving her body, he knelt between her legs. He inched back and watched as his dick slid out from her body. He arched up, easing back inside her velvet grip. Again, he pulled his dick slowly from her pussy, rubbing his head at her opening.

"Oh, kitten, if only you could see this sight. Damn, Diana. I can't get enough of you. I think mirrors may be in order."

"Come back inside me. Please, Shawn. Do it."

His latex-wrapped shaft was wet from her juices, and the sight of them joined pussy to cock almost shattered his will not to shift and mount her. Leopard to leopardess. He plunged back inside Diana and ramped up his tempo. Her soft whimpers gave way. She cried out his name, giving him leave to take care of his needs. Her second heat orgasm drenched his cock and balls. Her pussy clenched around him, alternating a relaxing and contracting grip. The rings of her muscles rippled as if seeking to siphon the semen from his balls.

Diana had an energetic force field about her that made him want to tear off the condom and deposit his cum into her body. Not fucking, but true mating to produce offspring. This went beyond a physical connection into the sphere of a mating bond he craved with her. The leopard in him sought a perfect mate, never before had he experienced this urge to fuck a woman to make a baby.

He slammed into her one last time and shuddered as a burst of semen left his cock. Twice more he spurted and his balls tightened up against his groin. Her pulsating pussy milked the cum out of him. He eased from her body and tore off the condom. He lifted off the futon with leopard grace and deposited the used condom in the wastebasket.

Her figure curving over the futon whetted his appetite all over again. This was going to be a long night and he was just getting started. Her glazed expression brought a smile to his lips.

"I know I haven't knocked your socks off yet, but is there even a dent in the insanity?"

She reached out her arms to him. "More than a crinkle; the haze of heat twisting my thoughts is much less. Thanks for rescuing me from *crazyville*."

Chapter 4

The searing hunger that had raged inside her body eased from the point of pain. Her thoughts cleared and she sipped a long, calm breath. She stretched, unable to remember if they'd shifted partially or not at all.

Shawn's mind-blowing fucking made it difficult to think backward. His cock was magical in her world. Now was not the time to do a body check for bite marks.

He returned to lounge next to her on the futon. His skin was as spotted as hers. He gazed, unblinking, with leopard eyes. His dilated pupils shone reddish-black at her.

Oh shit. She touched her neck and inhaled a shaky breath. They had protected sex. His semen hadn't come in contact with her skin so there was no way they'd mated or bonded. But he'd definitely marked her. Maybe this type of marking didn't count.

She didn't know what to think. His erect cock glistened at the tip and she didn't care about the details. Not yet at least.

"Your scent is delicious. Let me taste you," she murmured in a husky voice.

Without waiting for his response, she crawled over Shawn, rubbing her body over his skin. The feel of his male hardness perked her hunger. She bent over his waist, running her hands over his body.

Shawn trailed his fingers over her breasts. He drew his tongue along her legs, easing them open under his hands. He followed a leisurely path, slowly traveling toward the place where her legs connected to her body. He pushed her legs apart, spreading her pussy wide open to him. She felt him blow on her. The cool air made her opening pulse. His hot mouth found her. He licked her from one side to the other. Shawn came back to her clit where he sucked on her with a maddening intensity.

He thrust his finger into her. She had to taste him or give into to an unfolding climax.

"Mmm. Will you come in my mouth?" She took hold of his cock. She licked the rim, tasting him, and sucked him across her tongue.

He gazed up at her. "Baby, is that what you want? Or this?" He pumped two of his fingers into her.

"So close," she murmured against his crown, then wrapped her mouth around him. Removing his fingers, he tongued her opening. Hard and deep.

The waves of another orgasm were building, making her shudder. Diana pulled his cock out of her mouth, sucking the tip, savoring the texture and taste of his cock driving her to the edge of insanity as he licked her slit. She convulsed under his mouth. His actions delivered her to a cliff, suspending her over a sea of desire. A hunger broke free, urging her to act.

"Let me please you. Shawn, how does this feel? Tell me." It was a wild plea erupting from her leopardess nature. She didn't comprehend this drive to please him. She was the one insane and in heat.

"Perfect. Do you like the feel of my tongue between your legs?" His voice mirrored his tongue—rough, hot, commanding. She squirmed under his dominance. A force within her wanted to snarl and roar and hiss.

"Yes. But let me taste you. I need to know your essence."

He held onto her, pulling her bottom across the sheet. "No backing away. You agreed, Diana. Tonight, you're mine."

"Shawn, one taste," she begged amidst her spiraling loss of control. The hunger was returning, broiling her skin. "Please, do anything you think will help." She consented without thought, intoxicated on the overload of sensory pleasure. She relished in being his for the night.

He smiled shamelessly at her and complied, adjusting his hips and fanning his fingers across her jaw. "Open your mouth," he growled. "Be careful of what you wish."

He glided his cock into her mouth just enough to tempt, and he withdrew, just enough to tease. She clasped his shaft between her hands, preventing the removal of his crown from her mouth. Her throbbing pussy moistened with each of his strokes into her mouth. Craving him so badly, she couldn't think straight and, finally, Diana gave in to her physical nature. She sucked him hard as he pumped into her mouth.

"Oh, sweetheart. That's it, kitten. Now, my turn." He slowly ran his tongue over her clit. He sucked on her bud, squeezed his fingers over her bottom, and probed between her cheeks. She moved her fingers along his cock and held him between her lips. Replicating his hold on her, Diane squeezed the rock-hard muscles of his ass, pumped her mouth up and down his shaft, and opened her thighs wider.

Shawn and she groaned simultaneously. They synchronized their movements and she submitted to him, fully trusting that he knew what to do with her body. Her desire spiked. She excitedly took him down her throat. He shuddered and she did it again. Diana let go of all thoughts. Instinct took over. She used her tongue to stroke the ridge of his erection, absorbing some hidden knowledge in perceiving what Shawn desired.

As he licked her and suckled her without mercy, her bliss drove her to bring him to the same cliff. She used skills she'd never known she possessed to drive him wild. She teased and nipped at his sweet spot, underneath his head, licking and sucking, and pushed past his dominance. "Suck me harder, sweetheart." Shawn's voice was an inhuman, hoarse whisper. He stopped tonguing her pussy and held her head. He fucked her mouth, pumping and thrusting across her lips.

She adored the feel of his cock in her mouth and did as he instructed. Diana ran her claws across his flesh.

He followed suit, rasping the tips of his nails over her skin. Shivers broke out from the tiny pain-pleasure scratches over her skin. His muscles quivered around her. His scent filled her mouth and head. She could savor him without fear and, at this moment, had to taste his orgasm. A savage hunger tore into her.

Previously, her mouth had been a safe spot on her body where an alpha's semen couldn't cross her physical barrier. Yet now, her whole body convulsed and shifted, a sign of error in her judgment. This man was different. Her leopardess nature pushed outward. She told herself she must absorb his musky scent and taste if only to recognize his marking in the world beyond this room. He pulled out of her mouth and her leopardess mind quaked in frustration, on the edge of claiming her mate.

"No," she roared. Her pelt rippled and she shook, flexing feline muscles. Spontaneously she'd let go and shifted. The experience was more than exhilarating. On all fours, she crouched next to him on the futon. Her long tail slapped against the wall. Never had shifting felt this powerful. She licked his face, stared at him from behind twitching whiskers, and she flicked her tail, snapping his leg.

"Diana, reel in your leopardess nature. Come back to me." His whispered command eased her nature. "Now, sweetheart." He rubbed his thumb on the ridge between her eyes, then petted the side of her cheek. She could feel his essence without responding to the content of his words. Deep within her, primitive instinct was a force that drove her, and she responded by purring and rubbing up against him, marking her scent over him.

Shawn's voice lulled her. She calmed instantly. Acquiesced. Her animal and human forms flickered.

The scent she released as leopardess would be near impossible for him to resist. She dropped beside him, blinking, and lowered her lids. For him, she began the process of shifting back. She hissed, and then moaned, curling up next to him.

"I'm sorry," she said, opening her eyes and contemplating him. This was the first time she had shifted in front of an alpha male for over a year. Was Shawn taken back at her lack of control? Her fur receded, emitting sparks of energy over the length of her skin, tightening and smoothing into her human form. Her claws got caught in the futon. She tugged each curved spike free, then focused and steadied her nature. "I understand if we shift during sex, things will get away from us."

"That's an understatement. We'd lose control. Short and simple, Diana, we would mate. I think if I come in your mouth, I'll shift. I was borderline a second ago. I don't know if I can control myself without being fully conscious. The human forebrain controls the leopard nature. You said you wanted your independence, but you're absolutely wild, too. Have you ever been trained? In the very basics?"

"Trained? As in controlling my nature? You can see I lack any measure of resistance. I left home when I was young. So, no. Nothing. Are you appalled? "

"You're an alpha leopardess, darling. Rare, and a prize for a male. If you can harness your power, I can only begin to imagine the things you'd be capable of doing. Didn't anyone ever explain what all this means?"

"Not really. My husband and I were alone. We ran away from home when we graduated and made our own way in the world. My parents were against our getting married. They prohibited us from coming home. We never went back."

"I don't doubt it. Females such as yourself are usually placed in arranged marriages. Your power is untapped, so you can't just go around and have sex with any Tom, Dick, or Harry. And you can't go this long without relief." Shawn ran his knuckles across her cheek. "I do know that we're a good match in bed."

"I don't agree about being an alpha leopardess. You might be mistaken there. But for argument's sake, where does a woman find a trainer?"

"Diana, I'm right. You're a full-blooded alpha leopardess. An alpha male would train you. Or another alpha female can provide training, if you're open to such experiences. There aren't many alpha leopardesses here in Denver, though." He grimaced, seeming to contemplate her for a silent moment.

"But you're alpha and a male and leopard," she said.

He exhaled. "That I am. Are you saying you'd allow me to train you?"

"You know I don't have many choices, now do I?" She nodded at the dawning of her understanding. He would be perfect and he couldn't back out after marking her.

"There are ways to remove scents. Not that I want to."

"Then what's the problem? Tell me, Shawn."

"With any training between opposite genders, there's a risk the pair could shift and mate for life. Those bonds are unbreakable if a pregnancy occurs. You'd have to be willing to risk a lifelong commitment and children if you couldn't control yourself. It's risky, but the rewards are great. Especially for someone like you. You'll have to work hard not to give in at the wrong moment— regardless of who trains you."

"I won't shift again without reason. Ever. I get the risks." She promised, unable to synthesize his talk of rewards. *Did he mean great sex?* "And what about you? If you shift, there'd be no way to fuck safely. Am I right?" she asked.

"Diana, I already want to mount you like an alpha. It's my primal nature to mate with an alpha female to produce babies. Twins with you, more than likely. I won't lie to you. Your scent is driving me crazy, but I'll control myself. Every cell in my body wants to bond with you. But I won't. I've more in my life to keep me on my toes morning to night. So, don't worry, this isn't something I take lightly."

She didn't know if she wanted him to control himself. Tonight they'd discovered their mutual attraction was more than skin deep and could be controlled by their human nature, not their animalistic forms.

"I understand the depth of risk in trying to set limitations around a potential leopard mate."

They gazed back at each other as humans, understanding that, if left unchecked, their desire would result in two potential alpha leopards who wanted to act. Badly.

Her two natures were beginning to yearn for the same thing. One man, one leopard, one future. The tearing of a condom wrapper roused her from her blurred scrutiny of him.

Shawn's sheathed cock nudged her slit. She licked his chin, giving in to the urge, and rubbed against his face. "I'm crazy for you." He crawled over her body and they purred loudly, rubbing and nuzzling against each other.

She relaxed from the rhythmic vibration coming from his chest. Then tears flooded her eyes. How was it possible to feel so lost, on the brink of shattering, and at the same time feel orgasmic ecstasy? Her leopard third lids cleared the tears away before a droplet fell.

He wiped her lids and kissed her lightly on the forehead between her eyes. "Baby, I'll train you. Hell, if only because together we're an amazing team. Design by day, mind-blowing sex at night. And I don't want to let you get away just yet."

She knew he was teasing her, attempting to put her at ease, but his expression said more. Much more. She purred in response.

This man she admired above all others had agreed to help her. She smiled, still hungry, yet not alone. Did this mean she could bestow her scent upon him? She didn't know if he was involved with one or more other shifters. Just because he didn't work as a club stud didn't mean he was unattached.

Diana flexed her hips, moving her bottom under Shawn until she found his hardened cock between her legs. "Let me get on top of you this time."

"Claiming your right?" he asked, rolling over onto his back, and then pulling her to sit astride his torso.

Diana toyed with the sensation of power he'd given her. She pressed her knees down into the futon and rose upward. She took hold of his cock and pressed his crown within her folds. "Shawn, oh my God, you feel so good against me."

"Use me to satisfy yourself. What a turn-on. Let me watch you play." He rose up on his elbows, gazing at her stroking his penis.

She rubbed against the top of him, gliding her slick lips across his head.

He cupped her breasts, thumbing her nipples. He squeezed, plucking each nipple into a hard, aching peak. He pulled her closer to him. He latched onto the tip of her breast with his hot, moist mouth.

She stopped to gasp, and then slid across his crown. Using his cock, she teased her clit, rubbing the head of him from one side of her slick slit and then back again. Her pleasure expanded in all directions. He sucked her breast, at first tenderly. Then, he let his teeth scrape across the edge of her nipple. She snarled a warning.

Diana pressed his slippery head at her opening. She inhaled and sank down in one movement, thrusting herself down his cock. She pushed up and lowered herself, pivoting her hips, riding him. She held onto his shoulders, giving into her hunger and riding him hard.

He growled, "That's it. Baby, fuck me. Fuck me, Diana."

Diana submitted by action of her pussy. Her thigh muscles tightened from raising and lowering her hips, riding him up and down. The pounding of his cock into her depths, hovering at just the right angle, ensured the head of his cock grazed across her G-spot. Each swipe of his stiff penis unleashed orgasmic bursts deep in her belly.

Her legs began to shake, and the pressure built within her core, layer upon layer until a dam broke loose. She threw back her head, yelling, "Shawn, I'm so close. Take me over the cliff."

Shawn held onto her hips, drawing her hips back and forth over his cock as she straddled him. He took over, plunging into her, going as far as he could. "Give it to me. Diana, I'm fucking you hard. Come for me."

Her orgasm exploded, filling her completely before bursting apart. Her body unleashed a torrent of pleasure, deep within her pussy, and soaking Shawn's cock with her juices.

She yearned to shift into her leopardess form and submit to this man with the depth of her being. Instinct told her it would require him to place her into a mating position. At first, he'd overpower and secure her from behind, bending over her body and allowing her to submit. He'd mount her and take her several times in rapid succession, claiming her whole, body and spirit. There was nothing free or easy in being mated to an alpha male leopard.

"I've got you, darling." He scooped her up against his chest and turned them one hundred eighty degrees in midair. Spilling her onto the sheet, he stabilized his body, doing a precise push-up from the futon instead of crashing into her body. He rose on his knees, lifting her legs over his shoulders. His cock remained embedded deep inside her pussy.

"That was impressive. Quite the athlete, aren't you?" she murmured in a husky voice.

"You make me wild. I'm going to take you, alpha-style. Don't shift if you want to retain your independence. This should help your heat." Shawn flexed his hips back and then thrust from tip to base into her, extracting an unexpected yelp from her mouth.

He repeated the movement of his hips, slapping against her flesh, pumping his ass into the air only to plunge down fully into Diana. She dug her fingers into his shoulders, her body clenched tight into a spring.

Shawn slammed powerfully into her. Over and over, he plowed deeper and farther until his thrusts made her teeth rattle. Her insides unfurled and she floated in an orgasmic haze.

"I'm going to come. Tell me when you've orgasmed," he panted.

"Shawn, now," she cried.

He twisted her hair around his hand, exposing her neck. His eyes flashed golden and gleaming. A snarl crossed his lips. Shawn opened his mouth and clamped down on the pressure point that existed below the surface of her skin. A force within her joined something beyond her body, something male and dominant. She cried out his name, bucking her hips against him, and he released her neck.

"Fuck," he groaned, freeing her from his bite. A shudder racked his body. He pumped, increasing the force of each thrust, hiking each plunge.

Shawn pushed through his *more-orgasm*—that's what his climax was to her. She swore the more he pumped, the more he came. Shawn continued to bury himself repeatedly inside her body, making her think he existed in another dimension.

"Baby, I don't know what you do or how you do it." He lowered his body, falling onto the sheet next to her and pulling her body against him. He kissed her lightly on the shoulder. "This was the best sex I've ever experienced. I swear I could fuck you forever."

For several minutes they lay entwined, no need for words where their heartbeats filled in the gaps.

"Did we almost mate?" she asked, unable to comprehend all that transpired over the evening.

"I'm sorry I got carried away," he murmured against her hair.

"Shawn, I'm confused. Why did this happen? We've known each other for more than a year and nothing. What does *this* mean?" She touched the space on her neck, puffy under her fingertips.

He pushed back a few inches, lifted her hair, studying her neck. "You're somewhat marked physically, both times we joined. Then there was the thing with our…"

She stared back at him. "Is that what I felt? It was like being outside my body. I know this sounds crazy, but were you outside your body at some point?"

He nodded. "I'm sorry, I didn't keep my word. The craving for you was overpowering. Mind-blowing on a level I've never experienced. It will take discipline and some planning to maintain our control."

"But what does *that* mean?" she whispered.

"You're right. We almost mated. Somewhere between fucking and mating. Any male from any clan—that means any shifter who wants to fuck or mate with you—will have to openly challenge me. No one will touch you."

"Why so much power with a bite?"

"You don't know, do you? Not a thing about my ties to Denver or the western part of the US?"

"Only that you own more companies than God, so it seems."

"Things are changing in our world. The one between shifters and humans and the *others*." He glanced over to her and she nodded understanding. He spoke of the recent rise in crime plaguing not only Denver but the entire United States. Shifters were openly challenging humans and seeking positions of power and rights that so far had not been afforded to them. The *others*, beings who resided in shadowy existences, weren't so menacing or outrageous. Not yet at least.

He continued speaking, "I've been authorized to sit and hear cases involving shifters. A council has been formed so that humans aren't the only means of judging shifter crimes. The council is harsher in some ways in dealing with shifters. The human justice system isn't prepared to do more than lock shifters away in compounds. At the least, the council is open to hearing cases with varying degrees of punitive measures while also helping those shifters who can be rehabilitated. That's where this idea of training shifters to control their urges has arisen."

"Is that why you were chosen? To act as a type of judge?"

"I suppose. My ties run deep in this part of the world. The council believes shifters may seek justice instead of vengeance if there is a fair and impartial place for them to vocalize their concerns. This council isn't about blind punishment. Shifters are being sought to bring cases of alleged abuse and victims can seek a remedy. Never has there been a place for shifters to seek this type justice. This could mean a laying down of arms, if it works. If not, things will return to an eye for an eye."

"I hope not. Our kind has existed between two worlds. What you're doing requires a tremendous amount of time and energy. When on Earth do you sleep?" Diana half-laughed, but in reality a cloud of worry hovered over her: one more thing on Shawn's plate would be an unwelcome burden. "How can I ask this of you, when you're already doing so much?"

He shook his head, lifting her hand, and then studying her fingers. Shawn shifted his gaze to her face. Underneath his contemplation, something smoldered in his eyes. "Baby, consider yourself part of my clan. You'll sit at my right hand. No one will take that spot until our connection is broken. Not to worry. We'll figure out some way to loosen the ties if that's what you want. I know there are ways. But for now, you're mine." His clasp around her waist shortened, pressing her breasts up against his chest. His satisfactory purr rumbled in her ears.

Her brows tightened. "And that woman who came up here before? Is she also part of your clan?"

"No. She's works here and has her own mate. I've not marked another woman in years. There's no other single female carrying my scent. Only one. You."

"Again, what does all this mean in terms of us or me?"

"Let's just say you're under my protection. Nothing overwhelming or mysterious, a mere deviation from the plan."

"A glitch that prevents any man from approaching or touching me within what, a two hundred mile radius?"

He growled back at her. "Over a thousand miles from the Pacific Coast toward the East. Is that so bad, sweetheart?"

Her chest pounded. He would be listening to her heart race in this enclosed space. This was not simple fear. It was no use pretending this revelation was anything but unnerving. "I'm concerned about our relationship at work. What about my scent, Shawn?"

He inhaled deeply and his gaze fixed upon her. "Me too, kitten. Me, too. How about we renegotiate our deal from before. I'll be your stud if you continue to kick ass in the design world. I want you to come live with me. I'll be infused in your scent."

"You mean we'd work together by day?" she asked.

"And at night, we'll explore a whole different world. You and me, baby. I know it's a lot to think about."

Shawn was beyond breathtaking in the way his hard, sculpted muscles moved. His upper body bore an intricate inked pattern and without the ripping hunger devouring her mind, she studied him. Before he was a shifter, her boss. Simple. Now, he was the man who had brought her intense pleasure. Complex. Appealing. Her chest purred.

She reached out and traced a black line running down his shoulder. She didn't recognize the swirled patterns crossing his skin but imagined the design was his creation. "Mmm, I don't know. What if we can't keep our hands off each other at the office?" She couldn't promise him she'd have strong willpower at first. Maybe after training, yet she didn't even know what that encompassed. He arched an eyebrow and shot her the most licentious look. "Sweetheart, I'd not complain if you tempted me to break our deal. Are you thinking you want to me to take advantage of you on a design table or copier? We could renegotiate our relationship over and over again until you're satisfied. I'm not looking for an out clause—only 'the way-in clause'. I think you'll need my undivided attention for a long fucking time." He journeyed from the futon, depositing one used condom into the waste bin, and snagging another packet. Shawn's leopard stamina showed no signs of waning.

"Are you always ready for action?" she asked.

"We joined during your cycle. Our forged attraction binds us to keep fucking non-stop. Your heat is *our* heat cycle. Baby, you pull every one of my strings."

He removed the condom from the packet and rolled it down his cock. He pushed her back against the futon, spreading her legs, and climbed over her body. Shawn nuzzled her neck, sucking at the point where he'd marked her.

"Mine," he whispered against her ear. "Let the training begin, kitten." He thrust into her. "Baby, you feel so good around me, I don't know if I could ever let you go."

"Shawn, you're a wanton and wicked man," she moaned. "Please keep training me like this. Hard and fast and deep for a long, long time."

Chapter 5

Shawn fought the rock-solid urge to dive cock-first into the softness of Diana's body. He'd spent the last two hours slamming his dick into her body without denting his desire to do it all over again. Starting right this second, if he didn't get hold of himself, and fast. The more he had buried his rod deep inside her, the harder it was to put any sort of distance between them, even for a moment. She smelled so goddamn good. He ground his back molars to keep from piercing his lips. A low snarl of frustration slipped away. This was simply sensation. Here he was on a mission to teach Diana to control her impulses, and he was two seconds away from crawling between her legs. Again.

"Come away with me. Away from here. I promise, I'll get you through your heat but not in a room like this." He kissed her incredible mouth, wanting to pull her up and carry her downstairs into a waiting car. One call from him to his driver was all that was required. He was about to suggest as much until he saw her tightly-furrowed brows. "What are you thinking?"

"I've told you about my past," Diana stroked a single finger along the ridges of his chest. "Why aren't you with another female such as yourself? Obviously, it's a choice that you're single."

He wanted to dismiss his entire past, except Diana deserved an honest answer. If he demanded that shifters brought before him on charges tell him the painful details of their lives in a roomful of council members, he'd better have the fortitude to share his less than savory past with her.

Gazing into her eyes, he was mesmerized. Truth serum couldn't have been stronger. Holy shit, talk about not learning the first time around. In Diana's orbit it seemed he had yet to learn how to temper himself, even after surviving a fouled-up relationship with another woman whom he had once trusted. His stomach juices turned to battery acid or something equally caustic.

"I met a shifter, years ago," he began. "Her name is Mia Velarte."

Diana stiffened in his arms. She met his gaze and asked softly, "Is she located in Vegas? A designer, by chance?"

He sighed. "Yes. She has a firm there. She is partners with Frazier Jenkins. Once, a long time ago, we all worked together. *They* left town together and now live together in every sense of the word. Nothing they do surprises me."

Mia had played him like a drum. She beat him at a game he'd believed he had mastered: love 'em and leave 'em. Only, that little number Mia had performed for his benefit had carved out his chest, leaving him empty when she stole from him. Injury to insult, she had also been sleeping around with Frazier.

Diana's eyes had gone round as saucers. "I know of her firm. But not your specific connection." Her eyes were filled with questions.

He inhaled a breath, preparing to address why he kept his circle of friends small. And why trust was a hard commodity for him to share. "That tie was severed a long time ago. For years since Mia, I've walked around hollow, until tonight. Mia and I were engaged. It wasn't the type of relationship that was love at first sight. We worked as a team and I didn't want the hassle of my family's expectations of choosing the right mate. I hate to admit it, but I just wanted to get past that issue. Mia seemed like as good a choice as any. For all practical purposes, it had made sense to propose to Mia. She was someone I was willing to marry and settle down with, checking that benchmark off my to-do list. I'm not proud of thinking in terms of business. Perhaps I got what I deserved. But I never expected to be blindsided."

"Shawn, don't be so hard on yourself. Things happen in life, and hindsight is always twenty/twenty or better."

"I guess." He tenderly traced the edge of her jaw, and then twirled a strand of her dark hair around his finger.

Back then he'd been proud, and unprepared for his girlfriend to stick it to him using their engagement as a ruse to get what she wanted before leaving. Back then, he'd allowed himself to trust without looking over his shoulder, thinking he didn't have much to lose. His mistake was refusing to consider trust had to be earned. Not in some cases. All cases.

"Does that mean you'll never consider mating? Are you some type of confirmed bachelor?"

"Is that what you think? Feels more like bachelorhood selected me."

Mia had proven that wide-eyed women were not all soft curves and warm sighs. He'd given her access to his business and his emotions, believing she'd be a good partner in life. Maybe not the type for whom he'd crawl into a corner and cease breathing if she reconsidered his offer.

Mia had shown him a side of life he hoped to never repeat.

Except here he was, swan diving into oblivion with a woman who nearly had him wrapped around her finger. Almost.

"If you'd asked me that before tonight, hell, this very morning, I would have agreed whole-heartedly that being a bachelor fit my lifestyle. Now, I honestly don't know that to be true." Shawn tightened his grip, taking hold of Diana's wrist. He pulled her next to him to chase away the bad taste that thinking about Mia and Frazier produced. His gaze trained on her curves, moving in an unhurried trail from the tip of her knee to the turned-up corners of her mouth. He couldn't help but stare as she wet her lips.

"Shawn, you know I'm not like that."

"Yes. I do. But you must know, there's still bad blood between us. It wasn't just my fiancée sleeping around. Mia and Frazier took company files and left with a hefty portion of my clients. Frazier Jenkins, my ex-cousin and ex-partner, went with her."

Diana covered her mouth with her hand. Telling her the bloody truth, he didn't experience more than a twinge in his gut, and the lack of discomfort pleasantly surprised him. He felt he could share almost anything with Diana, pour out his soul if needed.

His brain sent a warning siren to take care. He'd already lost at love and friendship. Two people had had the power to stab him and they made no bones but went right to work. Both broke the mold of backstabbers. 'Gone to Nevada to start fresh' was what Mia had written. Frazier had disappeared without so much as a "fuck you."

"Honestly, I never would have been as accepting as you've been. My God, you're remarkable. Is that why the council selected you? For your inner strength?"

"Back then, I was anything but gracious. If the council had known what was running through my mind, they never would have selected me to so much as judge a pie contest. I used every connection I had to obtain information on Mia and Frazier. In hours after they'd left, I had a list of their contacts, right down to where they had planned on setting up shop, bank accounts, and even their suppliers. If I'd acted, I could have shut them down before they'd begun. And what I found out gave me the means to do more than bodily harm. I wanted to teach them a lesson. I lived and breathed vengeance."

"But they're doing well enough and have made a name for themselves. They're on several design boards. So, you held back. Didn't you?"

"It wasn't about the money. I didn't need whatever business they planned to siphon. No, it had been on principle."

"What stopped you?"

He'd flown out to Nevada to settle the score, except Quinn had found him and prevented any action against Mia or Frazier.

Shawn laughed bitterly, recalling how out of control he'd nearly been. "You've met Quinn and Tristen. You could say they handled me quite well, considering my condition. I couldn't talk about it but that hadn't fooled Quinn. My friend can sniff out trouble in any form."

"They are very imposing figures when they come into Matrix."

"That's precisely why they work for me and are helping in this appeals process the council is setting up."

"So, for the good of others you didn't react? That takes a tremendous amount of self-control. No matter how you view your initial emotions. If anyone can make a justice council work, it would be you."

"Honestly, Quinn and Tristen had threatened to hogtie me if I refused to return with them. They found me in Vegas waiting outside Frazier's hotel. Nothing happened."

Quinn and Shawn had reminded him of what was at stake: his leadership in establishing a council to rule using balanced scales of justice and, when required, punitive actions that were based on judgments handed down. Not rash decision. Not mercenary action. And certainly not retaliatory action.

The crimson haze had lifted enough for him to agree—for the good of a million shifters—that he had enough meat to his character to step back from his own pain and frustration. He'd left with Quinn and Tristen without saying much of anything. He'd allowed them to cart him off and they'd ended up getting drunk. A truly wasted time and he hadn't remembered much, except Quinn had retained the presence of mind to get him to a healer before his leopard nature would demand action.

He let his gaze wind down Diana's body before returning to meet her eyes. "So to answer your question, I made the mistake of a random mating with Mia. No ceremony or celebration. It just happened. Lucky for me, when she left for Nevada, I set out to be cleared of my ties to her. Thanks again to Quinn and Tristen. As well as Fin. It was he who knew of the healer. Otherwise, I believe I would have gone off the deep end just knowing I had intact mating bonds to Mia."

"I'd heard that was possible. The breaking of mating bonds, but thought it was some type of urban myth. How do you know you're completely rid of your connection to her?" Diana's gaze drifted downward to her lap.

"Because we both know that Matrix has clients in Vegas and I go out there routinely." He lifted her chin, fighting the urge to kiss her. He'd wanted to get them inside his car downstairs, and enjoy her body all over again. Until it was more than apparent she needed the whole truth, and he needed to be rid of it in a way he'd never felt before. "You realize that the graphics community is small. I've seen both Mia and Frazier at professional events. I'm fortunate the healer wasn't a quack. I was assured the bond was severed and I believe it was."

Eradicated was more like it. The process had nearly killed him in the treatment. Mated leopards had bonds wired into their DNA. His alpha leopard nature didn't allow him to mate and forget. Some shifters who weren't full blood were able to fuck a circuit around town and around the globe. He wasn't one of them. He owed his friends big time for helping him find his way back to sanity. For years his DNA had been unmarked.

He sniffed, inhaling Diana's appealing scent. Now, he was close to losing his head and his DNA. Would his heart follow? Years ago it hadn't and that had been the key to getting his life back. He'd never lost his heart or soul completely to Mia. He'd been solo for so long…

Maybe that's why he couldn't let Diana go through this alone. Being solo was a desperate business and he'd had friends to help him. He'd taken time off to get his head screwed back on, and then it was business as usual for the last six years.

"No sense in crying over spilled milk. Right?" He stroked Diana's silky skin. "We've so many other important things to keep our minds…and bodies occupied."

She pushed back from him, staring up with a serious expression making him stop pulling apart her legs and teasing a whimper from her. His cock throbbed, wanting to plow into her full force. He patiently groaned in silence.

"From what I've learned, mulling over the past doesn't help. I think we've both been through a lot in life. I feel as though I can trust you. I hope you don't regret tonight."

"Hell, no. Not one regret in agreeing to see you through your heat cycle, or my agreement to train you to control your leopardess urges. I might learn something about myself."

He'd mastered the art of Zen Buddhist meditation to live with pain, frustration, and the desire for revenge. Tonight, he learned there was so much more to life. The type and depth of the exquisite sensations he'd experienced with Diana were all worth the wait. Worth what he'd been through to get to this moment. In business, he'd learned to control his decisions and achieve his goals on a level that made company operations seem effortless. He'd gone from hotheaded to levelheaded, and had reaped the rewards. His family had backed his change of perspective enough to hand over control of the southwestern shifter territory.

Now, with Diana next to him, he inhaled gazing out the window to the rising moon. Not yet truly full. That was hours away and a time when leopards prepared to mate. Indeed, his future had changed in the one night.

"I always knew you were busy. But never at this level," she said.

Diana uncrossed her incredible sexy legs giving him a tempting display of what he wanted when her slick, pink folds came into view. She slipped on a pair of white garters, lifting and stretching one leg into a pair of stockings. She was about to slip on her panties sitting next to him, His cock stiffened, and he broke his gaze away from her pussy to address her face.

"So, you've decided then? I've given you the whole ugly side of my existence. Will you still allow me to train you?"

"Without question. Even more so after what you've shared. *Simpatico*. Isn't that the term for us?"

"Yes. And no. You've little bedroom experience. Would you agree to my full training? It would require your full trust."

What would she do if he snapped one of the elastic lace ribbons? He'd bet that Diana would enjoy learning to bend the rules in life and romance. Her innocent lip bites had him enthralled and reminded him of the untamed creature underneath, while an angel appeared before him. "Forget the panties. I want you riding next to me without having to figure out this lingerie puzzle you've got going on. And that goes for anytime we're together. I get complete, unencumbered access to your body. Every day. In any way. Understood?"

"Is that necessary for training in self-control?" She arched a brow, lowering her gaze to his erect member.

"Absolutely crucial," he groaned, fingering the edge of her panties. "Defy me, and these will be shredded from your beautiful hips. I'd love to paint your bottom a shade or two of red in the process of training. We can begin tonight if you're so inclined."

Chapter 6

His finger skated along the inner valley between her thighs. "We've a car downstairs."

"Already?" Diana asked, enjoying the show of Shawn getting dressed. His muscles rippled in the red light. Still sitting on the bed with her thighs parted, she easily perceived the direction of his gaze. So carnal was his expression, she fought touching herself, and relished his reaction as she closed her legs when his low growl filled the room.

"Jesus, such a tease," he choked, buttoning up his shirt. "I always have one ready. Finish getting dressed. I'll be right back. Just need to speak with the Den staff."

He pulled her against him, his mouth as hot and demanding as when he had taken her the first time. His hands squeezed her breasts until her nipples were hard as stones and she shivered.

"I'll be ready," she said.

"Excellent. I'll be back shortly for more of this. Remember my instructions." He brushed his lips over hers. Heading toward the door, he turned down his collar, and then racked his long fingers through his dark hair.

She still questioned how on earth she'd missed that Shawn was one of the owners of the Downtown Den. He must think her naïve, or that she lived in a box. Shawn had promised to destroy her file and contract for emergency services. No one need know she'd requested stud services to get through her blazing heat cycle except him.

Several minutes later, she jumped at the sound of three rapid knocks on the door, and then he entered carrying a glass. "Here, something for you to drink. A special mixture of fresh fruits from the restaurant. All natural."

He'd come back in record time and she'd managed to change into a dress more suitable for traveling. The one she'd packed for the next day when she'd believed the evening would end and she'd return home. She gazed in the mirror, brushing her hair, and worried about what she'd find. Amazingly, the rosettes were less visible on her skin and her canines had receded. Her lips were swollen but resembled human lips. For all her shifting during the evening, she appeared more like her old self than she'd been in days. Sore in places from Shawn's mouth and body, but it hurt in a satisfying way, and she couldn't help the purr rumbling in her chest.

The fruity concoction soothed her throat. "This is really good," she murmured, running her tongue across her lips. "Do you want some?"

Whatever he'd planned on saying stalled. The searing look he gave her made her heartbeat skitter. "No but you're a vision," he said, his voice exiting his mouth low and hoarse.

She took another sip and then set the glass down on the sink. "I think I've got everything." She reached for her overnight bag, yet he was lightning quick in coming up beside her.

"Let me get that. The car is outside, around back." He took hold of her elbow escorting her from the room.

She glanced back at the metal collar and chain lying on the floor. It was only supposed to be for a night. No crossing of boundaries. Where was she headed with her boss, a man she admired, and now, an extreme lover she craved?

Together they walked toward the rear of the building and down the plush carpeted hall and into the stairwell. They passed by a young man with linens in his arms. He glanced down as he stood back, allowing them to pass. Diana's head snapped up at the faint scent the man exuded. Shawn tugged her arm, pulling her out the back door, and she quickly forgot whatever thought had passed through her mind.

Up ahead, Fin stood outside the car. Diana flinched upon seeing the shifter she knew from Matrix. He was one of Shawn's crew who stopped by regularly during the week. He opened the door to the backseat. "Ms. Hambre," he said softly.

"Good evening," she returned.

He smiled at Diana in a way that calmed her nerves. Tight-lipped as ever. Fin had never said much other than greet the staff at Matrix before disappearing into an office, either Shawn's or his own. From what little Diana had gathered working at Matrix, Fin drove Shawn and acted as a bodyguard of sorts. He was a shifter with the strangest eyes. He didn't give off any scent, a sign that he masked his markers, allowing him to move within society as a mystery, matching his already puzzling personality. Humans didn't have the ability to perceive shifters, but other shifters could. As well as the others, and Diana refused to think about those beings. Yes, she appreciated that of all the possible drivers, Fin had been chosen. Assuredly, he'd keep her secret of being with Shawn.

"Everything good for the drive?" Shawn asked Fin.

"No problems. Tristen's up ahead and reported the highways are clear."

"Let me know if any of that changes."

Shawn helped Diana into the backseat rather than allow Fin, and then he climbed in after her. "Looks like we're all set. Nightcap?"

"Please. How far are we going?"

Once the car exited the Den's front gates, he poured two cognacs and said, "We have a hike. I'm taking you to my home in the mountains. No one will disturb us."

Diana curled up next to Shawn, his muscular arm curving over her hip. Without warning, he pushed her down, helping her until her shoulders were against the cushy leather backseat of his private car. His body landed, swift as a mantle, across hers. He buried his head in her hair spilling down her neck. Anticipation thrummed in her body.

"Your scent makes me impatient," he growled. Finishing his drink, he stowed his glass. His hand moved up her thigh, making every nerve in her body come alive under his touch. "Finish your drink, kitten."

Diana handed him the glass, moving under him, her hips flexing instinctively as her body sought Shawn's hard domination. She yearned for his ability to tamp down her hunger. Her leopardess flickered and hissed. "You're teasing me."

"Kitten, never assume I tease. I'm quite serious when it comes to you and your needs."

She bit the edge of her lip, feigning physical control when she longed to spread her legs for him. Shawn's mouth found the sensitive spot on her neck and he sucked her skin, proving his point. *And hers*—she fought the urge to shift.

Her breath hitched, jarring each time he sucked and released, sucked and released the skin between his teeth. Good heavens. The man knew how to drive her wild. Diana dug her fingers into his tight ass, moving her hips against him and over his erection, titillating herself in the bargain. She shuddered, both cherishing and cursing this torturous lesson.

Her schooling had begun the moment he'd walked into her room earlier. She'd asked him to train her in the ways to rule her leopardess urges. Yet, pulling her nerves taut enough to snap and break as a lesson in control seemed improbable at this moment.

His hot hands pulled her hips against him. The car's motion, coupled with his expert fingers, had her speeding along a narrow highway. Inside a path that ran deep between her legs; the place he'd visited while fucking her over and over. Outside, they drove past the outskirts of Denver and headed up into the mountains. The change in air pressure caused a pop in her ears.

The car seemed to hug the side of a sheer cliff, rolling upward along a curving, mountainous road, swathed by a silver-streaked sky visible from her upside-down view out the backseat window. Sunrise was only a few hours away. She reminded herself to relax, absorbing the rhythmic vibration from Shawn's rumbling chest that provided a continuous massage during the trip to his home.

Diana ran her hands across his muscular back made up of ridges and hollows, enjoying touching the sinews he bunched and released while pulling up her dress.

"Did you heed my directions?" he asked in a voice that made her go wet.

"I don't remember. What did you say?" She pretended innocence and opened her eyes wide to him.

His eyes flashed a golden threat at her defiance. He spoke softly, his tone all the more dangerous. "Shall we also include discipline in your education?" He slammed his mouth down upon her and nipped her lip to remind her who dominated.

"You make misbehaving a temptation."

"Have no fear. Part of your training will allow me to completely discipline you, if ever I see fit." His half-lidded gaze didn't hide the fact he meant business. A pity he'd not shared this side of himself with her a year ago when she'd first come to work for him.

For all she knew about him at work, his life beyond Matrix Design continued to amaze her. Working under him, she was a head graphic artist, while he was an industrial designer and her boss. Shawn had given her the freedom to explore her edge in the world of retail design, advertisement and branding.

Then there was tonight, where she had been under him again—only this time she had been a leopardess in heat. Again, Shawn had prompted her to explore an edge, this one far different than work, consisting of an aching hunger.

She had given in to him without reservation, opening her legs wide for him and his leopard nature while his cock had expertly plunged deep, and then deeper, into her body. He had worked her over almost ceaselessly during the past six hours. Her body bore bruises, and the flesh between her legs was swollen and tender from being repeatedly fucked. Shawn had promised they'd continue to work together—and fuck together—if she desired.

She sighed and his fingers tightened over her waist, pulling her closer. Insanity is the feeling she got from this raw, overpowering sex with Shawn, and it was also what had prompted her to get into his car, riding with him to God knows where while giving him total domination over her. Still, no argument that his body felt right, even if it was exhilarating and terrifying all at once to give complete control over to him. Lock, stock, and barrel.

She inhaled his masculine alpha scent that now saturated her skin. He brushed his lips lightly over her mouth and unexpectedly sat up, leaving her reeling in hunger and need. He tugged her upright on the car seat, his gaze moved down to her chest and he smiled, eyeing her erect nipples pressed against the front of her dress.

"Not much farther," he whispered, "and then I'm going to show you some tricks to control yourself. Ever play with toys before?"

"Never. No," she whispered, crossing her legs. "Self-stimulation doesn't work when I'm in heat and besides, I wouldn't know where to begin or what to use."

"Tell me what turns you on. Besides what we did tonight, what else do you like? I want to taste you everywhere…and I do mean everywhere."

She swallowed under the blaze of heat spreading rapidly over her face. Did he mean what she thought? Her pussy swelled, hoping he meant to deliver her to the brink, doing things she'd only fantasized about prior to this evening.

"So far, you've hit every bull's-eye. I don't know what to say."

He chuckled, kissing the side of her head. "Why am I not surprised, kitten? Jesus, you tempt me to teach you everything I know in one night."

He pulled her across his lap, his erection prodding her hip. He swiveled and adjusted her, lifting her dress—this time with ease—as he spread her knees apart. His hands turned her this way, angling her bottom until his hard cock rode against her opening. *Oh, if he'd only unzip his pants and stop this lesson…*

She glanced at the screen separating them from the chauffeur.

"Are you sure your driver can't hear us?" she whispered, almost incapable of caring as long as he kept pressing against her, grinding his hardness over her pulsing clit.

"Not a peep. Zilch. I conduct plenty of business, and it wouldn't do to have my plans shared with Fin. Privacy is a high priority in my world, and not just at the Den, sweetheart. You'll soon find out that discretion is key in my life. Now, let's see which direction your education shall take. Christ, I almost hope you defy me."

Now, his hot palm seared her flesh, already heated to the point of sizzling. She prayed this lesson was about to culminate with an orgasm. He teased her, tracing a line from the top of her slit downward. She held her breath, expecting him to thrust his finger into her. Her stomach tightened…*just a millimeter more…*

He stopped touching her.

"Shawn." She exhaled his name between clenched jaws. She longed to shift and claw and bite him.

"Shush," he whispered and wrapped his hand in her hair. He pulled her mouth a fraction away from his lips; his breath curled around her senses. He circled his finger over the tip of her clit, awakening every nerve in her body. He rubbed his cheek alongside her jaw and trailed the finger of his other hand past her opening.

He didn't stop but kept moving downward, touching her wetness. He dipped his finger lower, circling around her anus and making her buck.

"God, how I love the sounds you make in the back of your throat," he said.

Falling silent, she pushed against his fingers. Her mind opened, her body demanded she shift, and she dug her nails into titanium-muscled arms. Shawn repeated the circling movement several times, each time spending a few more seconds probing her ass. "I love your silky skin. You're so soft, wherever I touch."

She whimpered, aching to impale herself on his finger, and longing for him to continue exploring her body. Her nipples hardened and the space between her legs grew wetter. She arched against the ridges of his chest and pressed her knees together, clamping Shawn's arm.

"Kitten, you're almost there, aren't you? The scent of your sweet pussy is intoxicating. Christ, if your whole body doesn't tempt me with the feel of my cock inside you…"

Diana pressed her cheek against his shoulder. "You've got me ready to shatter. I can't hold on much longer. Please." She rubbed against him, her moist folds slippery next to his fingers. She teetered on the point of crying, snarling, and demanding. She needed to feel his domination or break apart in uncountable pieces.

His mouth found her neck again and he sucked her skin at a throbbing point, making her almost scream. Shawn moved upward, dragging his tongue over her throat. She panted, battling an urge to let him drive her over the brink. She closed her eyes, so near to soaring—so near to crashing. The old Diana shrank into oblivion. For a second or two.

"So sensitive. Tell me true. You've never had your ass fucked, have you?" He swirled around her opening, and then moved to her anus and pushed the tip of his finger into her.

She jolted upright at his unexpected exploration of her nether end and the truth of his words. Diana gritted her teeth. She was at the point of explosion, and anger flickered across her vision. "I've got to come. Right now." Shawn's eyes flashed danger and his hands moved from between her legs. His fingers dug into her arms and he growled, "No. Hold on for me. Don't you dare come, minx. I promise I'll smack your ass cherry red if you do."

Her gasp was audible. "You'd spank me?" Diana whispered, a shudder moving through her body. It felt as though she were falling, and he shook her by the shoulders. His fangs found her, dug into her skin as he held her pinned to him. The pain of his bite expanded in her mind, giving her space to stop from leaping in an abyss of delicious pleasure. His growl mixed with her moan and she inhaled in time to avoid an explosive orgasm.

In just one bite, he demonstrated his command over her.

He was perfect power. A raw force. In a matter of hours, he'd taught her more about herself than she'd learned in the last twenty-six years. Shawn wasn't just an alpha leopard, he was experienced to the ninth degree and the owner of a stud-club. Of course, he'd tasted every flavor of sex. She must be a bland version of vanilla in his never-ending sex sundae and the swirling parfait-flavored partners he'd more than likely have tasted. Even if he'd been hurt, the ability to find partners for sex as the owner of the Den had to be mind-boggling. Surely, he'd seen *it all.*

But it wasn't even that. There was a power he exuded. The council he spoke about and the changes he sought to help shifters were another facet to him that fascinated her. Who was this alpha leopard who sat next to her, acting like he'd nothing better to do than enjoy her company, and all the while, hundreds if not thousands of shifters depended upon him?

For the last year, he'd never appeared stressed out or overworked. He was the head of Matrix, usually appearing in tight jeans and open throated oxford shirts, a boss who ordered in take-out for staff lunches to kick back and toss around design concepts. His ability to bounce ideas had inspired her and others, and all the while he had seemingly been juggling more balls than she'd ever understand. And she had every intention of finding out just who this man was who extracted her will and had caught her in his clasp. Her breath fell all around her in gasps. For a few seconds, she peered up at him, positive that if she let him, he'd crush her heart.

"How will I ever keep up with you? Mark my words, you'll grow bored and I, for one, will say 'I told you so'."

"Never." A low unwinding growl seeped from his throat. "I look forward to being the alpha who will train you to harness your leopardess powers. Kitten, you're almost too good to be true. You make me want to forget myself. Together we'll create your experience, and you'll wear my scent. Only mine. All over."

"Shawn, I may be inexperienced as an alpha. But sex isn't long-term. Nothing lasts forever. Don't make promises you can't keep." He cupped her cheeks between his palms. Shawn lowered his face, brushing his mouth across hers. He groaned, and opened his lips over her mouth, devouring her will entirely. He pushed her hips over his lap, grinding himself upward into her crotch. She clawed his shirt, gouging the tips of her fingers into his shoulders. His body tensed before he bit into her lip—a sharp nip—and she cried out.

"If you play rough, you might get hurt," he whispered, before brushing his lips over her mouth again.

Diana felt the car slow as it passed through security gates. From the backseat of the car, she could see up the winding, well-lit drive the car followed, yet the grounds beyond were dark. She squinted, utilizing her leopardess night vision and suddenly the open spaces shimmered. She gazed out the car window at the silhouettes of trees and turned to look out toward the other window across the backseat. More darkness expanded over what appeared to be boundless land. Her focus returned to Shawn as his fingers crept back between her legs.

"We're home," he murmured, and captured her earlobe between his teeth. Biting down, he pushed two fingers into her pussy. "Tell me, do you like when I do this to you?"

"More than you can imagine." She whimpered and he curled his fingers, deeply thrusting past her entrance and finger-fucking her hard and fast.

"Right now, I want to be inside you. Would you let me?" he whispered. The car stopped moving, and the front door opened and slammed shut. "I promise I'll not, given Fin is right outside, but you too must learn to exercise restraint. Take control of yourself. See how your body and mind respond. Go to the edge… but hold back. You can do it."

Diana squirmed, unable to resist him or herself. He was doing more than testing her; he prompted her to wonder how this would play out. Or if she'd survive.

"Yes. God, I'd let you do whatever you want as long as you take me. Why do you keep delivering me to the edge and then pulling back?"

"You're right about this being about sex. But sex is power, make no mistake. Don't come. Hold on. Control yourself, kitten," he whispered against her cheek.

Shawn kept plunging his finger into her slit, curling and vigorously rubbing. He removed his finger abruptly, leaving her breathless and hanging off his shoulders. His cock continued to move against her bottom, a suggestive pledge of his intent.

"From my vantage point, you've got all the power," she gasped through her arousal. "We had better *mount* those steps, otherwise I might rescind my promise to keep from *mounting you,* right here." He softly murmured against her neck, twining his fingers into her hair, tilting her chin upward. "I'll make you come and when you do, you'll never question why I push you repeatedly to the edge. I'll fuck you so hard, you'll be sitting on a feather pillow. I make promises because I keep them."

She didn't know if he was serious or not, but Shawn Barclay's reputation in the business world had already been proven. He achieved his goals. Shawn was unconventional, not exactly someone who gave a rat's ass for what anyone else thought, but she believed his unwritten mission statement was damn close.

"I want to learn control. This last year has been hell. But I need to know the reasons why. I can't blindly accept even though I wish I could. Give me time."

"Time," he groaned. "Perhaps that's what we both need." He scooped her up and off his lap, and then he reached down to adjust his erection. He watched her, the corners of his lips lifted giving him an air of smug satisfaction. The chink in his near-perfect smugness was a fleeting look he gave her containing a glimmer of vulnerability.

To her surprise, Diana realized she was learning he wasn't the emotionless wall he attempted to present to the world. She framed her hands on either side of his jawline, capturing his face furrowed by his knitted brows. She pressed her forehead against his, unable to fathom what made him take on such a pained expression.

He whispered, "I've never been this close to losing complete control myself. You push us both."

She rubbed her nose alongside his and laughed. "You bring out this side in me. Don't blame the leopardess when it's your leopard nature that makes me hungry. If anyone is pushing, I'd say it's you."

He tunneled both sets of fingers through his hair. "I'm captivated with your mating scent. In a matter of hours, I crave all of you. I can only imagine the level of hunger I'll experience after a few days or weeks in your company. This isn't something we can lightly put aside like a hobby."

"You have that exact effect on me." She released him and tugged her skirt down her thighs, focusing on him, not her trembling fingers. By mistake she scooted forward on the backseat, and the friction of the padded leather against her sex made her arch and gasp. She quickly bent over, retrieving her purse that had fallen onto the backseat floor. Uneasily, Diana swung the strap over her shoulder, aware that Shawn's gaze followed her every movement.

With an arched brow, he asked, "Shall we?"

"You tell me, *sensei.*"

He stared for half a second and then threw back his head, laughing, and damned if he didn't slap his knee. The sound hit her square in the chest. The ring in his voice, the crinkle at the corner of his eyes kept her pinned, awaiting his words.

"Aha, my luscious grasshopper. I think you shall teach me a thing or two." He opened the car door, pushing off the seat. "We're finally here and can unwind," he murmured over his shoulder.

Fin greeted him at the side of the car door, touching his cap. "Will you need the car again this evening?"

"No. We're staying here for the next few days. I'll relay that to Tristen as well." Shawn held out his hand to Diana in the backseat. He bowed to retrieve her arm, all the while his eyes searching her gaze, accessing her depths with his pensive expression. His brows knitted as he sought her reaction to seeing his home for the first time. No wonder—it was unlike anything she'd ever seen. The house sat far back from the road and they'd pulled up directly in front, giving her a car-window view of a home that defied definition. The house design combined styles of architecture into something unconventionally breathtaking. An original three-story structure with more glass than she'd seen in any home in Denver. What must the heating bill be like?

The porch lamps flickered, casting and recasting shadows along the cut granite block walls. Her fingers squeezed Shawn's muscular arm. "Never have I admired such an uniquely designed home. The glass and angles. Your hand?" The tension eased from his arm and he exhaled.

"Yes. I'm interested in your reaction to the interior. I think we share the same tastes on several levels," he murmured.

"Excuse me." Fin's voice came from behind them. They both turned toward the driver.

"Shawn, is there anything else for this evening?" Fin's quiet Midwestern accent always made her smile, but tonight her grin froze on her face.

There beneath Fin's jacket, dull gun metal riveted her attention. He had a holstered weapon at his shoulder. Fin was his usual self, dressed in all black that spoke to military experience. His demeanor had always struck her as trained but still on guard. Same with Shawn's right hand man, Tristen. She reminded herself, this was the same Fin she'd seen around Matrix, and carrying a concealed weapon was far from unusual. But why would he need one? Was crime running that rampant in Denver?

As Shawn's driver, she'd wondered about his duties. He was a staff member present at almost every Matrix function; yet it had been all work, design presentations, and no play. Him in the background. Watchful. She couldn't recall him speaking during the meetings. His affable nature had always been pleasant enough whenever she'd greeted him.

Again, more questions about Shawn and what his life entailed.

"Thanks for the safe journey," she murmured, her gaze sweeping past the man's blank expression, but then her attention backtracked. He acknowledged her with an incline of his head, same as usual. Yet Fin's expression wasn't really blank and it was the first time she noticed. Was it the dark that made his eyes change color, going from a colorless grey to a flash of hues sparkling from his irises? The effect reminded her of a rainbow forming, but then instantly dissipating as though a trick of the light.

Wolf, she'd always assumed. She blinked, unable to place his shifter type or level. And then it was the heat in Shawn's fingers crossing into her body that recaptured her attention. Her chest expanded as Shawn tightened his grip on her. He turned back to his driver. "Fin, we'll be fine. Get the Jeep ready for tomorrow."

"Very good, I've some maintenance work I can attend to on it." The man bowed and shut the door.

•••

Shawn tucked her fingers into the crook of his arm and pulled her with him toward a set of wide steps leading up to the front of his house. Massive Doric columns rose from the veranda, framing a set of equally stately arched doors. The outside of his home challenged her brain to find a home that compared in size and stature. His home pushed the boundaries of form, capturing elegance and even simplicity, but on such a grand scale that her gaze kept moving and marveling.

She wondered if she was ready for what he had in store. So far this evening, he'd tamed the insane inferno that had dwelt within her body and doused her heat with several rounds of mind-bending sex. So far, he'd marked her and revealed that, without her actual consent, he'd ensured that no other male would seek her out. Since the moment Shawn had told her she was an alpha leopardess, she continued to doubt him given her lack of control.

All he asked in return was her trust. Confusion still jabbed at her. She'd traded a cold metal collar for blazing heat that held her prisoner all the same. Thinking about where this was leading only heightened her unease. Shawn had nothing to lose; after all, she was replaceable both at work and in his bed. Her heart began whispering that he might not be.

He'd brought out a side of her that literally roared. She had shifted into a snarling leopardess—almost out of her mind—and then consented to his whispered command to calm and shift back into human form. She'd never known such *powershifting*. He had proven his mastery over her tonight. Alpha leopardess. Never before had she questioned anything he'd told her.

The nagging echo contradicted her desire to trust him. What on earth would a man like Shawn be doing with a female who wasn't an alpha? It didn't make sense and the details were too risky to contemplate when, at every turn, his hands, his mouth, and his cock kept tempting her to put aside worry. On the ride down the other side of ecstasy, she contemplated just what's she'd agreed to in his arms.

Warring was ridiculous, other than a form of self-torture, when here she was in Shawn's company and in a setting unlike any place she had ever visited or imagined. Climbing the steps, she inhaled and gave into the yearning to *let go and let Shawn* take care of her needs. Right then he took her hands, pulling her closer to him. She gazed up into his golden eyes that grew darker, boring into her. "Diana, before the end of the week, the only promise I intend on keeping is mounting you and claiming you fully. Unless, of course, you tell me no."

The words he said liquefied her bones, for she was certain he told the truth. She swallowed and they commenced walking, moving toward the entrance.

"Well, we'll just see about that. Won't we?" Cocky is what she strove for, blatantly ignoring her heart pounding harder and harder with each step closer to the door.

He reached across to her, hoisting her up within his arms. "Really, I can do that. With pleasure."

Chapter 7

The *snick* of the doorknob connecting the lock in the jamb rebounded off the foyer walls, floor and ceiling. Shawn set her down beyond the front door.

Gripping her face within his hands, he murmured, "Kiss me."

Between the hammering in her ears and his feral glimmering eyes, Diana trembled, standing on tiptoe and pressing her mouth against his, opening to him.

He pushed her against the wall, grinding himself into her body, moaning, "Mine." His kiss consumed her fear, casting it aside and leaving in its place another vast expanse of desire, layered and demanding. And just as fast, he reeled in his passion, leaving her shaken.

"Another lesson?" she asked, seeking to steady herself by leaning her shoulder into the wall.

"Yes and no. I want you, but first we should eat. Can you make the rest of the journey at your own speed or should I hoist you over my shoulder?"

"I'm not that undone by the events tonight. No matter how hard you've tried. And yes, you are amazing, don't get me wrong, Mr. Barclay."

"You're welcome, kitten. Make yourself at home. Mrs. Wells, my housekeeper, is asleep, but anything you desire or need she'll make arrangements to provide when you meet tomorrow."

She allowed a tight smile to form on her lips. *More training*. She'd asked, and he was delivering. No way would she give him the opportunity to see her unravel further, otherwise he might think her a mouse instead of a leopardess. Earlier he'd told her how, while in Tibet, he'd learned how to give in to pain and suffering, absorb these qualities into his body by relaxing. He'd said that to fight pain accomplished the exact opposite of relief.

Diana softened her gaze, letting her fingers trace the rich textures of his home. Wedgewood blue saturated the foyer walls, bordered by gilded molding and painted wainscoting. "I bet you're responsible for the design of your home. Both inside and out."

"I had plenty of help. But the overall scheme is mine. Just remember, all roads lead back to the main drawing room."

"I won't even ask," she murmured, imagining a multitude of nooks and crannies just from what she saw in the front hall. He led her forward into a room and immediately she took in the many doorways from which one could exit the room. "On second thought, do you get lost much?"

Coming forward into the room, she sucked in her breath as the walls opened into a receiving area with soaring ceilings. Her eyes didn't remain still; her gaze jumped from architectural detail to detail. Each item within his home had required exceptional taste in the ability to envision the overall effect. A chess game in architecture and interior design. She wondered what this room would be like during the day. She envisioned the space with the sun spilling inside from tall windows, and the various glass insets within the walls. She held onto his arm, gasping. "The cupola… where did you manage to acquire the fused stained glass?"

"Hand-made in Arizona."

"Amazing," she whispered. Just as his club had gleaming floors, the alabaster flooring of his home was played out in a varied pattern where the floor was set in ever expanding and seamless alabaster. The furniture was low, modern, and off-white. Yet nothing was strictly angular, but more organic in curve and shape. The room held several warm hues of white, never rising to beige or grey, yet the undertones were more than inviting.

She moved alongside Shawn as lighting preceded them into each area. "Interesting. The way the lighting comes on automatically."

"Programmed sensors; absolutely love them. I never turn on—or off—a light switch. Energy efficient to some degree, except neither you nor I require much illumination, do we?"

"So far, no." She stopped walking. Before her was a large oil painting on the wall. The portrait had to be at least four or five feet tall, depicting Shawn and a young woman, eerily positioned with eyes so golden and bright they seemed to stare down at her and follow her movements. She walked forward for a closer view. "Shawn, this painting is so lifelike of you."

Diana returned her gaze, up at the woman with raven-colored hair. Who was she? Her coloring was darker than Shawn's, but there was no mistaking the leopardess features steely under the woman's beauty. The artist had captured the essence of their shifting nature. A cold tingling passed over Diana's skin; more like a slow chill that lingered in the crevices of her body.

"And you wonder who she is, don't you?" He inhaled, his face tightly drawn with his features hardening as each moment went by. "Shannon."

She couldn't help but flinch. The raspy tone of his voice made her gasp. Was this the reason he'd kept apart from women?

"My sister. What a handful back then," he said, gazing away from her as soon as their eyes met. "Are you hungry? You should be, after the energy we expended downtown. First, let's eat and then to bed." His voice sent a heat wave across her skin and spiked her hunger for him. The thought of food, not so much.

"She's very beautiful. Are you close?"

A muscle twitched at the corner of his jaw; his eyes once again took on a pained expression. "We were. Once. This isn't a story told in a few sentences. Later. Not now."

"Of course." She'd entertained enough edgy clients to know when to shift gears. This seemed like his Achilles heel. She had no right to poke around in his wound. "Your home is beyond belief. Do you return here each evening?"

He smiled at her, the warmth returning to his eyes. "As often as I can, but that's not enough."

It must have taken at least an hour by car to reach his home. From what she gathered, he worked non-stop as owner and head partner in Matrix Design, and she was still rattled by her surprise at finding he owned part of the Den.

She didn't want to think what that meant since he'd served as her stud, and his leopard sexuality would demand he act, not sit on the sidelines. She'd already known before tonight that he owned several restaurants, businesses related to retail design, a public relations firm, and many real estate holdings in Colorado, California, and Arizona. It was all too complicated, coupled with his responsibilities to the justice council. She cast a fleeting glance back up at his sister's portrait, taking in the young woman's proud, haughty stare that more than likely had taken generations of alpha leopard mating to perfect.

"I wish I had a reason to force my hand but time waits for no man—or leopard. Sleeping at my apartment is easier. But enough about me. Come here, Diana." He held out his hand to her and she crossed the floor. He wrapped her shoulder under his arm, pinning her close with his hand hooked around her waist. With his other hand he lifted her chin, his thumb tracing her jaw while gazing into her eyes. Her skin flashed heat under his amber perusal. Up close in this lighting, his eyes weren't simply golden. Ice blue splinters in a sunburst pattern were distributed through his irises.

"Let me have you any way I desire during your stay with me." His sensuous tone aroused her as though warm oil was being drizzled over her naked flesh. "Give in to me without reservation, holding nothing back. Without hesitation. I'll protect you, and you'll be with me during this cycle. And the next, and the next.

You are the woman I'd treasure. The leopardess I'd come to at night. As often as I could. Anything you desire will be yours."

But he hadn't said the words she wanted to hear: *I'd come back here to see you every night, or you'd come into town to be with me.* He wanted to put her up, a cosseted erotic novelty, a stop along his varied route. She wondered uneasily, how many points did his route have? "Shawn, it's impossible to answer you if you keep posing questions with your cock rubbing up against me."

"What is it that you desire? I thought it was to learn how to deal with your nature. I'll give you that and more. Much more."

"You're using my state against me. You can't keep changing the game plan."

"Why not stay here beyond this cycle? Don't you already work flextime? I'll build you a studio right here, anything you desire. I want you safe. Protected. Not gallivanting around Denver. You know as well as I do, running wild has to stop. Things will have to change." His voice ramped up; a controlled roar if ever she'd heard one.

"Wait…are you saying I'd not work at Matrix anymore?"

"No. Just that we'll extend Matrix to a satellite office here. I've always wanted the freedom to work from home a few days."

She hadn't been off the mark. *A few days.* He'd be free and she'd be…what? Captive on a mountain with a stern-looking driver. "I appreciate the offer and your wish to look out for me. You must give me time to think. Let me get past this heat to answer you with my head, not simply through a haze of lust. Perhaps by then you might want to rethink your feelings."

"You won't deny me tonight. This is mine," he snarled, his mouth taking possession of her lips. His tongue moved apart her mouth, seeking her out.

She moaned under his assault, snaking her arms around his neck. His breath and words dispelled her resistance and coaxed her into agreeing to each and every one of his suggestions. Had he not been holding her, her knee joints would have unhinged and she'd have plopped to the floor at his feet. And that's what she feared. Him towering over her, wielding all the power, and she would be nothing but a glorified employee—*with benefits*—unable to resist him.

All he'd have to do was roar a command and her leopardess self would come bounding.

He bit down on her bottom lip. "I'll do anything to get you to agree. I want you. I act from what I feel. You in my household waiting for me *is what I desire*. You'll be safe and we can make love all the time."

Waiting. Is that what he really desired? She'd pegged him correctly.

Diana slowly looked around. The irony of Shawn having delivered her from a locked metal collar bolted to the wall of a stud room to standing in his home, another form of imprisonment—albeit, a gilded comfy cage—struck her. It was difficult to determine the reality of anything that happened during the evening for her or him. Only distance and the ability to ponder objectively might enable her to make a sound decision, but linear thinking wasn't available right then and there.

"I don't know if that would be the best choice for me." She drew in a serrated breath. There could be many people tucked away inside this home for all she knew about him. The home wasn't simply large, it was sprawling.

They moved through another room with more sofas and tables, then down a hall past a dining room with a table that easily seated twenty people. He was so seamless at Matrix. Not once did he flaunt his lifestyle or his level of wealth.

Her heart thudded. Holy Mary, Shawn would hear her heartbeat with his leopard perception. Predator to prey. She listened to the silence of their passage; she could hear his pulse race but with a familiar tempo that her leopardess perception recognized as encouraging. He was attracted to her. That was truth. For all her trepidation, she must now question her own wishes, and how to structure and build her life now that her walls had been breached by him. Shawn had given her a gift by turning her darkness inside out.

Yet with his gift, he'd made her aware of a fragility that had never existed. With Cole she had never felt this powerlessness.

Shawn made her want things she'd learned as a girl to put aside and forget. Her family would have looked at him with greedy eyes. Her heart saw a man who held her fixed in his gaze for the moment. The future was as uncertain as ever, yet she wasn't alone any more. To never have known this type of shifter existed would have saved her from heartbreak. Now, that was too late.

A flock of fleeting thoughts teased her, then darted away. *His strange, inordinate interest in her.* If she refused him, he might fire her, leaving her without a reference and alone. Or worse, take him up on his offer and she'd be tainted professionally for sleeping her way to the top. Both choices had bad endings. Doubt stabbed her own heart double-time.

"Don't look so worried. Nothing need be decided upon this second. I want you, Diana. I'm prepared to do whatever it takes to convince you this could work out splendidly."

"And you don't fear the issues? What if this is all hormones? Nothing but a sex-crazed phase?"

Go back to her old life. Emotional hues of despair, sorrow, had changed to bright-warm-clear skies of not being alone. Say no and go back to a dismal existence. Diana shook her head. The soft echoes of the home and her thoughts converged.

She was haunted by confusion and realized that it might take an exorcism of emotions to clear away the detritus of her spirit. Her best game plan involved passive resistance in the form of completely noncommittal responses. She tried to change the subject in lieu of giving in to the man who asked too much. He opened doors into far too many areas within her, and now this request shook her to the bone. Following him, she was nearly lost, unable to find either the way in or the way out.

"Because it's not."

She refused to give in. "This house is unbelievable. I imagine balls, dinner parties, a time when salons were held. How many rooms are there?"

"Last count, eight bedrooms and thirteen baths. Two living rooms and all the other usual areas. I've a few that remain empty. I stalled and didn't want to commit until the moment was right. I thought the *right* feminine touch would come in handy."

She sharply inhaled. Did her *sensei* read minds and the future? Was he such an expert player that he'd infer what she wanted to hear? No lies, only suggestions. She nervously laughed. "Understandable. I imagine furniture shopping could get mind-numbing after, say, the ninth room."

"Surprisingly, when it's your own, it does get old rather fast. Paint chips and textiles took me down. I cried uncle after a year."

"You've only been here a year?" She didn't want to think back twelve months. Her life had been utter hell.

"The land has been in the family for generations. I marked the foundation years ago and then it sat. I've enjoyed being footloose and fancy free, enjoying the perks until that lifestyle suddenly was no longer appealing. Anyway, we're here now. Enough to keep us satisfied. If not, we'll get whatever you desire."

"For now, I think if I could get some clothing, I'd be set." She refused to think about this tantalizing offer he tossed about so glibly. The odd truth—that he wasn't bonded to a mate—had her wondering. More than likely, half of the available shifters in Denver, even the United States, considered him an eligible bachelor. Toss in available women who didn't know he was a wereleopard, and the numbers went exponential.

An alpha such as Shawn would bond to an alpha shifter. Those shifters didn't put up with other females mating with her consort, just as this man wouldn't permit his bonded mate to copulate with another male. This cycle must have gotten to his brain as well. What in God's name was he really asking her? In her world, this meant ties and lineage if she was an alpha.

It was one thing to run away from home with her childhood sweetheart. It was a very different thing to mate with a clan alpha. From what she could tell, he was childless; that was one scent impossible to mask. Based on his sexual prowess, Shawn's all-too-powerful *more-orgasms* would result in a brood of cubs. The thought of having not just one child but several to care for hit her full-force. Her career would be effectively over.

This was crazy, to take his asking her to live with him as anything more than a temporary arrangement. She nibbled her fingernail, imagining how beautiful his children would be. During a heat cycle, this was not helpful thinking!

The room blazed hotter, her skin shrunk, and she pulled at her neckline. Think, she told herself. Nothing to get boxed in over. This wasn't a life sentence. She was free to march out the door. Fin would take her home. She was here of her own accord. Her erratic thoughts were just the product of her heat cycle.

"Would you care for something to drink?" he asked.

"Yes, please," she said, shaky and acutely aware she needed to gather her wits. *One step at a time. Easy as pie.*

He pushed a swinging door and they entered into a huge kitchen that more than likely was the size of one of his restaurants. "A full gourmet kitchen. I believe you mentioned you loved cooking when we first met."

"Your memory serves you well." She stopped talking. *Good God, it was the largest kitchen in a private home she'd ever seen.* "I've got one word: luxe. This kitchen is out of control."

Intriguing how he'd combined different textures to create a modern, warm atmosphere. Natural stones and woods. Industrial stainless. Hand-blown glass. From the intricate tiled floors to the smooth granite counters, unending horizontal surfaces begged her gaze to continue skirting the room, only hesitating to note the polished white cabinets, ultra-modern chic lighting, and the several sinks. Over the island were gleaming copper pans hanging from an ornate wrought-iron rack attached to a ceiling higher than those at his club. She followed him as he stood and pulled the handle on a veneered Sub-Zero. Escaping mists from the freezer surrounded them in a chilling cloud as he removed a bottle of vodka.

"Here, please put this on the counter," he said, opening the refrigerator where he pulled out a wrapped tray. She set the bottle down. "Let me help," she said, reaching for the refrigerator door handle.

"Thanks. I hope you enjoy smoked salmon. I remember you eating some at that breakfast during the holidays."

She peeked at him from under her lowered lashes. "How did you even remember that day? You were surrounded by your clients."

"Most of us generally live in contradiction. We ignore what's important and attend to the details that are meaningless without context. I've always leaned into the light where you're concerned."

"Leaned into the light?" she asked, uncertain what he meant.

"Paid attention to you," he murmured, a hot glow emanating from his eyes.

Her skin rippled with pleasure. He would have her groveling if she didn't pace herself. Beginning right this second. She contemplated the small bowls on the tray.

"Everything looks delectable." She couldn't say for sure what she'd eaten at the meeting he described, but she vaguely remembered having tasted lox and cream cheese. But the Beluga caviar, Greek olives, pickled beets, and tomato and onions drizzled with balsamic vinegar and oil was certainly appetite inspiring. Everything she'd naturally select was here. Not one item wasn't something she had come to relish—her ultimate brunch.

Shawn moved away from her, the source of ember-like heat going with him. He opened a cabinet and removed two plates. He set them at the counter before padded leather barstools. She followed his example, placing the tray near the plates.

"What else do we need?"

"Just silverware and glasses. If you turn around and count two cabinets over, you'll find them. Get the tumblers. Do you mind?" Arrogance as a style looked good on him. The set of his jaw and arch of his brow made the space between her legs ache to be dominated. He moved and opened a drawer, removing flatware.

She opened the cabinet, noticing that the wood smelled of wax and lemons. She gazed across the neat rows of crystal, far different from the jumbled mess in her cabinet of unmatched glasses. She lifted a crystal tumbler. Not the lightweight kind. This one rested heavy in her hand. Waterford, she'd bet on it.

She set one glass down on the counter rather than run the risk of dropping it, and shut the cabinet. She turned just as he opened the bottle of Belvedere vodka.

"How do you feel?" he asked as he watched her from behind half-closed lids.

Jesus, she almost dropped a glass, unnerved by his expression. Was she on the menu and no one had informed her?

"Nervous, but hungry. You were right. I'm starved."

"Come sit and let's take care of one hunger, then another. And there's nothing to be nervous about."

"Said the spider to the fly," she murmured.

"Sweetheart, there's nothing insect-like about you. Delectable, yes; creepy-crawler, impossible. If anything, that mouth of yours is more like a slice of heaven wrapped around me, as is your pussy.

Drink with me to how I will fuck you in my bed. The things you'll learn." He handed her a drink with barely a finger of vodka. Shawn raised his glass, his gaze locking with hers. "To enlightenment."

"And easing the pains of hunger. Thank you for taking me on during this crisis and clearing my head."

He smiled across at her. "Diana, I can't pretend. I desired you the moment we met. I respect you immensely as a graphic artist. For all you've been through, you needn't fear this is one more act of craziness. Not with me."

They clinked their glasses and he flipped the crystal tumbler back, pouring the entire serving of vodka into his mouth. No wonder he didn't fill their glasses. He drank Russian style.

She watched him over her rim, the vodka slipping over her tongue. She swallowed the shot of smooth liquor, setting her glass down. Diana stood next to him with his dark good looks as he poured more velvet-tasting liquor to accompany his equally smooth words..

The idea of going clubbing with him, tossing back shots, and listening to music when she was past the haze of a heat would be a treat. He'd be hard to resist while dancing with his hot, hard body bending over her, bending her to his will. He gazed back at her, his face serious, begging the question of why the sudden change in his affect.

"What are you thinking?" she asked.

"How to finish this meal in a hurry."

Chapter 8

During their meal, he kept thinking of what her life had been like this past year. With his staff, he kept all his interactions above board so they'd never discussed her life outside Matrix. There was no crossing of lines or muddying the waters at Matrix or at the Den, not after his *learning by fire with Mia and Frazier.*

"Let me tidy up." Diana began to stack the plates in the dishwasher. Shawn came up behind her, bracketing her hips between his hands and rubbing his stiffening cock against her tempting ass.

"Don't worry about all this. Come. It's time for bed."

She swayed her bottom against him, and it was either take her here in the kitchen, or get her upstairs. His housekeeper might not know he'd arrived home and wander in without warning. He clenched his jaw, his desire to mount Diana swimming in his mind. "Now," he snapped, pulling her body back from the counter.

"Okay," she said gazing up into his face with her shimmering eyes and pupils nearly fully dilated. The scent of her filled him, and he interlaced their fingers, leading her out of the kitchen and down the hall toward the backstairs.

He held Diana in his arms, having picked her up at the bottom step. He couldn't resist touching her whenever possible. She was his, whether she realized it or not. The idea of her running unchecked in the middle of Denver had him seeing red. He wanted to spank her bottom for shifting without a care for her own safety, and in a public park. No way would he ever let her do that again. His gut spasmed at the unsettling thought: what if she had no intention of letting him do more than train her?

He started up the stairs. "Diana, you must promise me, never shift alone again?"

"You said I'd have control. Right? I'm not worried. You're not going to start acting like a brood hen?"

"Don't force me to impress upon you the severity of this problem."

"I've taken care of myself up to now. I do understand. I've no desire to end up in some lock-up facility." Her flippant tone said otherwise.

Oh, hell. He wanted to shake her good. Tristen and Fin would be assigned to tail her if she refused his offer. *Note to self: hire another bodyguard.*

Time would tell if he was right on first bite—for her, not him. He was certain. He wasn't in full control when what he sought involved the volition of a strong-willed woman. Diana might not understand what it meant to be an alpha leopardess at present. Yet, just from her attempt to go it alone for over a year, she had already proven her strength of character in his book. He had enough sense to admit that his inability to take her without a chase excited and, at the same time, bothered him. To be conflicted in claiming a woman like Diana would demand correcting, and fast.

He found it inconceivable that her parents had refused to let her come back just because she'd married a man not of their choosing. Now, as a widow, would she go back to her family?

Christ, she was an alpha leopardess he'd have been proud to bring home to his parents if they were alive. He didn't want to think along those lines. Not tonight.

Diana had asked him questions he realized that were doorways to grounding them and deepening their connection. They'd shared their pasts and pain, but it was only the first night he'd let her into his world. Regardless of having known her for the last year, he'd been her employer and had kept his distance, all too aware of his attraction to her, and unwilling to risk crossing any lines that would make her uncomfortable.

Bringing her home, to this house and into his bedroom, very much satisfied both his human and leopard natures. "Are you tired?" he asked, brushing her hair back from her face.

He lifted her chin, gazing into the most beautiful eyes he'd ever seen. His words became glued to the back of his throat. If he lost this woman, he doubted recovery would be possible. Jesus, what could he do to ensure she would be safe? *Everything possible.*

Her fingers had crept up and held his face. "You look worried," she said.

He inhaled, unwilling to articulate these thoughts just yet. "Concerned. You're a handful but even so, I may have tired you out. All I want is to tear off your clothes and toss you across that bed." He brushed his mouth against her rose-petal lips.

"Mmmm. There's nothing we need to solve tonight." She moaned against his mouth. Her breath caressed his tongue and he returned for a second taste.

If she refused to listen to reason, he'd take things into his own hands. Starting right now, with her body, he turned her face to give him better access. "Open for me. No holding back." This time he kissed her with the intent to have his way in his own bed.

Shawn set her down in the hall outside his room without releasing her. He pushed her back into the wall, plunging his tongue into her mouth, delivering and taking with each tangle of his tongue. It was impossible to get enough of her. He ran his hands over her shoulders unzipping her dress. He brought the material down her waist, enjoying the feel of her skin over her lush hips. Jesus, to draw out this experience would be explosive.

Opening the bedroom door, he guided her inside. "Take it off. Everything you're wearing."

Slowly, she worked her fingers letting the dress fall around her legs. She stepped free, unhooking her bra, and undoing the garter belt. She removed her shoes and then one by one, he watched enthralled as she rolled down her stockings in the most provocative striptease he'd ever witnessed.

"Beautiful," he said coming up in front of her. He cupped her ass, hiking her hips up to his so he could press himself into her, closer to the soft wetness he sought.

Lifting her up, he spread her thighs. "Wrap your legs around my waist," he murmured against her mouth.

He continued exploring her body while his fingers traveled toward her center. No panties, just splendid warm skin, the way she should always be for him. He found her pussy, lightly traced her folds.

She sucked in her breath, quivering in his arms the moment his fingers found her slickness. "I hope you're not teasing me. Is this another lesson?" she asked.

"Fuck, no. I think we've been good long enough."

She pressed her pussy along his finger and whimpered. Damn, if she wasn't the most sensitive creature. His cock thickened as his craving to possess her surged; a primitive instinct to join with her shook his core. He rubbed her silky folds up and down his throbbing erection. He carried her toward the bed and deposited her on top, then gazed down at her breath-stopping beauty. Biting back a groan, he knew he couldn't lose his head. She required him to take the lead.

"Spread your legs and touch yourself for me. Show me what I desire." His voice lowered, close to drowning in his need to dive into her body.

"What? I don't know—"

"Don't…" He marched over to her, pushing her back against the mattress, and bent over her, placing both of his arms on either side of her body. When he spoke, he did so slowly to make his point. "Don't argue with me. Do exactly as I've instructed. If not, I can find a way to motivate you to do as I say without argument. And trust me, I'm only too happy to begin tonight."

He didn't move and waited. A silent exchange occurred between them, concluded by her small nod. He backed off and tunneled his fingers through his hair. Her scent had his lust ramped up. It was taking more and more not to come at her like a savage beast and take her. For all his talk of being just and even knowing the history of shifters like his sister, he was pushed to the very edge between man and beast when it came to Diana. "Like this?" she asked, coyly seductive. She opened her thighs, her movements unhurried. She slid her hands down from her raised knees until her fingers met.

"Diana, you can't imagine how this feels, seeing you open before me." He watched her fingers moving, pressing down on her mound. She arched and moaned, opening her knees and giving him a spectacular view of her pussy and that sumptuous ass. The sight of her slick center pushed his leopard nature to the forefront. He snarled, staring at her. She hesitated, glancing up at him and her lips parted into an innocent 'O.'

"Oh, baby. Don't stop," he commanded, as he almost tore his own clothes off.

She lowered her legs to the bed, her knees and legs together. "Are you sure you want to watch?"

"That's one. Shall we go for more? Perhaps you like the feel of a hand across your bottom. What did I say before?" His fingers twitched, toying with the fantasy of spanking her, and then driving his cock into her wetness.

Slowly, she opened her legs, sucking her finger and stopping before opening her folds for him. Her lips were wet with her own arousal and soon he promised himself he'd taste her creamy slickness. He inhaled, the scent of her pervading his body, invading his soul, down to the smallest atom. She had imprinted her form upon him.

He stroked his cock, aware that in the next few seconds he'd plunge into her, taking them both over the cliff. Never had he been so thoroughly turned on by a woman. He wanted to conquer her hunger while quenching his own.

Diana's finger dipped inside her opening and a snarl tore from his mouth. He could feel the wild leopard inside himself demand that he take her. He came down onto the bed as if he'd pounced. "I've got to have you."

He turned her over, bringing her across his legs. "This is for questioning me." He lifted his arm and smacked her soundly on her ass cheek. Diana snarled and tried to move off his lap. "Did I say to move?"

Again, he spanked her. The sound of his hand was loud in the room. "Any more arguments?"

"No. None," she whispered. He tossed her onto the mattress, her legs splayed, the memory of her rosy ass heating his arousal past scorching. This was how he'd wanted her, from the moment he'd laid eyes on her last year. Completely under his control. He followed her on the bed, moving over her body, dragging his cock between her legs while she arched, moaning his name.

Diana lifted her hips, rubbing against him in the most primal form of submission. "Please," she whimpered.

"Turn over," he growled, hardly able to form the words while staring down at her body. Every fiber in his being screamed to mount her. Take her. Own her.

He wrapped his hand in her hair and bared her neck to him. He took care not to clamp down tight. His dick swiped across her folds. He wrapped his hands on either side of her hips, lifting up her ass as he knelt in between her legs, her body a soft, yielding fit. Then he was at her opening. In one forceful thrust, he took possession of her.

His cock throbbed deep inside her body.

"Shawn, a condom." Diana's voice quavered.

Fuck. He came out of her and in one swift motion he pulled open his nightstand. Nothing. He went into the bathroom, nearly mad, slamming cabinet doors. The leopard didn't care about protection. Hell, the beast preferred if he'd put aside all promises and do what nature demanded. She was an alpha and a worthy mate. His skin tightened and he fought a primal nature that burned his self-control. Take her, and then he'd be done with this blistering craving. He'd own her forever. *Except she'd never trust him. Would she?* Just as he'd been burned, he couldn't do that to her. Not Diana.

After grabbing a fistful of condoms from the bathroom, he returned to the bedside tearing open a condom wrapper with his teeth. He tossed an additional handful of condoms onto the nightstand.

Christ. He surveyed Diana in a position of subservience on the bed. No wonder he could barely contain his need to possess her. With her ass in the air, his leopard nature was being pushed to the brink. He flung the open condom packet down on the nightstand.

He had to reduce the fire of his desire to possess her. To take her from behind on the bed urged his primitive leopard nature to take her completely. He had to wait out his lust until he was fully in command; otherwise, he risked taking her in a way neither of them desired. If and when they mated, it would be by mutual consent. Not him, taking her from behind her back, stealing her will without permission. The leopard in him let loose a roar that he tried to choke back.

Diane's face swung around at the explosive sound that echoed in the room. "Have I done something wrong?"

"No. On the contrary. I need to take care. We're both near the edge. Sweetheart. Come to me. I want you to stand up and hold onto the railing. I'll be right behind you."

"Stand by the footboard?"

"It's time we fucked down your heat to a manageable level. For both of us, Diana. You've got me as hot as you are. We need to fuck hard if we hope to get past the urge to do what our leopard nature demands, but I can't be close to your neck or pulse points right now. So, you're going to hold on while I'm in back of you. I'll have you by your hips. Christ, I need this more than you do at this point."

"Because this is too like leopards mating?"

"Yes, we'll do the stance in this position, but under no circumstances are you to shift. I think we can trick our inner natures into subduing this urge. It'll get worse before it gets better, but we've got to let loose some steam before we run."

She swallowed, staring at him. "We're going to run? As leopards?"

"Yes. Tomorrow. But tonight I'm going to deliver like a club banger would have you." He held out his palm to her.

Her breasts swayed, nipples erect, and she grazed one tip across his rib cage gliding past him.

"Here. Or here?" She motioned with her hands.

"Stand closer to this side so you can hold on onto the bedpost. Widen your stance and bend over." Her fingers didn't reach around the post. He doubted she'd hold on for any length of time.

"Let me get something to tie your hands."

Her brow shot up. "Is this what you wanted all along?"

"We can't risk you falling down or getting hurt. We don't need another complication. Not with our run tomorrow."

"I'll agree to being tied to a post. Running free…"

He took one of his silk ties from the closet. "Shush. You'll do everything I suggest or I'll invoke my right to discipline you again. Baby, I'd love to throw you over my lap and spank that beautiful bottom of yours for more than a couple of swats. Don't tempt me to give you another preview. You know that by the end of your training, I'll know you inside and out. Darling, bend over." The look on her face was priceless.

He came up next to her, taking hold of her hand. "Place your palm here. Don't move your hand. Give me your other palm. Thread your fingers together clasping the column." He lifted her interlaced palms upward a couple of inches. "Do you wish to say something?"

"I don't understand why all of this is necessary. That's all."

"It is if I say so. I'm not going to have a repeat performance of you shifting. I think this involves a little quid pro quo. Trust me?"

She nodded with eyes big as saucers. The slow slide of her tongue along the edge of her lip made him see stars. "Baby," he groaned. "Give me your mouth." He held out his engorged cock to her. If he wasn't careful, he'd get lost in her hot mouth.

"Oh, you need me to help you. Nice change of events, Mr. Barclay." She knelt in front of him, her hair tickling his legs. Jesus, the feel of her mouth almost brought him to his knees. Diana danced her tongue around the precum dripping from the end of his head.

"Suck me harder, kitten." He pulled her hair away from her face so he could see every swipe of her tongue. She returned his gaze, fire in her eyes so bright he swore the flames licked his crown. The feel of her wet lips enveloping his cock lit every one of his nerve endings. Heat spiked up his spine, tightening his balls. He fisted his hand in her hair and tugged. Her eyes widened, a tinge of anger flirted within her eyes, and color tinted her cheeks, but she didn't stop sucking him. Oh no, if anything she took him deeper and sucked him harder. He closed his eyes, enjoying the way she delivered with that those succulent lips of hers. Electrical pinpricks raced up his spine and in a second he'd jet his load down her throat. "Damn I'm ready to explode," he panted. "All right then. I'm going to tie your wrists to the bed. You're incredible, even if you've a temper hidden down deep."

He noted she was beginning to chafe, a sign of her leopardess nature wanting to emerge, wanting to lead. In pushing her, she didn't back down all the way. Retreated was more like it while gathering for her next move. At Matrix, he'd given her near complete freedom in design creation, yet she'd always held back. He might suggest an idea but, so far, they'd both been on pretty equal footing. He suspected it was one reason she'd been so low key. Not once had she asserted her position or attempted to buck under the weight of authority. This was a fine line they'd both have to learn to dance. A give and take based on mutual and complete trust.

His lips twitched at the thought. "You've not had much experience in the yoke of constraint. Have you, kitten?" He looped his tie around her wrists. Soon, no doubt, the leopardess would show herself. Then he'd brandish a firmer hand with his little debutant shifter.

He finished making the square knot. "There. Not too tight? Turn your face this way and open that amazing mouth of yours." The moment her tongue flicked across his dick, he shuddered. He gazed down at her, the head of his cock inside her mouth, thrusting over her tongue. He tangled his fingers through her hair, framing her head. "Get ready to take me." He held her head steady and he rocked back and forth on the balls of his feet. He stopped just as his spine started to tingle.

"Your turn." He pulled her upright. "Bend over and hold on."

He knelt in back of her, pushing her legs wider apart. Her perfect ass was right in front of his face. He spread her ass cheeks, giving him a full view of her sweet, tight, puckered hole. He dragged his tongue up and over her opening, licking her up and down. She trembled under his mouth. He thrust his tongue into her slit, making her rock.

"Shawn, I'm going to come if you continue. Please, babe."

He wasn't prepared for the effect of hearing her endearment. His heart thundered. Without warning, a pattern of dark spots came to life over his skin. "Christ, hold on darling." He stood between her legs, lifting her body, fingering her clit. "Diana, hold onto the post and don't let go. I've got to fuck you right now. Close your eyes. Don't disappoint me. Eyes closed."

Shawn didn't want her to see him in this condition. He tore into a new condom packet and sheathed himself with latex, grunting at the feel of his palm. Pinpricking points spread like a rabid rash. His sweat glands shut down in anticipation of the appearance of a coat of fur. He positioned his cock at her entrance.

Groaning loudly, he surged into her pussy with one hard, body-slamming thrust. The feel of her made him stop moving, afraid he'd lose control. All the while, he was aware that stubble had formed across his skin. He focused on his breath and delivered another earth-shattering pound into her. Then he stopped worrying that he was hurting her when her ass arched and flexed up to meet him, thrust for thrust.

Setting a rhythm, he stroked her waist as she rocked back to him. Fuck, he rode her hard, his balls slapping her ass. The burning in his lungs escalated and spread across his skin, but a desire like none he'd ever known spurred him onward as he held back from shifting. Barely. Diana clutched the column between her hands. Her body glistened in sweat and then he noticed her skin was under the same attack. They were mirror images of one another, leopard and leopardess shining through the human forms. Her body was breathtaking, every muscle outlined under feminine curves and she took what he dished out. He was almost out of breath from fucking her past this heat. She slowed and shuddered. Her pussy wrapped around him, squeezed and then hugged his cock. She shuddered again and he buried his cock deep inside her.

Not wanting this to end, he continued thrusting into her narrow folds, unable to contain himself, and then a snarl broke from his mouth, signaling his descent.

Shawn released his hold on her, running his hands down her spine. "Sweet Jesus, the things you do to me."

He untied the knot and picked her up as she swooned against him. Thankfully, her eyes were closed. After laying her on the bed, he switched off the nightstand lamp and went to the wet bar in the corner of his bedroom. In the darkness, their breathing came out in gulps.

"Here, drink this," he held out a bottle of mineral water to her. "We definitely need a fully stocked wet bar inside this room," he murmured, settling down next to her on the bed. He closed his eyes to the darkness, focusing on an illuminated triangle behind his mind's eye. Right in the center of forehead, the place he'd learned to find a calming peace during meditation. He stroked the outline of her face, memorizing each curve and plane.

"That was incredible," she whispered.

He opened his eyes, staring into her red-hazed, dilated pupils. *What must he look like to her?* His heartbeat resembled something closer to a mallet striking a wall instead of an insane power tool gone haywire. Shawn opened his arms to her, cradling her against him as he rubbed his cheek along the top of her head. Her body had cooled remarkably and he'd dulled the razor-edged, insatiable appetite to mindlessly fuck.

If he could gain some control over her, enough control that she'd not question him openly. And perhaps more importantly, silently, she'd accept his advice. Then they'd be safe to flee up the side of the mountain. The freedom to roam would allow Diana to test her leopardess nature without losing control as she'd done in the past, going at this solo. The question was how to push her to openly test the boundaries they tenuously treaded. As leopards, this was part of being in a pack. Learning the pecking order. Up to this point, as an adult she'd learned a small part by being with a partner outside a clan. Eventually, if things worked out between them, he would take her to meet his family. But only if things worked out. Christ, what would Shannon think? Or any of his family? It had been a long time since he'd returned to his clan to share anything other than business news.

She'd have to learn he was the one who commanded. Sure, he'd be the one to dominate, but in reality it was she who held the power. He tilted her chin upward. In the darkness, his mouth searched for hers. She licked his mouth and then kissed him, enfolding him within her arms, a continuous purr emitting from her chest.

Most definitely, she held the ability to wrap him around her little finger if she ever got the idea into her beautiful head.

Chapter 9

The filtered rays of the morning came through the large windows in Shawn's bedroom. Several immense oaks were outside, dappling the light, and creating a whirling pattern of shadows whenever the breeze caressed the branches.

She'd refrained from stirring in bed, preferring to observe Shawn as he slept. His arm had curled around her waist at some point during the night, keeping his hold on her. She longed to touch the dark hair that fell over his chiseled face. During sleep, he appeared much younger without the thoughts that she supposed worried him incessantly. Her chest tightened. He did so much and it wasn't something that was publicized, giving him credit for being more than just a rich bachelor or the gorgeous entrepreneur who made the social section of the newspaper. She sighed without thinking and his arm squeezed her.

"I didn't mean to wake you," she whispered, and swept his hair from his brow.

He opened his golden eyes, still unguarded, and smiled radiantly at her. "I'm glad you did. I haven't slept that well for years and might have piddled the day away in dreamland. We've much to do today." He stretched, and she watched as the sheet dropped; his muscles rippled over his shoulders, arms, and down his belly.

"May I take a bath?" she asked.

He pushed her back against the pillows, bringing his body over hers. "Only if you want company."

She innocently asked, "Why, is there another shifter here who can help me bathe? You must certainly be tired. Perhaps you can catch up on your beauty sleep."

He growled a sharp warning. "Don't play, kitten. I don't share what's mine. I'll bathe you this morning and we can talk." The tip of his stiff cock probed the mouth of her pussy. She could feel her own desire heighten. Again he demonstrated lightning fast reflexes and bounded off the bed, pulling her with him. Shawn effortlessly hauled her up against him, his erection a vivid reminder of his hunger this morning. "Still want to play?"

"Inside a warm bath would be heaven," she said.

"Give me a second to run the water." He lifted her hand, kissing her palm, and tugged her into the adjoining bathroom.

She'd seen it late last night, but in daylight it was breathtaking with a vaulted ceiling and skylights. The bathtub was located in the center of the room with vanities on either side. Shawn used the dimmer to adjust the lighting and pressed a button; soft music flooded the room. "Pick your pleasure," he said, pointing to a tray of bath gels and soaps.

Diana selected a sandalwood and rose combination. She walked over to the bathtub with water gushing from the double spigots, and squeezed gel into the steaming water. The scent filled the air as thousands of bubbles foamed over the surface of the water.

"The water feels just right. May I?" Shawn stood and held out his hand.

She nodded and he gently lifted her up and placed her into the tub. He sat on the edge, peering down at her. "Your skin is so beautiful tinted pink by the warm water."

"Join me," she said softly.

"Scoot forward." He settled in back of her, and squeezed water over her shoulders using a natural sea sponge. "Pass me the gel," he murmured, his beard bristling over his jaw scraped against her shoulder.

Soon, he had her skin invigorated with the wiping motion of the sponge and the aromatic foam covering her upper body. This was the first time she'd enjoyed this type of luxuriating experience. "I've never been pampered like this before."

"You deserve to be. Each and every day." He rinsed the soap off her skin, and his body tensed. "But what we'll do tonight is far from pampered. I'm going relish chasing your lovely ass up that mountain and down." A low purring rumbled deep in his chest.

She glanced over her shoulder and up into his face. Shawn would be right next to her tonight. Nothing to freak out about. "You're certain that us skittering along a ledge is safe?"

"Yes. Trust me, Diana. It's the reason I brought you up here. I own this whole bloody mountain top. Fin will drive us down into the valley." His voice burst past the back of her head. She scooted forward and he immediately recaptured her, pulling her against his chest. His cock lay against her bottom, a rigid pole. His arm caught her along her rib cage, under her breasts. Inside the bathtub he reclined, placing both of his legs over hers and locking her against his hard plank of a body.

"And what if I get away? I can't promise I'd run back up the mountain. I don't know what my thoughts are when I'm in leopard form."

"Well, doesn't that sound a bit alarming? You should know what you think at all times. It's not as though you morph and body jump. Your brain is still your brain."

"Sure. This is my brain on human time. And then there's my brain on leopard time. It's like there's a wall that's erected. I don't know that I'm the same as you. What if I'm different? Some sort of ADHD for leopards."

"That's nonsense. I promise I'll make it so. The trauma you've been through since leaving home has taken its toll. Even if you don't remember everything, you'll remember where you belong."

"How?"

"You've got to trust me."

She played with his hands, threading their fingers together. "I already gave you my trust."

"Yes. In word. But we'll begin today and see how much you really trust and how far we'll need to go to teach you I can be trusted. Kitten, trust isn't something that people can just give away. Even if you wanted to."

His insistent hands were down between her legs, making it impossible to sit still. "You've a fascination with my ass. Why is that?"

"Because I want to possess all of you."

"That's only physical."

"By giving yourself to me and letting me care for you, it's one way that you'll learn to trust me. I've got to have you. All of you." He sucked her earlobe between his teeth and bit down.

Her clit throbbed at the feel of his body and each of his movements made it hard to think. She was nearly unraveled. "What do you mean? This sounds like an excuse for kink, not an exercise in whether you've got my back."

"Really, a lot of what goes on in BDSM clubs originated with shifters. Being tied up, bound, learning to yield and to submit. It's all about power and trust. It's just not exactly the diluted version of what is offered."

"I've never been to one." His tanned fingers crept over her skin, weaving a tantalizing trail, and she sat mesmerized by the things he said and the sensuous way that his hands caressed and squeezed her.

"Do you like it when I'm rough with you? Like last night, spanking your ass." He took her breasts in his palms, her nipples pinched between his fingers. She closed her eyes, struggling to control herself. "I want your ass. I plan on taking it and filling it. I want you wrapped around me."

"I see," she whispered. She told herself that Shawn was a good man. A man she'd known for a year. He was demanding, but no less from himself. Everyone at Matrix respected and admired him. Yet she'd not known this side of the man. The part that wanted to possess every inch of her body.

Last night when he'd spanked her and then brought out the silk tie, his eyes had flashed with a challenge. This would be the type of man who'd enjoy the chase. The question of aftereffect still plagued her. How much domination would he have over her?

"What about control? After the chase, what will be my position? Complete submission?"

"Hardly. There's not trickery here. If I wanted a mate, the last thing I'd want is to gain such a relationship without mutual consent."

"I don't mean to imply you would. I've seen the ill-effects of arranged marriages between shifter clans."

"Diana, we all have. But I've no desire to be part of that tactic. Ever. I won't take by force something a precious as a female's gift of bonding. It's archaic."

"Those types of arrangements still exist. They did in my family." She'd seen those types growing up. She'd feared those types, and it was why she didn't hang around to be bartered off to the shifter chosen by her father. The memory of an arranged marriage had kept her from ever returning home. To this day, the image of that wereleopard her father had selected as her mate crouched in the recesses of her mind. His laughter resounded at the forefront of her memory, and still had the power to make her skin crawl.

Diana shivered, recalling how the shifter had slyly whispered vulgar suggestions to her, alluding to what their life would be like once he had her in his power, so sure in his control over her family. From the moment she'd met the frightful shifter, his eerie eyes had followed her with a rapacious hunger and a lascivious grin that her family either failed to see, or simply ignored.

But inside of her, his attention left her cold and troubled. More so after she'd overheard him bragging about how he planned to subdue her and his abominable ambition to control her, making her nothing more than his submissive slave. She'd tried to complain to her parents, but they accused her of being selfish. She couldn't go through with the arrangement, not with a shifter whose eyes were empty, cavernous pits.

If it hadn't been for Cole, she'd have run away on her own. Cole, with his gentle laugher and soft voice, didn't scare her. Cole was all comfort. Her friend from childhood. Gone for good.

"Tell me your thoughts," Shawn whispered against her neck. "What troubles you?" He turned her body around so that she lay over his chest and torso.

"It's nothing. Just the past," she murmured.

His cock was hard under her abdomen. He pulled her up by her biceps until her mouth was against his. "Tell me or I'll tickle you." He lowered her onto his broad chest; his hair was matted wet over his nipples, and he ran his fingers lightly down her spine. She tried not to breathe…not to think, but he knew. His fingers tweaked a spot right over her hip and she jerked without meaning to, letting out a squeak.

"I know your sensitive spots. You've more than just this one." His fingers deftly moved over a line riding from left to right above her bottom. She shuddered, her nipples tightening, and she flexed her hips, slamming against his balls.

"Christ," he swore, throwing his leg over her hip.

"I'm sorry. Oh Shawn. Please tell me what to do."

He sucked in huge gulp of air. "Nothing. Well, there is something. If I could just…"

"What, tell me? Please."

"Help me up. And then if you'd let me find some comfort in your succulent bottom."

"You're teasing me. Do you know how worried I was? Shawn Barclay, that wasn't funny."

"It was worth a try. I think you need to take one for the team, kitten."

"I think you need to take a cold shower."

"Baby, you're only hours from letting me have my way with you. We can do it nice and easy, or we can do it leopard-style. But either way, I will own your ass. It's mine." He bit his lip in such a provocative way that she almost wanted him to take her right then and there.

She crossed her arms over her chest to prevent him from seeing how erect her nipples had become from just his words. "The water's getting cold."

"Well, we mustn't let you catch cold. Come." He pushed up from the bath, his arm a band of steel around her waist.

He lifted her easily, reinforcing her conviction that if he ever hankered for anything from her, she'd have no easy way to deny him. She hooked her arms around his broad shoulders.

After he took her in the manner he described, she'd be marked in another way by him. Little by little, he was casting his scent over her. She imagined he wouldn't wear a condom, and although not fully mated, she'd wear his scent. Another layer added to the bite and serum he'd infused into her bloodstream. His semen would cross another barrier. She didn't know if she feared the penetration of his thick cock; hard to believe it would fit where he wanted it to go, or the fact that she'd be further linked to him in a way that required an expert healer to sever.

He set her down and removed a bath wrap from the warmer. "Let me cover you up. Your skin is chilled. Now, Diana." His tone snapped her focus back to him.

"What if you decide that we're temporary? We hardly know one another."

He enfolded her in a soft, warm, terrycloth heaven. When he came back around her body, facing her, his urbane expression grew darker by the second. His eyes captured her attention, going deeper than his words.

Without touching her, he connected with her. "I know. Down to my core. And yes, we do know each other. In the important ways that get muddy when people start out in bed and then have to learn to be civilized. A lot of game-playing goes on. We know each other in the ways that matter. I respect you. Jesus, I admire you more than ever. As a matter of fact, we have a business meeting planned. Don't we? Just because we're not downtown at the office, do you still want to meet? Let's go down and have our meeting as planned. Perhaps not as formal or as professional, but the outcome will be the same. Do you agree?"

"Who will be downstairs this morning?"

"Not a soul besides staff. Would you rather meet up here?"

"No. I just wondered."

"Mrs. Wells will be about. Tristen should be around this morning. As the day goes, he more than likely will make a few appearances with something he wants to discuss. Business is never far away, and I have several corporations to run regardless of my personal commitments. Quinn may do a webcam meeting. Fin will be about. I meet with them every day. They're not strangers to you." His voice softened finally.

"Barely. What will they think when they see me here? That I'm sleeping my way to the next level?"

"That I'm the luckiest son-of-a-bitch in the world."

"That's you. Not me. Shawn, be serious."

"Fine. They'd say *you're* the luckiest woman on the planet. You must realize that of anyone who is part of Matrix, those two aren't going to judge you." His somber expression left her silent.

She had known Tristen and Fin since she'd begun at Matrix, and it was only now that she had understood that with Shawn's other professional interests that maybe Fin and Tristen's shadowy existence was linked to the justice council more than Matrix. That made much more sense and explained why they weren't exactly staff.

And now that she thought about it, there were others at Matrix, people who seemed to hover around Shawn without an apparent purpose, routinely coming and going. Other than conversing in hushed voices, Shawn and his mysterious staff's interactions were not part of her interest at work. Not when she'd been bombarded with preparing for a client presentation, working on a design, or trying to figure out how to keep sane on one side of a heat cycle. She didn't have time to spend at the water cooler gossiping and so she'd never actually paid them much mind. Until now.

She didn't hobnob with many of the office staff to begin blatantly asking questions. Her less than social overtures to other Matrix staff were a valid reason why she wasn't invited to more extracurricular shindigs. Now, she was glad. Fewer nosy work friends to keep at an arm's length.

"What shall I wear? I mean, if this is a business meeting."

"Come in your birthday suit. I won't complain."

"Even with Fin and Tristen roaming about?"

"I don't think they'd take notice." He looked at her quizzically. "They're partners."

"O-o-o," she strung the vowel sound. "I didn't know."

"You don't seem to take notice of others much outside of your projects. That laser focus of yours keeps you insulated."

"If they aren't part of my world, then I don't have the time to do small talk. It's not part of my repertoire. Is that a problem?"

"Not exactly for me. But you might want to work on that personality trait if you plan on getting further along in your career." Smirking his full lips, he moved past her, tweaking her nipple.

In the silence of the space left by his passing, she inhaled sharply. He had turned up the heat on her slow burn. She clamped her jaw shut, observing one alpha male who was quite full of himself this morning. *Well,* she mused, *they'd just see about that, Mister Fancy Pants.*

She silently snickered, realizing as he swaggered past that he wasn't wearing any pants. She swung around, not about to let the sight of his tight ass get away. Shawn was a product of Mother Nature's best efforts and very much worth watching.

She followed in his wake, certain that his sudden shift in attitude was linked to a greater plan. Early on, she'd gotten a sense of how his mind worked as her boss. He didn't simply see the issues before him, he saw the ripple effects. He constantly prodded his staff to see cause and effects play out and to be two steps ahead of the client. Either he'd lost his keen analytical ability or he sucked with getting a woman—this woman—to bend to his will, if this was his new plan of the day. Right now she wanted to arm-wrestle him and make him bend.

"I don't think that's any of your concern. I can handle myself. Just show me the ropes. After this week, we might just go back to business associates. Right, boss?" She gazed up at him, meeting his eyes that pierced her.

Without a word, he crossed the distance dividing them. "Don't underestimate what I may or may not feel. I promised to help you. What you need isn't a short-term fix. This isn't a type of bandaging situation, solved with a down-and dirty-bang. I've seen good people who let their natures get in the way. They think they look like humans most of the time, so why not live in denial? Things can get crazy. Fast. One day someone will punch the wrong button and you'll be all leopardess, out of fucking control. And then what? You're an alpha. Untrained, you're a time bomb waiting to blow." His voice was a deep rumble in his chest.

Her head snapped up. The image of Cole flashed before her eyes. What Shawn said was true. No matter how much he pushed, he was teaching her to withstand, not react. Again, she'd reacted without thinking. "You're right. I get that these are lessons. That's why I'm here. No argument. I don't want to shatter apart. Not because of someone else."

"Get dressed, kitten. We'll go down, eat, and then we can decide how the rest of the day will play out. You may find that your heat is roaring and need to extinguish your lust. How do you feel right now?" He ran the tip of his knuckle under her jaw.

A wave of chill bumps broke out. At the mention of lust, her body blazed into a wildfire, engulfing her in a conflagration. The flesh between her legs went hot and wet. Definitely his impact on her, all right. "I need you. Right now."

"I knew you were getting edgy for a reason. I'm about to lose it, too. Ride my cock. Fuck me, baby."

She glanced down. His ever-ready erection saluted her. This time it was she who hit the sheets first. She knelt on her heels waiting for him. He was right there, next to her. Shawn punched a few pillows before settling back against the headboard, one knee bent and lounging in a sexy repose in wait of her.

"Let's start with this." Diana handed him a foil packet. The feel of his fingers brushing across her palm unfurled her claws from the tips of her fingers.

The sound of the condom unfurling down his shaft held her rapt attention. His cock stood straight up from his balls that lay tight against his groin.

Shawn was too gorgeous for her own peace of mind. She eased his knee down on to the mattress, and then straddled his legs before taking hold of the base of him. A few swipes of his flat, broad cockhead against her erect clit made her dizzy.

"God, you feel so good." His cocked pulsed against her opening, like a live wire connected to every nerve in her body.

Then, all at once, she pushed down, moaning as her swollen tissue stretched around his crown, and then she lowered herself, taking in the length of him.

If he'd fucked her hard last night, she was about to give him an encore production. Excitement spiked her pulse. Being on top, she relished each time he groaned or gasped. She ground her hips against his steely body, lowering her chest so her breasts could trace a pattern across his chest. He was so powerful under her, and his roaring groans spiked her desire.

"Does this feel good?" he asked, letting her control how deep he went into her body.

"Awesome." She ground herself against him, taking his bottom lip between her teeth.

His hands cupped her bottom and then he lazily traced a finger around her clit as she lifted up. Slipping lightly downward, she poised, and his feather touch disappeared.

He sucked his finger, watching her intently, and then his finger swiped across her anus. Her breath caught. She lifted up and his finger returned, and this time went straight to her ass. One of his fingertips stayed put, the other probing her as he pushed in and she lowered herself.

The pain made every nerve cell come alive. Her pussy clenched. She lifted up and had to slam back down on him. His finger pushed into her. She couldn't stop moving up and down on him; closing her eyes, she gripped his shoulders.

"Do you like this?" he whispered in a gravelly voice.

"Babe, you're driving me wild. I'm going to shatter apart." Her body swayed, and then her climax hit full-blast.

Her orgasm enveloped her; spasms wracked her pussy, tightly wrapping his swelling his cock. He flexed and shuddered, his hands driving her hips down as far as she could go against him. Shawn pushed her backward before he continued to drive himself into her. Ramming his way into bliss, he rode out another *more-gasm* and he moaned, kissing her face.

She was accustomed to his way of climaxing, in which he made certain she'd found release to the point that her brain no longer functioned, yet her body responded, climaxing again and again.

He groaned, "Kitten, I've got to have your ass. Soon, or I don't know if I can survive this. I've got to release my semen into your body. Pussy or ass, you're mine."

Chapter 10

He sat at the head of the table with her on his right, exactly as he'd imagined. He ran his fingers along the wooden surface, smooth-grained from years of beeswax polish. If his parents were alive today, his father would be seated here, his mother at the other end, and twenty or so guests would be seated in between them. The mahogany dining table had been in his family for several generations. He'd grown up coming to this table in his parents' home.

Diana was a first in many ways for him, including being the first woman to visit here and occupy more than a single night in one of his apartments. Her scent swam in his veins. If he stopped after her cycle, he doubted they could ever return to staring at each other over a desk, calmly discussing retail design as though this had never happened. He scratched the side of his jaw as he watched her movements.

Her refusal to wholeheartedly accept his idea of living together twisted his clear thinking. They both very much felt the same way. Or was that some illusion he'd harvested from fantasy? Now he was frustrated he couldn't achieve the last objective: having her safely here. With him.

She ate her food daintily, as if she had all the time in the world. There would have been no complaint from his parents on this arrangement, if there was a future for them. His parents might have balked at her severed ties to her own family, preferring to have the traditional daughter-in-law arrangement, but that would have been the only flawed part of this equation.

And who knows, had he been the one to seek her hand, perhaps her family wouldn't have cut her off.

He tenderly picked up her hand, inspecting the lines along her palm. "No spilled milk issues?"

"None," she smiled over at him. "See anything good there? Tell me what's going to happen."

"Yes, in your future there seems to be a move. High elevation…a home with lots of light."

"Too funny," she whispered. "I meant the far future."

His future. Her family. After helping her sort through her issues of heritage, it would be right to help her heal her familial wounds. That issue was for another day to belabor; no use in delving into the realm of spilled milk in her past. Or his. Right now, he shelved the idea of getting her back in contact with her family, knowing this argument he would return to when he'd cut through her reservations.

Shawn's reverie was dissolved by the expression on the face of his housekeeper, Mrs. Wells, whose curious gaze sparkled with unspoken words. Mrs. Wells refilled their cups. "There's coffee on the sideboard if you'd like more."

"Are you here all day?" Shawn wiped his mouth, remembering his plans.

"Yes. I saw your note about a delivery. I'll take care of the set-up of the furniture that's been ordered. The corner room on the east wing?"

"Yes. Have the furniture remain on coasters, in case there's some wrangling."

"And dinner tonight?" Mrs. Wells asked.

"Something that we can heat up when we return. We'll be out for a while."

Mrs. Wells nodded and exchanged a smile with Diana before leaving. Even dressed in a simple blouse and skirt, Diana, with her hair hanging loose and her unaffected countenance, struck a chord and reminded him of his mother and sister. Shannon would easily welcome Diana. They'd shared a similar fate. But where the hell his sister was at the moment was a mystery.

He'd been wrong in suggesting Diana should take an interest in those around her. More than likely, her reserve came from being deep in thought. His sister had been hell-on-wheels as a socialite. Not exactly a success story.

He met Diana's steady gaze. "I've ordered office furniture. I realize how important a connection to your work is and I don't want you to feel stressed during this time. Just the basics to set up a place for you to work and get you going. You'll let me know what you need."

"Thank you, I'm running on a deadline that's getting shorter by the day."

"If you mean the Ikashi account, not to worry. They've sent over another revision pushing out the due date. A somewhat more complicated design and one I'm certain you'll handle without batting an eyelash. The room will be ready by lunch and then you can take a look at the revised bid. Does that work for you?"

"When did you find out? I'm glad I mentioned something."

"My kitten's claws are showing. By phone. Before breakfast, while you were dressing. I have no plans on holding back from you. Not in business or here in our bedroom."

"My phone reception is awful. I checked and wanted to speak to you. I'm glad you brought up business. Did you plan on keeping me sequestered if I misbehaved?" She studied him before her mouth curved up into a teasing grin. "Am I given a choice of what works or shall you exert your will, leaving me little room but to agree now that we've crossed the boss-employee boundaries? I need structure is what I'm saying."

Damn. What he wanted her to do with her voluptuous mouth. The momentum and tension brewing between them didn't seem to lessen over time. Right now, he wanted her more than last night. This was very much a hot cycle, never mind heat.

"It's my job to oversee. I don't step on toes. Least of all yours. I fully intend to give you what you need to make this arrangement work. But we have to talk openly. First and foremost."

"I get that about you. I always have, yet now you do seem… possessive."

He looped his fingers with hers. "I promise, where work is concerned, I'd never second guess or countermand your design principles. But in the bedroom, I'm in charge. Nothing has changed in that regard, kitten." He rubbed his fingers across hers. "Is that agreeable?"

"More than agreeable."

"Good. We'd better begin preparing for our run. If you're through with breakfast, we can begin training."

"You've hardly eaten a morsel. Aren't you hungry?" She reached out stroking the top of his knuckles.

His pulse pounded at the thought of chasing her up the side of the mountain. If he didn't stop thinking about the things he'd do once he caught her, he might just give her a preview.

"I'm fine. I don't think eating will help the hunger I've got brewing." He spoke between clenched jaws. Her touch infused him with the need to possess her. He'd acknowledged it without entirely acting upon it until now. He curled his hands into fists. Each second in her presence was a fight to maintain his self-control. Training Diana…hell, he doubted he could teach her to tie a shoelace at this rate. "Join me, and you can see for yourself. Am I correct, then, that this will be your first time being pursued?"

He got up and held her chair. The sweet smell of her—now mixed with his own scent embedded in her skin—intoxicated him.

"Yes. My husband and I were childhood friends. We escaped our families' expectations together. He protected me. He never would have hunted me."

"Yet you've run freely this year. And still not one chase?"

"I was lucky within the nature preserve. No leopards were present. I've escaped the plight of many leopardess shifters." The amused curve of her lips coupled with the glittery look in her eyes kept him in rapt attention. "Sweetheart, make no mistake. I will track you down. If I have to move heaven and earth, I will."

"I've no doubt. Actually, from the moment we met, I fantasized this is where we'd end up. It's also what I feared. Now, I see there's really no choice."

"We both put a good faith effort into avoiding each other at work. As shifters, I think we knew the risks each presented to the other. You still have a choice. Diana, I want this to be what you freely desire."

"I only meant that once we connected, and with what we've experienced, it would be hard to forget you. Don't you feel the same?"

His gaze lowered when she brushed aside her hair, away from her neck. Several bite marks were revealed. By tonight, he would make many more marks over her body, if she acquiesced by agreeing to let him claim a part of her. Biting one's mate was a time-honored leopard tradition if they were to be bonded. She had a choice to keep this simple or take their relationship to the next level even if wasn't true bonding. The thought of mounting her assaulted his calm.

This chase could be an exercise, a foundational step in her alpha training. Or…the second-to-last step for both of them. Considering their past experiences with lovers and mistakes, going slow together made sense regardless of what she might wish.

"This is our destiny. We're both alphas. No other type of leopard would bring us fulfillment or push us to boundaries where we need to…grow."

"Me. Yes, there's no question. But you? Shawn, what do you need?"

"You're not the only one who has bad memories and issues with trust. But you are the only one who must learn that to gain power, you must let go of the walls that box you in and keep you small. Before you can stand tall, you must be comfortable bending, adjusting, learning to put aside your ego. You will follow my directives without question. They are for your own good. We're not going on some well-charted walking path up the mountain. Where we'll cross has been worn, but only by strong and able leopards. This isn't some pseudo-challenge I've arranged as a token ceremony. You'll be pushed to use the prowess of an alpha leopardess. There are sheer drops, and plenty of places where rock ledges can give way."

Flinching, she stared back at him, blinking once. "And you're confident that I'll possess the required level of proficiency?"

"I'd never suggest it otherwise. All I'm asking for is your trust." Footsteps echoed in the hallway down the hall.

"Is someone here?" Diana asked.

"That should be Tristen. He's here to help. Diana, you've nothing to fear. I put my trust in Tristen for years. I told you the extent that he helped me. I want your trust. I know it takes time."

"My trust? That's more than obvious each time we discuss tonight. This feels more like blindly leaping without a parachute."

He laced his fingers through hers and looped his arm over her shoulders. "If you feel you can't do what is asked, all you have to say is 'no' and I won't push you. There's still time for us both to step back. I don't want you to give up, but I also can't be the one to dictate how your life unfolds. Only you can determine which road to take and what bridge to cross. I'll help you in all ways except making the decision."

"I do trust you in all the ways that are important. I just need some time to learn how to trust myself."

Tristen met them in the outer entryway. The man stood almost six foot four, with a severe expression. The way Tristen's eyes flashed under a brooding stare expressed his concern. He jutted his chin out, settling back on his heels, waiting for them.

"Good to see you, Diana," he said in a monotone voice. Tristen leaned forward, extending a thick arm for a handshake. His buzzed hair gleamed platinum, framing his skull.

Shawn shook his head at Tristen's robotic address. "No need to be so dour."

"Says you," Tristen retorted, pulling open the front door. "It's going to be a clear day. Near perfect." He stepped onto the porch, putting on a pair of sunglasses. When Tristen descended the front steps into the direct sunlight, glare lifted from his colorless hair like a halo. "Tonight as well. Excellent conditions are expected. Fin's changing the oil in your Jeep. We'll be on our mark come nightfall."

"It's a short walk to the place where we'll begin to train." Shawn kept his arm around Diana's shoulders. In human form, her thin bones were fragile beneath his hand.

This wasn't the first time he'd participated in the ceremony for paired leopards. What he'd do with Diana was like a chase between leopards to be mated, but she was learning her nature, not coming back here to be his mate. His chest squeezed for a second on that thought. There was no arguing he wanted all of Diana, but he still felt unsure about taking the leap into forever since she refused to commit.

Christ, right now she seemed one foot out the door if he didn't watch his step. "Your family much for the traditional mating chase?"

She blinked before she turned away. "Yes. They're very conservative about all that stuff."

"We used to prepare for days for a bonding chase with family and friends. When my parents were alive, this was a time for partying and a celebration that rivaled a wedding. At least a week was set aside and the culmination of the paired leopards' run marked the beginning of a union."

Nowadays, these traditions were less about the journey and more about the destination. Many couples were more interested in posting photographs about where they'd gone, as if this was a human honeymoon. Some couples agreed to forsake the tradition altogether, opting for a church wedding where the actual mating was done on the wedding night.

Shifters had learned to adapt and fit into society. Their kind didn't roam neighborhoods in primal form. Except for ones like the hard-headed shifter next to him. He snorted. For Diana, a conservative shifter, that would be much the same as walking down the sidewalk naked.

There was no way to remain silent on this issue. "You've a real blind spot as to your own needs. There's a shifter time and place to cut loose, and that's the reason why Quinn and I opened the Den. Do you realize there are shifter kidnappings? Under-reported, of course, but still the practice goes on."

"We've all heard of the female shifters who go missing."

"That's a slight understatement. You don't believe they run around wild only to be captured or killed, or even worse, sold to deviant animal shows?"

"I think many things happen. Females may run away and be taken advantage of. I appreciate everything you've said. That's why I'm here."

He worried that if Diana couldn't or wouldn't go through with this training, she would run the risk of wildly shifting and ending up as another shifter gone missing, never to be seen again.

They walked in silence, their feet crunching the gravel path in back of the house, then headed across a smooth expanse of lawn into a line of evergreen trees. Once inside the shaded wooded area, the temperature of the air dropped remarkably. Diana's skin cooled under his fingers. "Where are we going?" she whispered.

"Just up ahead. There's a small building that we use for meetings."

Tristen snorted without saying a word. Diana's soft curves swayed and bumped against Shawn. She rubbed her cheek against his thumb at her shoulder. "Mmm," she said softly.

He slowed his walk, uncertain if any of them was up for this task. The rivers would be running high, currents twisting and tumbling, speeding along, keeping boulders hidden until a body slammed and broke against them. She'd be lucky to get by with just getting her paws damp. His mind raced, conceptualizing every possible scenario, and what might be done to lessen the chance that she'd succumb to the elements. Fuck, this was a fabulous time to reconsider.

As though Tristen could read his mind, he turned. "She'll be fine. If you can undo your death grip for a couple of hours, *dad*?" The wolf's scowl was obvious, even behind a set of wraparound sunglasses.

Shawn retorted, "You're one to talk, *gramps*." Tristen had proven himself over and over. Today, the wolf shifter was about to undertake accessing Diana's leopardess nature using sophisticated neuro-technology. He was the only key holder Shawn trusted to unlock Diana's nature. Someone else might leach her primal leopardess power, stealing a portion, but never Tristen.

Up ahead through the tree trunks, the side of the red building came into view. Constructed to resemble a farm building, complete with tin roof, the building had every modern convenience including enough technology to rival a small government. Tristen camped out here along with Fin, across the land on the East Ridge. Shawn didn't ask what they did and they never offered an explanation.

Tristen had established he was indispensable as his right-hand man and had become his friend over the years. Trained in neuropsychology, he'd stopped working in his field after coming back from Afghanistan. He had served a number of years with Fin as combat soldiers. Both Tristen and Shawn's parents were long gone. Shawn's respect had coalesced into a solid friendship with these two men and, together with Quinn, they formed a tight bond around Denver.

Tristen unlocked the door. He opened it and stood back, letting Diana enter first. As with the house, the building used motion sensors and automated climate control.

Shawn stopped in front of Tristen as the wolf shifter spoke in a low voice. "I assure you, Diana will have everything one might need to navigate over the terrain. Just give me a few hours. I've never let you down." Tristen's unblinking eyes held his gaze.

A low hum of white noise floated around them from several pieces of neurological instrumentation and machinery. Electronic equipment gave off an electrical smell. He watched Diana's reaction, the fluttering of her cat-eyes changing.

"What shall we do here?" she asked.

"Tristen has been instructed to work out a program to unlock your inner nature, freeing you from the obvious walls you have built as defenses. These are roadblocks to the decision-making required in your primal form. It's also why you can't remember anything when you shift; it is actually a type of psychological veil that keeps you safe from what you fear. This safety net will tie you up when you need to act instead of react."

"How will this impact my thinking when I'm not shifting? Or when I'm in a…cycle?" Her face glowed with color.

"You'll have access to memories. Right now those memories are sealed off. They exist, but you've no way to retrieve them. Soon you will."

She walked around the office, peering at the equipment and charts. "Is this another one of your businesses?"

"Not exactly a business. More like a service we're trying out. This is part of what I spend time doing. There are huge numbers of shifters who live on the fringes of society because they don't fit into a world of modern conveniences. You left your family and have been cut off. If you'd stayed, you'd have become an adult shifter and learned what resources were available. Instead, you've been out of the loop. My family has been responsible for governing the Western part of North America for generations. As you know, I'm responsible for a newly-formed board that assists shifters seeking mediation when conflicts occur. This is one step."

"This is so far from justice, graphic design, restaurants, retail engineering, and a mating club. Is there anything you don't do?"

"It's all related. Design in another form, a resource in a necessary form."

"And Tristen? I don't understand his position here."

Shawn inhaled. Tristen had moved up ahead into the room where'd she enter as one type of leopard and come out a very different type, if the program took hold within her synapses.

"Before the war, this was his specialty. He got out of the medical field when things got complicated. Now he's agreed to help as a personal favor. Tristen designed a type of neuro-deprogramming method to get behind the barriers a shifter erects. Once he is behind those barriers, he inserts hundreds of hours of brain training to make your thought patterns flexible. There's nothing nefarious or evil. He limbers up your brain, to become just like when you were young. I'll be here to monitor your progress as Tristen employs a series of exercises while you're in a REM sleep."

"Brain games. If he finds the memory of where I lost my keys, can he take notes and let me know?"

"This training doesn't provide a movie of your thoughts. More like a map and insertion points. That's all. I promise."

"I hope you have an excellent memory for all the promises you've made."

Shawn stopped outside the room, lifted her hand, and ran his lips over her palm. "I do. Each one is tattooed deep within me."

Chapter 11

Diana woke back inside the bedroom. She'd been dreaming of running, jumping effortlessly, powerful muscles bunching as she leaped through space. Only this time, the freedom she'd experienced was exhilarating, without boundaries. She blinked, trying to recapture the totality of the dream in lieu of a patchwork quilt of images. Her mind drifted away from the dream as she moved into wakefulness.

She sat up, naked under the sheet, and glanced about. The long shadows within the room indicated it was late afternoon. It had been morning when they'd begun the mind training. She didn't recall anything after lying down on a chaise lounge that made her think of a dentist's office.

Tristen's voice had lulled her into sleep using some sort of hypnosis while she distinctly recalled the feel of Shawn's hands on her skin, the scent of him, and his soothing words comforting her.

Absent was the perception of sorrow that had infused her life by being alone as she had been these last months. A wave of guilt washed over her. Cole was dead. Shouldn't she still feel a deep, abiding remorse? She rolled back onto the pillows. This shouldn't be the end of her guilt trip. She shuddered under a wave of uncertainty, pressing her fingers to her temples. In the last week, her life had twisted and turned. Tonight, another major stepping stone lay before her. Only this wasn't the type of step she could slip upon—not high in the mountains surrounding the bedroom in which she was safely seated.

The door opened and Shawn leaned against the doorframe, as he'd done only one night ago. As before, his appearance made her breath catch in her chest. The light spilled in from the windows and he wasn't cloaked in shadows. The lines of his face were in plain sight. A five o'clock shadow gave him a rugged, dangerous appearance.

"Hello, stranger," she said, scissoring her legs.

"I didn't want to disturb you, but I had to find out if you were awake." He peeled himself off the wall, sauntering toward her with more catlike grace than she'd ever witnessed from him. The air—once static—swirled about them both. She inhaled his scent, caressing her from head to toe, raw and lustful. A skittering snarl, one she'd never imagined possessing, tore from her lips.

Without any time to think, her claws sprang outward. Her skin reacted like a wool sweater put in hot water. He was coming for her. Her leopardess perception sensed a chase was imminent. "What do you want?" she asked in a low voice. The leopardess inside her sought the means to make her way from the room, yet longed also to stay, in order to submit. Primal and too powerful to resist. Then an entirely different urge overcame her like a volcanic eruption.

She wanted to feel him behind her. Mounting her and grinding into her body. Unsheathed and spraying his seed inside the walls of her womb. The moon would bathe the mountain in light tonight. This was the pinnacle of her heat cycle. What he'd tried to describe and couldn't.

"Kitten, I'm going to have you. Just a taste to make certain you find your way back. I promise it will be quick."

"No," she retorted, without giving his offer any thought.

"You will give into me. Do you want me to get Tristen or Fin? They wouldn't be pleased to assist with this part. But they would. You don't seem the type to want an exhibition. Not the first time."

"Are you saying you'd let them participate?"

"They'd never touch you. No man would dare without risking a challenge. But they will do what they're told. Especially if it means saving you. I think Tristen is quite taken with you in a scientific-subject way."

All the while she kept her eyes on him. Every one of his movements was loud and clear: he wanted to fuck her in a way she'd never experienced. Until meeting him, the things he'd suggested were beyond imagining. If they were going to mate for a lifetime, her leopardess *knowing* realized that she had to make him earn the right. Was that where this was now headed?

"I thought this was just supposed to be temporary?" She swallowed, uncertain what she desired.

It was right to give her alpha the chase they both deserved. One where her mate could prove himself. And one where she in turn gave him something to remember. This was her whole future. Not so simple as a chase, followed by simple sex.

There were the tales retold to children of how mates outgunned or outmaneuvered until the last second. An alpha would want a story worthy of repeating. This was a sexual coming-out party, with only two guests.

"I'm not tricking you, Diana. This isn't a secret ceremony. I promise you, you'll own your life by the end of tonight. And I will claim a small part of you. If you want to break our ties, you'll still have that doorway. This isn't a leopard bonding, sweetheart. I'm training you as you wanted."

"I'm not going to give you what you want just because you ask nicely. Shawn, all female leopards know the rules."

"We discussed this already. I give you my word. You must know what markings to keep track of as you find your way. Without the scent, you'll get lost, or worse, tricked or trapped. Plenty of poachers would love to bag a big cat. I will have you to protect you, but I won't screw my own chase. Baby, I want to let you run just so I can get hold of you. I promise, only a few strokes and that's it. When your cells absorb my precum, you'll be set. Let me have you, Diana. Now." His voice thundered, making her flinch.

And then he was on her. His linen pants and no shirt were no barrier. His warm body against her stymied her bolting. "I can't," she panted bewildered.

"You will." He became naked, rubbing his body over hers. His cock was harder than she remembered, if that was even possible. He pinned her body, his knees pressed her thighs open, and then he bit into her shoulder at the base of her neck. A feeling of being paralyzed overcame her and she couldn't move. Teeth—or rather, fangs—sank into her skin and he released his grip on her arms.

A bottle appeared and he squeezed something into his hand. This was heaven and she could do no more than lie under him. Cold liquid bathed her ass opening. His fingers gently swiped her pussy. Had she been able to utter a word, she would have called out for him to do whatever he wanted.

Then his fingers were at her ass, pressing, swirling between her cheeks, creating the most delicious torture. He bit down harder as the pressure from his cock increased against her anus, and he worked himself into her with just the tip of his crown.

All too soon, she was opening to him, while his hips flexed and then he breached her opening. Pain—red-hot and scalding— assaulted her nerves and she reached to scratch him. His hands caught her wrists, hauling her arms above her head. The head of his cock nudged inside her anus without doing more than titillate her. Shawn gyrated, pushing little by little past her sphincter muscles, and then plunging his head inside her again. The pain made her buck, trying to get him off her. He came out of her for a second before he rocked back and this time pumped into her with greater force. One thrust and he was inside her, not far but enough to make tears flood her eyes.

Closing her eyelids, she froze, overwhelmed. Taking in his length and size were tearing at her. Together they lay without moving. Then warm lips were at her throat instead of teeth. Shawn licked her skin, making her body tingle. His mouth reclaimed her, pouring murmurs into her mouth as he kissed her, releasing her wrists and wrapping her with his arms.

The burning stopped and all that remained was the need to have more of him. Pleasure so sharp, so intense, sliced through the haze and she rocked toward him this time. Oh, the feeling was more than artful; it was sinful and dark.

Ecstasy she could no longer hide, bliss, poured around her, whispering to her to ride his cock. In response, he nipped her lip and arched up, sliding backward. She felt his head withdrawing from her, a moment of power, and then he was back, moving slowly, sliding into her, allowing her the chance to accommodate his cock. He withdrew so quickly, she shuddered and cried out, not in pain, but in surprise.

"Can you take more of me?" His hands snaked down, cupping her ass cheeks.

"Yes. I think so."

Just as soon as she'd agreed, he opened her wide to him. His cock rimmed her anus, firmly gliding and stretching her, pressure building with sinful heat, searing mixed with pleasure so hot she wanted to feel the length of him. Pushing her breasts against his chest, she threaded her fingers into his hair and pulled forcefully back.

Growling, he surged into her, his dick ramming, then stopping, and he withdrew, lowering himself over her. She pulled his hair again, wanting to anger him and make him slam back into her. No movement, only his shallow breaths followed by a curse.

"One more stroke, but that is all. If I give in and take you completely, then I've not kept my promise. Do you understand? Don't beg me or plead—one more stroke and then we've got to run. I've spilled enough inside you that you can pick me out of a crowded Moroccan bazaar on market day." All her thoughts tried to make sense of what he said. She struggled to understand this delicious sensation was not going to last, but downright stop. In one more stroke.

This was the ultimate tease. No wonder every leopardess tried to find her way back. Who wouldn't want to taste this pleasure again, knowing at the end of the chase her alpha would take her and bury himself deep in her body? Two exquisite sensations--stark, bright, and biting--to make her crave release in a way she'd never known. Well, she knew now, didn't she?

"Please, then. But hard, Shawn, fuck me good. Make me remember."

"Yes. You're right. But not from behind. I'm going to give you only what you deserve. Later tonight, I promise I'll fill you so full you'll never forget my dick in your ass."

Shawn curled his hands around her cheeks, hauling her up. She gazed up into his gleaming eyes, his pupils fully dilated, and her breath evaporated as if burnt from her lungs. What she saw bordered on savage and ruthless, utterly feral.

This was no easy task for him, and she understood that fact as if it had smacked her in the head. The glowing light emanating from his eyes captivated her with intensity, leaving her in no way uncertain he would find her tonight.

His body tensed, betraying what he wanted to deliver. She didn't dare move a muscle but couldn't help quivering from the heat in his eyes. The spark he produced ran deep in her body. Her pussy pulsed and clenched. The feel of his hard head rubbed her anus. He gritted his teeth, working a muscle along his jaw, and then he arched back, way…way back.

Before her brain took hold, his cock thrust inside her, and moved beyond her rim into her body in one forceful slam. His balls swayed against her ass, the muscles in his shoulders bunched, and his arms shook. Struggling against his own hunger, he snarled, revealing four large canines snapping at the air. Pumping without moving deeper, the complete sensation of pain twisting and teasing her wrapped her in bliss and exploded.

Her sex reacted with a deep-seated throbbing, making her gasp. The way he held her open made her want to push down, all the way to the base of his cock. But she couldn't be responsible for making him come undone. Heat spread in all directions over her body, flaming across her skin in a heat-cycle blaze.

Shawn came out of her and pulled her into a tight hug, holding her flush against his body. Hot kisses covered her jaw, face, and then his mouth found hers. His tongue tangled over and around her mouth until she returned his kiss with the fervor of a promise. She wanted him and now had to have him in ways she'd only imagined until just a moment ago.

Adrenaline dripped into her bloodstream. Excitement roiled through her veins. Tonight they'd run as leopards.

Chapter 12

Only a thin strip of will power kept him from thrusting into Diana's ass all the way. Fuck, she was tight and her flesh hugged his dick. He worked himself into her little by little, holding back, and then tasted supreme pleasure in one powerful thrust. Soft and silky, he slid his finger into her pussy, finding her wet and so ready to explode.

Tonight he'd capture her and then there'd be no mercy. This was the night that they'd both remember; and heaven-fucking-help them if they didn't remain together. No way another leopard would ever compare in their black books of carnal history. He was about to rank number one if he had anything to say about it. He might not mate with her, but he'd fuck his name into her DNA, mind, and soul before her heat cycle was done. After tonight, he'd always be a part of her, just as much as she was a part of him. He kissed the top of her head, rubbing his cheek along her, marking her with his scent.

Strange, too, that he wanted her scent all over him. Never had he even considered what it meant to wear a leopardess's scent. "Mark me," he growled. At the same time, he wanted to fuck her, unmercifully this time as the other times, but knew he'd have to hold back, keeping his semen boiling. His scent would grow stronger if he stayed hungry for her. He drew her nipple between his fingertips, tweaking her peak. "Now, Diana."

She laughed. "I wanted to see if you'd make me do as you wanted."

"Don't tempt me to teach you a lesson on top of what I already have in store for you. Seeing that pretty little ass of yours painted crimson would be too surreal for words."

He'd already marked Diana. Since yesterday, he'd fucked her without tiring. What he did bordered on savage brutality in needing to possess her, and he wanted to fuck her again. Shit, what he had in mind for later that night replaced any guilt he felt about his inability to hold back. Each orgasm exploded, rocketed through his body and out his cock, with hot, streaming semen leaving him shattered. Where the hell had his Zen sensibility gone? Right the fuck out the window.

He twisted, took hold of her roughly, and seated her on top of his lap. His cock pushed up between her legs. Achingly erect, he ignored the throbbing pulse of his member. Soon he'd be buried inside her. What was to come amounted to the erosion of any question from either of their minds—she was his.

Until another male challenged him, openly and where there were no morals or justice. Or if she left of her own volition. Until then, Diana would belong fully and completely to him. Only him. After tonight, every shift of her emerald eyes would display his possession. If it meant spanking her until her ass suffused with crimson color, then all the better that her memory would be Technicolor-brilliant. Every fucking detail emblazoned vividly within in his recollection and hers.

He wove his fingers into her hair and yanked. Automatically, this close to a run, she bared her teeth and hissed without thought. Both of them were a hairsbreadth from shifting. Teeth and eyes were already catlike. Their rosette markings were dark black against a rose-golden background.

"Kiss me one last time before we leave," he said, his voice harsh and demanding.

She sighed, pouting, and said, "Be gentle this last time."

His chest hammered. How did she know he craved the time when he could display the torment she imposed, leaving him unstable and vulnerable? He released his grasp on her hair, and rubbed his hands down her back, stopping to graze the swell of her ass cheeks where he was certain his relief would be found. Without warning, she slipped from his grasp.

She inched back away from him off the bed, cocking her brow, hands planted at her hips. "Should I demand you catch me first? Or better yet…make me." She turned from facing him, her body rippling in shredded, lithe beauty.

Her eyes flashed, mocking him to the core. To get hold of her required that he still his body. Even his thoughts would give him away. He centered himself, pushing forward even though he was seated. Calf muscles tightened, and he slightly rose up onto the balls of his feet. Behind half-closed eyes he noted the direction of her gaze and, more importantly, how she oriented her body, slightly toward the doorway. The fuzzy world receded, leaving her to become his locked-on target. One thought—and he had her. Reaching out to put her off balance while his body moved in the opposite direction, he careened into her direct path.

"No fair," she squealed. "Let me go."

"That was your second mistake," he said, lifting her arms above her head. Naked and open to him, she'd have no choice but to give in to hunger. He leisurely licked along the side of her neck where he'd already marked her heavily. As he lowered his head, he brought her arms down and secured them behind her. Diana's form rippled in his arms--graceful, fluid, serpentine movements to curve her torso across his upper body. He pulled her wrists firmly behind her, pressing her firm, high breasts up against his chest.

"Your first mistake was believing I'd be fair. When it comes to having you…baby, I'm not playing some game. If there are rules, I'll break every one of them to get to you. That's my promise. I get you in the end. I'll destroy anything—anyone—that stands in my way."

No more words. Syllables spoken were useless. He kissed her in a way that left them both breathless. He kissed her to remember. He kissed her to make sure she'd find her way back. He kissed hello, not goodbye.

• • •

Stepping onto the damp, dew-covered ground, he observed the earth was just beginning to cool in the evening air. He lifted his muzzle to sniff the air. Thoughts swirled around him, none of which he wanted to consider. In leopard form, he was free to just be. He snapped his tail, impatient for Diana to begin the ascent up the first level of cliffs.

He gazed upward along the western side of the mountain ridge. If she was going to complete her training, she'd need to make this climb unfettered and navigating on her own, defining herself as an alpha worthy of respect. Her scent and sound would carry across the air and then be carried further in messages by other Rocky Mountain shifters with access to this mountain range. The hairs all over his skin itched with the sense of wariness and need to protect her. He closed his eyes against the truth. If only this was a traditional chase for them.

Shawn peered into the night sky and panted to taste the air, thoroughly savoring wisps of Diana's scent. The experience was akin to sipping wine, her fragrance of leopardess musk so sweet and intoxicating. He held back from caterwauling. If he distracted her during a leap, she might miss her destination.

There, he heard her. Her low, muted growl echoing up the side of the sheer granite wall that lay before them. From the sound of her, she'd be somewhat north of his location. She'd more than likely been loping to have gotten that far from where Tristen and Fin had dropped them off.

A narrow, naturally carved path could be found if she followed her leopard intuition. Tristen had worked with her for hours, untangling her neural pathways he'd said were fried or burnt. He laid down new tracks, repairing what he could. Before leaving, Tristen had said Diana needed more work but she'd do fine, more than fine, tonight.

Shawn raced through the terrain, claws digging into the moist detritus, clods of earth spewing as he tore up the distance between Diana and him. Prickly rose caught in his coat, scratching his nose, and making him blink. At the end of a patch of shale, bristling reed grass swayed. He leapt over and into the gravelly stretch that brought him out into the open, away from the line of trees, a border defining where they'd begin climbing sandstone foothills.

It was a great warm-up for him, allowing the burn to loosen his muscles, and he readapted to leopard form. He brought his back paws to meet his forepaws, before bursting into a leap driving him upward onto a low-lying ledge. He inhaled. Diana had left her mark. His pulse skyrocketed from a rush of adrenaline. She'd made it to the first point, over two miles from their drop-off and was in front of him, nearly able to outdistance him. But he'd not really tried—had he? Rocky debris scattered under his paws. He left claw marks on the side of the broken boulders.

A canopy of white spruce covered the sky again, and the air condensed in the moisture-laden upper foothills. Shawn's speed increased as his step lightened. As his muscles worked out the knots leftover from his human form, he was pure power racing up the hills. A snarl let loose from his throat to let Diana know she was not alone. In quick response, her echoing hiss relayed to him she didn't need his help. Even in leopard form, his mouth pulled tight against his fangs before he had to choose between jumping right or left. It was not enough to follow behind her; he knew he must almost circle around, coming up on her flank, to overtake her as well as protect her. His best plan was to sweep forward without her knowing it.

This time of year was ripe for mating. Bears were thick as pine needles, as were cougars roaming higher up. Mountain lions stayed on the lowdown but wouldn't think twice about attacking a leopard out for a hunt coming upon a den or litter.

He paused, contracting his body, then, effortless in streamlined fortitude, leapt and landed on a nearby ledge ten feet to his left. Continuing to climb, he surreptitiously moved away from Diana. This action was both nerve-wracking and electrifying. Scanning the upward slope only yards away, Shawn quickly realized this was not a path he was unaccustomed to taking. In leaving her to the path of leopards, he'd taken another, unmarked course.

The clouds streamed over the sky. The darkness gave away again, displaying ledges that wound upward, rich with drops and missing sections. Rocks gave way without warning, tumbling down the hillside. He slowed his gait, squinting to follow the maze of centuries-old carved rock, not wanting to blindly head down a course only to dead-end—or worse, leap into an abyss that had nothing to do with the sweet softness between Diana's legs.

A crashing howl of wolves, Tristen and Fin were home. Alerting the mountainside to stay back. He shook his head at his worrywart staff.

Coming down the path, he ran over the last part of shale, noticing the change in terrain. Small rock and sandy dirt lay underneath his paws. He jumped up to the overhang above his head, then leapt again, zigzagging a hopscotch pattern until he was well into the rugged alpine landscape.

Water dripped down the side of the mountain, cutting away micromillimeters one at a time until gorges formed in these bedrock exposures. The side of the mountain twisted as his breath did, not from exertion but from the elevation. There were fewer trees up along this side of the mountain. A few stragglers, willows and a few heather trees, but for the most part low-lying scrub.

Rocks pelted his fur from above. Then more, followed by loose, larger rock from somewhere up the side of the mountain. He had to get off this ledge, and fast. He could jump down and continue a descent or try to reach the next ledge over. Without considering anything but getting closer to Diana, he leapt the twenty feet, tearing his claws into the side of the ledge as he struck the edge mid-belly.

His back paws scraped at air, then he began to slide backward. All he had was upper body strength to pull himself up and over the side. To move forward, he had to let go with one paw. He roared in frustration, snapping his claws up and then forward, hauling his lower body upward. Again he released his opposite paw, clawing madly into sheer rock, tearing grooves into the ground. His claws gripped and stopped sliding backward, and he pulled himself upward, his back paw latching onto the side of the cliff. He dug into the rock with his claws while using his tail for balance. One last effort to claw and hoist himself upward, and he stretched, coming fully on top of the ledge. He glanced back over his shoulder as a stream of rock and gravel fell onto the other ledge, followed by larger rocks, the size of bowling balls, which began raining and gouging the cliffs below. That would have been him buried under a ton of rubble had he not leapt. He turned and sprinted, moving upward along the ridge. Near the top, he stopped to gauge his distance from the house and Diana. Up here, along the western slope, Douglas fir spotted the landscape.

His attention riveted on a series of low-level growls. His ears tugged forward, twitched, and if he could forcibly capture the sounds at will he'd sit stone-still for as long as it took. A tiger salamander skittered near his front paw. He searched the landscape that lay in front of him, his fur ruffed in agitation. A snarl fell from his lips. He issued a growl, loud and deep, aimed to alert Diana. He listened. Nothing.

The sounds he'd heard were coming from the thicket in front of him, about two hundred yards off. Christ, he wondered if black bears would find her scent as appealing as he did. Fuck, those greedy bastards ate anything in sight. Some were mean-spirited, just for the hell of it. They screwed with campers for no other reason than they could. They were fucking alligators with mangy fur and he detested dealing with them in the realm of business or under the canopy of a pine forest.

For fucking once, he wondered where in the hell was nanny goat one and two who seemed incapable of leaving him in peace. He swore a vow that he'd nail Tristen and Fin's hides to the wall when he returned home. On that thought, Shawn savagely tore through the juniper and bitterbrush, not caring that his eyelids were scratched. He swept a heavy-handed growl from the back of his throat and he hurled it up and out of his mouth, aimed to gather the attention of Tristen and Fin to this emergency.

Diana was near black bears on a rampage. These wild bears had been spotted out along one of the Southern ridges. So far no one had been able to track them or capture them. They tended to stay hidden along the South slope and hadn't trespassed on his land long enough to hunt them down. Until now.

He disliked this form of profiling, but these bears were not part of the greater ecosystem of the Rocky Mountains. They were outcasts, scavengers, and had come from God-knew-where. They reminded him of human misfits, where being part of the group meant everything in an attitude of *either-you-are-with-us-or-against-us.*

A lilting snarl and hiss filled his head and white-lightning concern crackled up his spine. Echoes of bears growling ripped at his bowels, forcing him to race, not run, over the terrain. The wind was swimming over him, keeping his scent hidden. The sound of

Diana kept him from forging ahead thoughtlessly. He crept along the brush, totally hidden.

He could easily have leapt up into the pine tree at his shoulder to assess the situation. But then the bear clan would be informed of his presence, making them giddy with stupidity. Attention reinforced their actions, for most of them were based on a delight in thwarting authority.

Shawn being the owner of this part of the mountain would prompt them into further acts of violence and it wasn't his safety for which he worried. Before, he would have taken the proper channels to settle a dispute. Taking the higher road demonstrated that he believed in justice. That was before he had to consider Diana's welfare.

Well, fuck justice when it came to Diana. He'd deal in what he believed was fair. And that didn't include taking prisoners, names, or excuses. He opened a can of whip-ass and intended to spread it on thick. Shawn watched, ready to tear through the low-lying shrubs, but he didn't see Diana anywhere. Her scent was here; she was here. Somewhere. He studied the three large, male black bears standing with their backs to him. He padded through the thicket, noiselessly, and then he heard her before seeing her. The bears edged apart and, in front of him, Diana's voice struck him deeper than a blade to his heart. Hissing, her ears back, baring her teeth, she hunched her back up, head down, and eyes so heated sparks should have blasted forth.

There wasn't an ounce of logical thought that went into the hurling of his body through the opening in the trees; there was only one urge. *Diana.*

No time to wait and assess the situation as he landed on the back of the largest bear. He bit down, sure and hard, into the neck of the bear, and with his four-inch claws Shawn shredded the bear's face. From behind, bear claws swiped at him and he turned, and turned again, making the bear swing around in a bizarre and deadly dance. Repeatedly he ripped fur and flesh, and he refused to release the bear until the beast went down.

The bear sank to the ground at the paws of his companions. Diana crouched in front of the other bear, snarling and clawing at their movements.

Teeth bared, Shawn bounded in front of Diana, forming a dividing line. Bear blood splattered on his coat and smeared along the ground. He reared up on hind legs just as a scarred black bear rose as well. This time, both sets of his claws dug into a bear's body. He curled his claws, digging deep and deeper until his claws pierced through the bear's pelt.

The bear growled a snort of amusement, for Shawn was attached to him. The bear stepped back and Shawn had to follow. This was nothing short of extreme insanity—or genius. Shawn was lashed to the bear's torso, his claws embedded as sticky liquid oozed between the pads on his paws. The bear couldn't stop this mad backward saunter; he stepped back again, only this time Shawn held his ground. With the bear's skin taut under his claws, Shawn's leopard body coiled inward; his muscles contracted, bunched into a powerful mass before he inhaled, and a sound of tearing filled the air. Carefully uncurling his claws a titch more, and then with all the force he could muster physically, he brought his body down, tearing his claws through the bear's chest and belly. The bear's entrails spilled steaming onto the ground. The bear grunted, staring at the contents of his body dumping downward to fall in a bloody pile at his hind paws.

Diana's loud growl alerted him to the other bear's threat. He turned to see the bear lunge for Diana and take hold of her by the shoulder. She reacted by biting and snapping at the bear's face. Sharp canines reflected white in the moonlight, and fear woven with anger flared in her eyes. The bear pinned her to the ground, covering her body with his, and Shawn understood the bear's intent.

A bellow of rage built and released from his throat. Diana froze, their gazes locked, and the terror in her eyes was enough force to send him leaping onto the bear, knocking them both sideways onto the ground. He snapped his jaws, grabbing hold of a roll of bear blubber. Diana cried out in pain. The bear had intended on raping her but now their bodies were disengaged. Unheard of in the shifter world except by the most depraved beings. Shawn's claws sunk into the bear's face, taking hold, digging deeper until the bear released Diana from his bite.

Shawn snarled for her to move away from this beast, but instead she lunged for the bear, snagging her claws in the bear's hide. The bear swung around, his paw raised above her head. Shawn roared loudly, signaling for her to get out of the damned way.

The last thing he remembered was taking hold of the bear by the point above the jugular, and his teeth diving into the bear's fur and skin, the taste putrid from an unwashed body, and then blood filling his mouth.

He clamped down so hard that when he pulled his face away, a chunk of flesh was removed from the bear's throat. The hissing air of the bear's breathing through a pierced trachea came and went in a pattern of uneven breaths. Shawn clasped the bear again in his fangs, didn't stop until the animal ceased to breathe. He didn't recollect much of anything in his craving for revenge. Blinded by rage, he gave into the lust for carnage this beast provoked by attacking Diana. Shawn didn't go after the one bear who had played possum and who now limped off. The trail of blood seeped into the ground. He'd soon be dead from blood loss or predators. A just end.

Diana circled around him; he watched as though someone else was inside him. Never had he lost his control. His sense of self had vanished for a spell. The irony in teaching Diana to maintain awareness and a sense of logical, organized constructs while he'd become emotionally splayed open was vivid and ludicrous. He'd become so demented that he let loose a wave of violence, and in the aftermath was incapable of recalling his actions. Before him lay the dead bears, savagely killed by his own actions.

He felt his humanity return, felt the slackening of his body as though torn between leopard and man, not knowing which form to take—which form would help him find his way back.

Diana rubbed her cheek against him. Flicking his tail, he snarled a harsh reprimand. She licked his face, sniffing at his coat, and then returned in front of him to squint into his eyes. The leopard in her assuaged the beast in him. He head-butted her softly, incapable of relaying the depth of his anger had taken. That razor feeling had dissipated, leaving him numb.

She moved, her tail swishing from side to side. Her scent pervaded his haze, pricked him to get up, and follow. His leopard body tightened, preparing to continue his chase of Diana. Endorphins swam in his bloodstream and now a cocktail of testosterone and adrenaline followed, blasting away any remorse he may have felt. Diana was his full concern.

A rush of hormones bolstered him. Regardless of what line of thought he might wish to contemplate, his primal state was back to full alert with Diana his sole priority. She purred, walking into the clearing, glancing with green-golden, feral eyes back at him. After she rubbed up against a willow sapling, his coat tightened and his belly coiled.

He ambled over the ground, the dank smell of earth and pine needles replaced with her heat-cycle scent that cleared away the fog obscuring his thoughts, shaping them into a line of need, a primal urge to take possession of her. Now, more than ever.

Diana started off along a trail that would take her into the forest on the west side of the house. This time he followed close behind her, drafting her scent, and with every foot they traveled, his need for her grew. She ran onward, and he followed so close he could have pounced, landing on her back, and rightfully taking what he'd earned.

The lights from the house came into view and a scent of wolves filled the air. Tristen and Fin were on the prowl. Their bodies were black shadows racing in between the trees. Coming from behind, they were invisible both in sight and scent. They silently ran, flanking him.

With a show of teeth, he snarled, warning them to get off his ass. Shawn swerved, coming around right in front of Tristen. The wolf stopped and panted, shrugging his broad shoulders. Jesus, he didn't need a pair of babysitters at this moment. The thought blew a hole in his reserve causing him to slow, and brow-beat Tristen to back-the-fuck-off.

Diana certainly could do without a pair of red-eyed chaperone fly-boys. He'd question them tomorrow. Now, he had a woman that needed to be fucked, balls deep, over and over until she yelled his name.

Chapter 13

Upstairs, sitting in the bathtub by herself, Diana stopped counting the times Shawn paced in front of the bath doorway, making the luxurious whirling water hardly enjoyable. "Are you sure you don't want to join me?"

"You enjoy your bath," he muttered. Shirtless and dressed in unbleached linen pants, he cocked an eyebrow, belying his words. Anger crept and carried every nuance of his posture, his gaze, and the line of his lips.

He'd met her at the outbuilding where he'd taken her earlier today. Shifting in the shadows, they'd stood naked. "We'd better get inside," he said, his eyes dipping down her body. "My posse is close behind."

"Tristen and Fin?"

"My ever-present task force. Next time—if there is a next time—we're going to have a *Come-To-Jesus* talk. And I do mean you three will understand my intent. I'm not beyond having you all write the rules on sheets of papers until each one is memorized. Then, we'll see who forgets what." He spoke off-handedly, as though he was addressing the coming weather or what they might do on Sunday afternoon.

Together they'd changed into clothing, without further discussion beyond his growl to get her ass upstairs. Pronto. The gleam in his eyes was loud and forceful, getting her to move without argument. "Pissed" wouldn't adequately convey the bunching of his shoulders or the set to his jaw. Shawn wasn't someone she'd disobey if she could help it. Upstairs they'd disrobed and he ran her bath, helped her ease down into the water, and had gone off to shower alone.

After dipping below the surface of the bath, she held her breath, enjoying the tranquil feel of muted sounds, and being still in the water. The burning of her lungs forced her to come up with a loud rush, inhaling deeply.

"What in blue blazes are you doing?" he asked, kneeling at the side of the tub.

She wiped the droplets from her eyes, blinking up at him. Concern filled his face. "Just relaxing. It's serene under the water. Haven't you ever tried it?"

"Not in that manner. Are you coming out soon? I'll go down and get something for us to eat."

She sat forward, moving up and onto her heels still inside the bath. "I'm not hungry…for food." No sooner than she had uttered the words, Shawn hauled her body upward, against him. Her wet skin was slippery over his bare chest.

He held her, letting her toes only skim the floor, and he spoke in a growl. "If you ever disobey me again, I swear, Diana, I'll fucking lose it. I don't intend on laying down the law but maybe that's what you need. You've gone on too long just doing whatever the hell comes to mind. I understand you've had to fend for yourself. But you're mine now. I call the shots. And when I say to get out of the fucking way, that's precisely what I mean. Am I crystal fucking clear on this one point?" He tightened his clasp around her waist, unwilling to let her go without a response.

"You're upset about what? The bear thing?"

"God, you're either trying my patience or you really live in a dream world. What do you think that bear wanted to do? Have you over for tea? Make no mistake, in this world, shifters aren't following man-made laws. Some shifters live in the wild. They spend more time in their primal form than human. They exist as they see fit, without any mind to what's fair or just. The law of survival is the only rule they hold to and they take what they please. An animal that is bigger than you or more powerful than you, deserves your respect. In the world south of this house, in the depths of the Rockies, might doesn't give a flying fuck about right. And don't you ever forget that. Do. You. Understand?"

Her chest heaved, easier than before without her ability to lose control. She understood. Of course, who wouldn't; but she wasn't about to let anyone push her around. Christ, where had that sentiment come from? Logically she realized retaliation on the bear was lunacy in the making. But a primal force had not seen fit to step away. Not when Shawn had been in peril trying to save her. "I couldn't just step aside. Not when you were threatened. I acted out of instinct."

"Christ, Diana. There's just one thing that is instinctive. The rest must be born from logic. It's the reason we ran tonight. The things that went through my mind," he whispered.

Shawn pressed his forehead against hers. She took hold of his face between her hands. His mouth came down on hers. Hunger laced with need seared her mouth and she relaxed against him. He lowered her so that her feet touched the floor, his fiery skin molded to her from mouth to hip. A frisson of desire shot up her nerve endings, spiking her blood with the instinct he spoke about. His erection, snug and trapped between their bodies, assured her their instincts were synchronized.

This was no mystery as to how a night run would end; but for her, this was the first time she'd returned and a man hungered for her body. With Cole, they went to sleep. Both were too tired to do much more and she never remembered anything from her time in leopard form anyway. Adrenaline saturated her blood even now, a type of high, where everything came to her senses with stunning potency.

A raging river of sexual tension filled her and, whether she would admit to it or not, the danger kicked her excitement into overdrive. They had survived with only a few gashes that would heal. All shifter wounds on the dermal layers healed rapidly, leaving no scars.

"I've never lost control like this before. I'm not at all pleased with myself. The only thing that comes close was long ago, and I thought I'd managed to overcome those gut reactions. I thought you were going to be maimed by that beast." His warm breath caressed her face. "When I saw that bear cover your body, I swear…I honestly lost control. I can't ever go back to being like that again."

She pressed her body against him. Her fingers pulled the drawstring to his pants. The air cooled her heated skin and droplets from her wet hair pelted down, landing on him and leaving swirling traces down his hard-muscled stomach.

"I'm in charge tonight," he snapped, capturing her hand. His mouth crashed down on top of hers, and his tongue burst into her mouth, tangling with her tongue. Shawn's fingers threaded through her hair, angling her head, and he deepened his kiss. His other hand slid down her back until he cupped her bottom, bringing her secure up against him, leaving no doubt he would hold her there for as long as he pleased. His fingers delved along the crack, wedging between her cheeks, and she wiggled her hips.

A low growl emanated from his throat. He pulled her head back, staring down at her with his beguiling golden eyes, intense and all knowing. "Don't move a muscle."

"Do you understand my rationale?" she had to ask him.

"I understand why you reacted. But I don't want a repeat performance. Ever. Consider tonight a furtherance of your training. I promised I'd paint your bottom and I will." He released his hold on her scalp. "Get into bed. Now, Diana."

She bit back her response. A shiver escaped from her core and a thrill raced up her body. Anticipation made her skin tighten and tingle. She had to be insane. From the furious sound of his voice and what he'd already said…anticipation? *Really?* Heat-cycle lunacy was more like it. She should be fighting back, but the pooling heat between her legs wanted him to take charge. To dominate her. To make her believe she wasn't alone.

Had he been looking for a reason and she had unwittingly given him cause? She'd never been hit, forget spanked except by his hand. Ideas about violence didn't appeal to her and yet the thought of him spanking her again aroused something in her, especially with the erection he sported. This was a hard-core erotic fantasy, and no wonder the underground clubs were popular. This whole night had blown the doors off her imagination.

When Shawn came to the bed, she sat on the edge, not knowing if she should say something, ask questions about what he would use—his hand or a…She didn't even know the proper terms for erotic toys. She twisted her fingers, raking her mind over the limits of her pain tolerance. Being mauled was one thing, but calmly presenting her ass to a man who promised to deliver a lesson was altogether different.

She wasn't at all sure she was going to like this. Glancing up, she nearly fell off the side of the bed from his steely expression. Their gazes connected, blazing past her fear, lambasting the locked doorways, snaking around corners and pulling her to trust that whatever he wanted to deliver, she'd welcome.

"I want you over here. I intend of satisfying a side we both possess." Her heart didn't leap into her throat, it nearly burst out of her mouth as he hoisted her upward, his presence powerful and consuming. "Do you have anything to share?"

"I desire what you desire."

"Don't ever scare me again," he ordered calmly. All traces of anger had evaporated, leaving a steely quality to his voice. She stood, leaning against him, giving into his appeal, aroused and intrigued by the promise in his threat. He took her toward the nightstand, and eased her downward onto the bed. All sure movements as he arranged himself up against pillows, not once releasing his hold on her.

Shawn's hands turned her over and pulled her across his lap. She gazed at the comforter, his legs under her stomach, and he rubbed his hand over her ass. "How many times do you need to feel the heat of my hand?" he whispered. "Jesus, I want to bury myself inside you and make you scream my name as I'm coming."

His hand caressed her bottom, from one side to the other, dipping and teasing her.

"Please," she said, clenching under his teasing fingers.

"Then tonight will be explosive and new. I intend to teach you who you belong to. No one need question my authority. Especially the woman who will sit at my right hand. I intend on delivering twenty lashes with my hand. You will learn or we will revisit this lesson. Next time, there will be more. I want to hear you count each one. Once I have finished, I will fuck you as you need to be taken. After tonight, you and I will have reached an understanding. You asked for my help. You gave yourself to me. You are mine, Diana. You asked me to train you. Bestowed in me a power and an obligation. I don't take either lightly. You agreed to accept my dictates. Didn't you?"

He didn't give her time to process whether she agreed, disagreed, or wanted to leave. The sound bore into her senses before the pain assaulted her awareness. And then, boy, she got his meaning.

"But…" she stammered from the brand of his palm.

"But nothing. Count for me. Or that will be five more for disobedience."

He rubbed her sweltering ass cheek, calmly demonstrating his patience. "Well?"

"One," she mustered.

"I like when you follow my directions," he purred. "Your ass is beautiful. And mine." He smoothed his palm over her cheek and squeezed.

Releasing her, he delivered a smack, the pain spreading out from where his palm lay, and she closed her eyes, then hearing him cough, realized she'd forgotten her part.

"Two," she choked shakily, as tears moistened her eyes. No sooner had she spoken than another smack landed. This time on the opposite cheek, in a red-hot game of connect the dots.

The pain she expected was more in anticipating the snap to her skin. Her cheeks burned, blazing arousal, tempering her heat cycle. Unbelievable. *Fight fire with fire.*

Her pussy pulsated, and she tried unsuccessfully to shift. "Where do you think you're going?" he asked, so low and quiet that she stopped moving. And then he spanked her again.

"Three. Nowhere."

"Hush. Only counting is allowed."

"Then don't ask me a question."

Jesus, he landed a heavy-handed smack, proving he was allowed to ask anything he desired.

Her mouth sounded out the words, but she lost count of the actual bite of each smack. Unable to keep up with the ache of wanting him, each time he spanked her bottom and followed up with a caress, she pushed back into his hand, wanting him to do more than smack her ass. She wanted him to sink far within her, join with her, prove he owned her. Every muscle spasm testified to her need for him deep inside. Her skin over her ass was on fire, and so was the space between her legs. His hand was driving her over the edge. She nibbled her bottom lip between her teeth, unsure she could stand another second.

"Twenty." The word echoed around the room.

She slumped on top of his lap. Her bottom was a glowing ember, heated and ready for him. After the seventh smack, she'd nearly come undone. Unrelenting and driving, he delivered her further and further into an abyss, tethered to a thin line, and capable of falling at any second, and to her longing for him to hurl her into an orgasm, not leave her teased and ready. Each smack magically made her want him to do something edgier. Harder. If he would take her or make her do as he pleased. Her skin rippled and if she shifted, he'd not finish what he'd promised to deliver. So close to climaxing, she pushed her ass up. He pushed her bottom down.

"Did I say you could get up?" He spread her cheeks, and explored between her legs. She squirmed and he held her still. "You're so wet. So utterly swollen. Apparently, you enjoy having your delectable ass painted red?"

He thrust his finger into her pussy, making her suck in a breath. "Shawn," she gasped.

"Diana, don't come. Ride the wave. I've got to have you. Hold on for a little longer."

"I can't."

"You will. And you'll thank me for teaching you. Say it. Thank you."

"Thank you?" she echoed.

"Not a question. A courtesy. Louder and surer."

"Thank you," she moaned, feeling so close to the precipice she might plummet into a blissful orgasm. "Please, Shawn." Never mind her ass, her center was so heated and wet, the slick feeling made each movement an act of conspiracy against her self-control to hold back from climaxing. Her clit felt engorged, ready to explode. If he so much as licked her, she'd shatter.

If this was her lesson, she might as well receive a failing mark. She fought against climaxing, tried to find her inner core, and ground herself. Pulsations threaded through her body, and she inhaled, expanding her control. Barely.

Shawn didn't push or tease, didn't keep toying with her, but let her regain her composure, tiptoeing back from the edge of insane release. So close, she fought against leaping when her body demanded that she pounce. Her mind held her still, syncing and securing her.

"Come, kitten," he whispered, drawing her up to him, holding her close to his chest. She listened to his heartbeat. Strong and sure. His voice rumbled. "This isn't about punishment, it's about control. You did well. Now I'm going to do as promised to you before we set out. You're mine for tonight."

His hands held her back and he kissed her, soft and secure, and pushing her back onto the bed while his hands kneaded and reshaped her breasts, thumbing her nipples already taut and sensitive. Shawn kissed a path down her body and she arched against him. The moment he took her nipple between his lips, sharing his hot mouth on her peak, she cried out. Changing breasts, he licked and scraped his teeth, making her insane for him to suck her nipple. She channeled her fingers into his hair, pulling on his scalp.

"God, you're beautiful. Tonight you took my breath away. Many, many times." His eyes glittered, sharp as broken glass.

She lay there, nearly spent and uncertain what would happen next. With his sizeable cock pressing against her belly, she didn't fight the unfurling of desire. He wasn't asking her to hold back anymore. "I want you so much. I'm as hungry as the first time I fucked you." Shawn's voice woke up her brain. She flinched as his teeth scraped the tip of her breast.

She pushed against his chest and he sucked her breast deep into his sizzling mouth. Slowly, he was turning her over, dragging his mouth over her shoulder, grasping her firmly by the hips. He spread her legs and positioned himself between the V-shape she presented. Shawn's fingers separated her cheeks and she remembered all the pleasure he'd given her earlier. Automatically her hips rose off the bed as she pressed back against him, giving him easier access to her. Lifting her ass into the air, he held her firmly, his erection grazed between her folds. She snapped downward as though a frayed electrical cord had been touched.

His palm cupped, squeezed, and delved in between her ass cheeks and folds. "You're unbelievably wet." He lightly bit into her shoulder. Not hard, but with enough pressure to make her pussy clench down.

Shawn lifted up and off her, his tight muscles flexing, a rippling expanse down his torso all the way to the tip of glistening erection.

"What are you looking for?" she asked, still staring at his body. "Something to ease your discomfort." He opened the nightstand and removed a plastic bottle. He flipped the cap and squeezed a steady stream into his palm and the scent of cool mint essences swirled in the air. After rubbing his hands together, he touched the cleft of her ass and massaged her skin with his warm, moist palms. He avoided touching her inside her ass cheeks, leaving her moaning and craving him all the more. "How does that feel?"

"Heavenly where you spanked me."

"I don't think that will be the last time, kitten." He crossed to the bathroom and she heard water running. He came out drying his hands on a towel. He laughed and she understood his intent.

"You're teasing me," she huffed.

"It's working." Walking back, he appeared powerfully masculine and unquestionably ready to deliver on his promise. "Now, it's time."

Her pulse hammered a steady beat by the time he returned and slipped a finger inside her crack, stroking downward and passing over her entrance. The mattress shifted and the bottle of lubricant was squeezed again. His hands spread across her, between her cheeks, making her a sweltering, aching mess. Her breasts and nipples swelled, and her clit plumped, throbbing steadily under his caresses. She steamed inside, wanting him to just take her and stop teasing her.

He repositioned her, and then she knew instinctively there was no escape from him in his coming to claim her. He pinned her under him, his teeth sunk into the side of her neck, marking her.

She arched her spine, lifting her hips. Shawn pulled her thighs apart. He was fierce in his possession, and in one thrust, his cock burst past her ring of muscle, sliding deep into her ass. She let out a cry mingled with pain and ecstasy.

All her focus was on the feeling of him grinding into her body, taking up all her space, and then a snarl tore from her mouth. She bucked back, trying to shake him loose. Without knowing why she reacted, she tried to lunge but he held her firmly beneath him, almost shaking her with the force and command of his dominance. His cock stilled inside her, stretching her, his balls tight up against her. He pushed forward filling her fully, pain laced with sinful pleasure, dark and decadent, rasping, and then he began to pull out.

"Do you want me to stop, baby?"

"No," she said hoarsely. His hand fisted in her damp hair. Pulling her neck back, he clamped down on a pressure point, thrusting back inside her in one long, exquisite stroke. She moaned pushing back onto his cock. He released his bite, withdrawing himself only to take her again. As he clamped his teeth onto her skin, he slammed back into her ass, hard and balls-deep.

He mounted her as he'd promised, holding her down as a leopard would, and possessing her. This was a primitive show of leopard-to-leopardess ownership. She could stop him now, not go through with this. Her mind raced; she wanted him inside her body.

"Do you know what you do to me?" he asked against her ear. "You're in my blood. Baby, give yourself to me."

"Yes," she whimpered. "Take me."

She'd carry another layer of his scent. He wasn't wearing a condom and she knew he intended to mark her in a way that only once before had she allowed herself to be branded. And then only because it kept her safe from others. Not now. This intimate marking was pleasure and need, woven with something else.

Again, Shawn drove himself into her and she rocked back in time with him. No thought, guided by leopardess instinct and lust.

Shawn's body was over hers, wedged up behind her and he began moving faster, making his dick slide in and out of her ass. He moved in a hard, pumping motion, taking his crown beyond her opening, rimming her, pausing and then ramming himself forward, slamming his body back against her. God, she enjoyed having him fill her. There was no way to describe the sensation that he heightened by sucking her neck and sliding his fingers up and down her slit. Sensation poured over her body, saturated her, and she couldn't hold a thought.

The pleasure was intense, but he wanted more. He gripped her hips, his hands spread open her cheeks, and then he plunged so deep into her, she arched up, crying his name. Working his cock in and out of her ass, he forced her to take him, accept him, and allow him to mate with her in this way. Not the final step, but near enough.

"Shawn?" she cried out this time not in pain, but in wanting an assurance. "Is this what you want?"

"More than anything," he replied, nipping her neck. He withdrew, pulling his dick all the way out of her.

"How do you know you want this?" she repeated, clawing at the sheets.

"I want you. To possess you. Protect you." Immediately, Shawn withdrew from her and clasped her hips, flipping her onto the mattress without a word.

She stared back at his face, meeting his gaze that took her breath away. If she believed she'd witnessed the primal side of him before, she'd been mistaken. His eyes were wild, feral, and a color so fiery bright, orange-red light poured out from his face. He wasn't out-of-control as he'd been with those bears. No, what she saw didn't frighten her but held her in awe. There was a quality of ruthlessness in his claim over her. As though he wouldn't let anyone or anything ever come between them. He wasn't a beast, but an intelligent being, inspiring a deep calmness in the parts of her once ravaged.

No words, only feelings, swirled around and between them. He took her almost to the point of savagery, but that wasn't what this act was about. Primitive, a bit brutal, but there was no anger or rage. Only possession. He sought to claim her and he did; beyond body, he came for her psyche, if not her soul. She didn't know if she was ready for the ultimate form of mating. To be bonded to him. But it was enough that he came for her. All. Of. Her.

"Are you sure?" she asked.

Shawn pushed her back into the mattress. "More than you imagine. You are mine. I promise to make you feel safe and secure. I expect that you'll follow my command. If you don't, I will teach you for your own good. You came to me to learn to be an alpha and you will become that and so much more." He spoke, and the embers from his eyes warmed her and released her.

She nodded, running her hands over his shoulders. Shawn leaned over her, swiping his palm against the side of her face.

"And you? Baby, I'm about to come. Is this what you desire?" he asked, in a voice hoarse and low.

"Yes," she whispered.

He kissed her shoulder; his large hands gripped her body, turning her over. She rolled to face the mattress, his body moving over hers. He tugged her thighs open, and then his hands were back at her hips, pulling her upward. "No, only your ass," he said, "keep your head down. Relax. I'm taking what's mine." Tucking his crown up against her opening, he thrust forward, mercilessly claiming her. Completely. He ground himself against her, growling and making her ass burn and pulsate. Shawn began to pump, seating himself deeper, forcing himself into her body. She held back, even though she wanted to open to him. A wall cracked, but didn't come tumbling down as she'd expected. She closed her eyes, not fully understanding this need to keep herself protected. She fought against him, and fought harder against herself. "That's it, baby. I'm going to come," he rasped as he bowed back, driving himself into her deeper, further than before. "God, I'm going to come so deep inside you, I'll mark you from the inside out. Are you close to coming?"

"I'm already there. Yes, I'm here." She closed her eyes.

"Look at me. Diana, let me see your emerald eyes flash as you come. You're mine. All mine."

She nodded, staring back at him over her shoulder, and giving in to what she could release. Flinging open as far she could, he moved faster, harder and wilder than before. His sweat-sheened body powered back and forth against her ass. The sounds of flesh slapping flesh, rapid and sharp, filled the room. She kept her gaze trained on him, pushing back on his cock impaling her body against him. His shoulders bunched, he grimaced as his cock filled her, and he pumped a hard thrust. One. He exploded, releasing a body-wracking spasm and spray of hot semen inside her.

Shawn remained wedged between her legs, picking up the pace as his fingers found her clit. "That's it, baby. Come for me. You're *all* mine."

Diana's orgasm unraveled, making her go hot and slick; her climax had her dripping, sated as she relished Shawn's swollen cock that remained embedded deep within her. She tried to hold back from him, even though she felt more vulnerable than at any time in her life. He came for her at the Den and took without giving her the ability to stop him. Tonight was no different.

His mouth sought hers, and she let him in, kissing him, stroking him, holding him. His kiss was gentle, giving in to her, and had her floating. He positioned her against him, with her back resting right next to his chest, securing her in the crock of his arm. After tossing his leg possessively over hers, he whispered against her hair.

"Always. Mine."

Chapter 14

He could just stay here and watch her for hours. Diana had given herself to him. After a year of avoiding all thoughts of intimacy with her, he had her right where he wanted her. The added worry about how to keep her still plagued him, and after last night his concern ran deeper. That answer would take planning, an iron will, and much patience in dealing with his hardheaded leopardess.

Plans…he definitely had plans for Diana. With his cock straining for release, he turned her and gently opened her legs wide to him. She moaned once he began stroking her pussy.

Getting his fill didn't seem like something that would happen soon. After being with her for a week and fucking her from sun-up to sundown, his appetite had only increased. Today was the first day they'd return to Matrix and he intended to take the edge off in the only way he knew how—fucking.

"Good morning," he whispered into her sleepy face. He kissed her briefly and sat back to roll a condom down his dick. She gasped as he positioned himself at the mouth of her slick center. "Come on, baby, I'm not about to start the day without you."

Insofar as her training, Diana had mastered everything he'd sought to teach her over the last week. She could outdistance most leopards in her ability to run a course and navigate her way from one point to another. Her memory was rock-solid. Whether in human or shifter form, she retained the ability to recall events with precision.

He, on the other hand, was losing the battle to stay afloat, feeling more and more as though he'd booked passage on the

Titanic. Sinking fast in maintaining his own self-control where she mattered, he was prepared to be a son-of-a-bitch. No argument. A bit of guilt—not enough to put him off. No way to stop from wanting to possess her, even though she hadn't committed fully to him.

He had no intention of stopping, either. All he could envision was the day he'd bond with her and stop this hunger that threatened to tie his usually streamlined thoughts into knots. The only way clear that he could see was taking the final step with Diana.

But would she ever trust him if all he could do was break the one promise she'd asked? All she wanted was her freedom. All he wanted was her freedom. Or rather, her lack of freedom to run about wildly, as if time was always going to be on her side. She had a wild streak she tried to bury, but it came out and then there was no stopping her. For her safety, she needed guidance and a modicum of restraint. They both were after the same thing and he'd play dirty if that's what it meant to protect her.

It had been easy instructing Diana. She readily grasped any and all points. Whether abstract theories or physical challenges, she was the near-perfect alpha. Strong, determined, and single-minded in overcoming challenges. It was just that small part of her that tended to refuse to listen to reason if someone was in danger. He gritted his teeth. And that loyalty was exactly what spurred him to want her even more. *She was the perfect mate.* In confirming this, with every glance she cast, each sigh, and whenever she touched him, he become edgier to get to the finish line and do whatever needed to be done to seize his right to claim her entirely.

He could assert control to dominate her, simply because she'd allowed him intimate entrance into her body and she was marked as his on many levels. Apparently, she didn't know—or remember—that one small loophole in shifter mating. He could demand that she submit to him. But would he do that to her? His patience was ebbing as his craving for her increased.

Her history and his respect for her kept him from acting like a complete bastard in claiming her for her own protection. And her desire that he train her kept her near him instead of her returning home when the worst part of her heat was over. She'd remained in his household and he'd gotten to know her, as well as let her into his world. She said she'd give him her answer about a living arrangement, but she still remained noncommittal.

The day she'd try to sever their bonds, he wasn't about to fool himself—he'd stop her, not let her go; not even if it meant he had to keep her captive until he convinced her they were meant to be together.

He held his cock, poised at her slick opening, and in one forceful thrust, he slammed into her. Diana's eyes widened, her body flexing, and she took hold of his arms, moaning softly. He wanted to embed himself inside her.

Shawn growled, "I need you." Hauling her legs up over his shoulders to gain better access to her body, he pulled back on her thighs, rocking and plunging back into her. He was so deep, but he wanted to go deeper still. He worked his dick, thrusting hard, making certain she was aware who claimed her. Last night he'd fucked her up against the wall, and then he mounted her, hardly able to contain himself. Now was no different. Instead of sating his desire, each time made him hungrier to possess her entirely.

Well, enough patience, he was about to press his point. "That's right, darling. Open to me." His dick hardened the more he pumped. He wanted her filled with his semen, but that day wasn't today. "Look at me, Diana. Who do you belong to?"

A look of bewilderment entered her eyes as she gazed up at him. "You, of course."

"When I take you, I want to see my ownership in the marks I leave on your skin and deep inside you. Your eyes are so volatile. Come for me. I've got to have you."

Her gaze connected and held with his, and she nodded. "You've got me."

This morning he had no desire for lovemaking in this act of domination. He gave into the roiling hunger to fuck her forcefully as her alpha. This was their last morning together before heading into the office. He was pounding his cock into her as though it was the only way he could make her understand. She was his. With each thrust, her body rebounded from his pounding into her. She closed her eyes and he stopped fucking her to nip the skin at her neck.

"I said to keep your eyes on me. Don't make me stop and haul you over my lap. I will, even if it means you have to sit on a pillow today at work."

"You've got me, Shawn."

Fueled by a burst of worry and concern, egged on by his yearning to tell her his feelings, he let his emotions rule him and move him to pound against her. "God, you're so hot and wet. Are you coming?"

Her pussy enveloped his cock in the most erotic grip. "I'm there. So there."

His release came on with a hot spurt of semen, but he kept ramming into her body. He could do this forever and he didn't want to stop. Not when he had more to give her. The electrical snap and burn at the base of his spine rocketed up his back and then his cock throbbed with the force of semen spraying out from him. He yelled her name, caught up in a final jet-stream burst of cum in a release that bordered on agony and ecstasy. The sight of her wrapped around him, so swollen and red, her whole body heated, the searing glow in her eyes, made him want to do it all over again. He shuddered, and lowered himself over her body.

"When you look at me like that, I could call in for a personal day or two." This time he held onto her even when she wiggled under him, a sign that she was more than awake. He sighed, not wanting to let her go. A raw edge to his urge irritated him more and more, as though his skin had shrunk.

"I've got a client meeting this morning," she whispered against his cheek.

He inhaled. "Then we'd better get a move on." Christ, he'd wished she would just stay here; he could deal with her client. Why on Earth had he agreed to be a modern, democratic shifter? The hell with being just and operating with principles.

A fine attitude for the person in charge of a newly-codified justice system for shifters. Crap, if he couldn't control his own emotions, how the hell could he expect any other shifter to demonstrate self-control? He wanted her no less amongst the scales of justice. Bloody hell, when it came down to it, he wanted all of her.

He didn't want to watch her walk across the bedroom naked. That would be tantamount to torture. He punched the pillow, not knowing what else to do.

•••

On the ride back to the city, she sat next to him while using the laptop he had given her. Another dazzling brainstorm. Too late to take back the damned thing. He sullenly gazed out the window of the car.

"Are you all right?" she asked, squeezing his fingers.

"Just thinking about the day ahead. We've got a short staff meeting."

"Are we just going to enter the office together?"

"Yes. No one need know anything other than we met this morning. As far anyone knows, we were in L.A. meeting with clients this last week. And this morning, we were scheduled for a breakfast meeting already. I see no problem if everyone knows that you're mine, but I will respect your need for privacy."

"Thank you," she said, squeezing his arm and making his gaze linger, just to contemplate her mouth.

"At least let me get the door." The car pulled up to the building's parking garage entrance. He pressed the intercom, alerting Fin to drop them off in front. He walked around the car, opened her door, and almost closed it again when he noticed her skirt hiked up her thigh and her inadvertent display of a white garter belt. Glancing over his shoulder, he glared at the two men standing slack-jawed on the curb.

He helped Diana from the car, taking hold of her attaché case regardless of how high her brow arched. It was only morning and she was dressed for a business meeting, but, fuck, she absolutely took his breath away in the body-hugging suit she wore. Without the half-crazed look of a wild heat, her coolness made him think about licking her, and putting a sign on her that she was his. Their gazes snapped together, and he had a sinking sensation that his inability to touch her at will was going to test him in ways he could only imagine.

"Steady," he whispered, when she pulled back at his cupping her elbow. Several of the graphic designers from a competing firm stopped outside the door and stepped aside. Every one of those jackasses smiled at her.

The senior partner of Allister Art Designs walked up next to her. "Congratulations, Diana, on the nomination."

"Peter. Thank you," she said, smiling and gazing over at Shawn.

He returned the smile while the idea of hauling her back inside the car, fucking her one last time, took hold of him. He shook it off. Partly.

The doorman greeted them. "Mr. Barclay, Miss Hambre."

Shawn nodded curtly, unable to say a word, his throat so constricted it felt as though he was choking. He had little comfort in the knowledge she was his if every Tom, Dick, and Peter was going to make his move on her. This morning he'd arranged a small office get-together to celebrate her nomination. Next week they'd travel to Vegas. He'd booked several rooms and had scheduled this ceremony as a means to get her away, not expecting his staff to agree to travel. But, hell—everyone invited had wanted to come. A weekend in Vegas and he'd be flanked not only by Tristen and Fin, but by the entire Matrix staff. If this was any indication of what would happen next week, he needed to make plans quickly. He'd be put out, to put it mildly, if he had to spend the entire weekend watching men fall over themselves fawning over her. She deserved it. Sure. But he didn't like it.

As they reached the elevators, Shawn kept his distance once Diana's other side was flanked by the administrative assistant from his office. The woman chatted with Diana, and he took the time to breathe deeply and center himself.

They were here as business associates. After this morning she'd be his business partner, if she agreed. Only his business partner, as far as anyone was concerned. Until she consented to further disclose their involvement, he chafed at the thought of keeping their personal relationship a secret.

The elevator doors opened and he held back, allowing Diana and his other office staff to walk together down the hall a few steps in front of him. Surprising him, she stopped and waited, eliciting a smile from him. The first time he'd actually felt like grinning since they left the house.

"Don't want to walk with me?" she teased him.

"Right." He held the door for her. Up ahead, Tristen stood staring with a concerned expression. Shawn would have snarled, but he staunchly reminded himself that Tristen would never be interested in Diana except as a shifter he was helping.

"Tristen, what's up?"

"Just checking in before I make my other stops this morning," he said, all the while appearing to casually study Diana.

"Hello, Tristen. How are you?" Diana asked, busy with messages handed to her by the receptionist.

"Good. Everything going well, I take it." Tristen moved to stand directly in front of her. So close he'd clearly invaded her space, causing her to stop opening a FedEx she'd just received.

"Marvelous. If you'll excuse me…I've a meeting to prepare for this morning." Diana patted his arm, then glanced back at Shawn before sailing down the hall.

"Tristen, we're all busy after being away for a week." Shawn tore his gaze from her swaying hips, forcing himself to pay attention to Tristen.

"This isn't a social visit. I've some results I think we need to discuss."

"Then walk with me."

Tristen walked alongside him, lowering his voice as he asked, "How is Diana? Any headaches or flashes of light?"

"Why are you asking? You know something," Shawn said, as chilling apprehension crept up his spine. He waited for Tristen to enter his office before locking the door. "What the hell is going on?"

Tristen shrugged, shaking his head. "I don't know exactly. There's a break in Diana's neural responses. A consistent break that occurs when she's stressed. At first, I thought it was fall-out from the training and revamping her neural pathways. But each time she's undergone any type of training involving her limbic system reflexes, she snaps. It's some sort of short that occurs within her sympathetic nervous system."

"Speak English."

"Fight or flight. When she's stressed by an aggressor, she falters in her control. I thought maybe it might be some sort of hormonal imbalance, like too much epinephrine. But all the samples we took, blood and urine, indicate her neurotransmitters are within normal limits, except when she's threatened. Then her whole system goes haywire. She spikes—or her hormone levels do—and wham, she's ready to go off."

"I don't think anyone here is going to kick her in the shin. She'll be with me. Everyone here loves her. You know how sweet she is; if what you're saying is true, it would take a situation akin to a street fight to tax her system here."

"Right, or an aggressor. At least that's what I believe. I'm concerned. We need to keep a watch on her, is all I'm suggesting. We've forced her to live without the defenses, walls she built up that kept her from reaching her potential. There was a reason she had walls to her personality. Now, we've freed her."

"I understand. I get that we've allowed her to access her alpha nature. The good and powerful parts. I won't let her out of my sight. Consider it done. How soon can you repair this crack?"

The wolf shifter stilled. Tristen's eyes flashed red. Not a good sign. "I don't know that this type of neural gap *can* be repaired. She'll have to learn how to cope. Not impossible—that's what she did previously. Difficult to do in a healthy way, but she must at some point."

"Exactly what type of response would she have, to get you this worked up?"

"Not good. She's lethal. Imagine a leopardess protecting cubs. It won't matter whether she's in shifter form. She'll respond when threatened."

Every hair on Shawn's body stood up at Tristen's expression and this information. He remembered his own instinctive reaction when Diana had been threatened. It was nothing compared to a leopardess reacting in fear. That type of gut reaction would be savage in disposing of any threat.

"When we return from Nevada, let's get her set up and take care of this, Tristen. Whatever it takes."

The wolf in Tristen flashed near the surface. That only occurred when he was in protector mode. This was serious.

"I expect you and Fin to accompany us to Vegas."

"I've already booked our flights," Tristen said.

Shawn removed his hand from his pocket and flipped a circular disk up into the air above Tristen's head. The man caught the piece and opened his palm.

"One thousand dollars?" Tristen asked.

"Ten more chips for you and Fin when we return. Do whatever is necessary to keep her safe. I want Santo on this one. Get him prepped. Where the hell is he these days?"

• • •

Diana walked into Shawn's office to find Tristen with him. "Oh, I'm sorry. We had a meeting scheduled. Shall I come back?"

"No, I was just leaving. Congratulations on the nomination. We're all…proud of you, Diana." Tristen held out his hand. Diana hesitated; shyly, she reached out and placed her hand in his. Tristen shook her hand briefly before releasing her hand. He turned and left, shutting the door on his way out.

"Is now a good time?" she asked.

"Yes. Anytime is a good time for you to come to my office." He reached for her, pulling her into his arms, his mouth hungry to taste her. All he could think about was bending her over his desk. "God, what I'd like to do you."

"I'm not wearing panties," she murmured against his mouth, and lightly bit down on his lip.

"Jesus, why did you tell me that?" His hand rubbed over the upper curve of her ass. He pushed himself against her crotch, knowing this would incite his craving to plunge into her. There was a discussion planned and he couldn't very well do what he'd like, considering what he needed to talk about with her. He tugged her hand, taking her over to his sofa and pulling her down onto his lap. "I need your decision. Yes or no?"

"What's the question first?" she asked, her arms lightly pressing down on his shoulders.

"Partnership. I already asked, several times over the last week. And this has nothing to do with our change in status. I made the decision when I first scheduled our morning meeting more than a few weeks ago. I put off pressuring you since there were other *points* we had to cover last week." He fingered the button on her shirt that kept her luscious breasts hidden from his view.

The button released, giving him a tease of flesh. Inhaling at the sight of the tops of her breasts, he let his finger skim between her cleavage inside her shirt. "I want you in a more permanent capacity. You've worked hard. You're up for the Design Academy award. You deserve it. And, besides, I'm selfish."

"And it's all just coincidence?"

"I'm not joking. Look at the date on the first page. These documents have been on my desk for a week." He reached over to the side table next to the sofa, and handed her a three-page partnership proposal. Her eyes widened after reading the first page containing salary, bonuses, and benefits package.

She lifted her eyes to him. "Doesn't seem like a selfish move? I don't know. What about Gordon or Elyza? They've been here longer."

"Yes. They have. But you're the one with the accounts. They have other interests and don't work power-weeks of fifty or sixty hours. They might want to be a partner for status; they'd hate the requirements."

"Are you trying to scare me?"

"If you worked as I'd expect a partner to put in time, it would be a step down from what you've done over the past year. Which is why I think a partnership is a good move for you. It would afford you the freedom to pick and choose the clients you want to work with versus those on your roster."

She looked at him over the pages in her hand. "You make it hard for a girl to say no."

"That's because I want you to say yes. Say it." He ran his hands down to her hips and squeezed, pushing his erection up against her.

"You're playing dirty." She opened her legs, permitting him to grind up against the V-shape where he longed to embed himself. Moaning and fingering the collar of his shirt, she closed her eyes. "Yes. I can't fight you. Not when you're doing that to me."

"Good girl. We've a celebration planned for lunch. If you'd said no, it would have been a much less happy event."

"Did you think I'd say no? Really?"

"I never know for sure what you're up to. That's why you've got me locked up. You're unpredictable. Very beautiful, sexy, but damn, I never know what you're thinking."

She bit her lip, unleashing a devilish light that permeated her gaze. She captured his hand, guiding him to the hem of her skirt. She wiggled, opening her legs, and fed his arm beneath the material. "Can you guess now?"

His finger brushed across her moist slit, then he scissored two fingers, rubbing them over her folds. Pushing her hips forward, she opened completely for him.

"Oh baby, I know what you want."

Chapter 15

Earlier this morning he'd taken her, hard and rough. Waking to him between her legs, she'd enjoyed total sensation as he'd slammed into her. This act of possession was mutual. She wanted him as much as he seemed to want her. It would hurt if she crashed from the places he'd taken her in body and spirit. It couldn't go on forever. That piercing truth kept her in check and she'd held back from giving in to him completely, as he would have liked.

Diana sniffed the partnership documents. The odor was unmistakable. Quinn's scent marked the pages. After this last week, the mystery surrounding many of Shawn's staff had come to light. They loyally protected him. Nearly everyone around Shawn gave into his imperious nature, without questioning, and she'd been a witness to the staff at his home or Matrix supporting his decisions.

During her time at Matrix she had met Quinn, the wolf shifter who had come to the offices, and he was the first person who didn't follow Shawn's orders. He was an equal with Shawn. And from what she'd learned, he was also a close friend and Shawn's attorney. The man's rakish good looks said it all, and she'd stayed clear of him whenever he was present at Matrix. His scent spoke about dark, illicit cravings and his wolf eyes flashed satisfaction, which was more than she needed to know before becoming involved with Shawn.

If she was only one more person who gave in to Shawn, what would keep him from tiring of her? He was a powerful man and an alpha leopard, and for a shifter such as Shawn, the hunt was salacious. Too soon she expected his fascination with her to ebb, which was why she had him promise not to hook her into mating so he could be off in search of greener pastures with the waning of his lust.

Except he kept giving her these looks that made her heart melt. The tight edges she'd seen him wrapped in over the last year were gone.

"Let's put this aside. For a few moments." Shawn took the contract from her fingers and dropped it onto the low table in front of the sofa. Cupping her chin, he tilted her head up, angling her mouth just so, before he kissed her. He stared into her eyes, his expression serious as though he searched for something in the gaze she returned. He brought his mouth down to hers, this time his tongue gentle and coaxing. Shawn continued kissing her; his mouth was insistent, though not hurried or rough as over the last week when they'd been ravenous to connect.

He captured her mouth in a kiss edged by sweetness in the sigh he let escape as he released her. His finger pressed into her, slowly swirling, and then he curled the tip, pressing and rubbing against her G-spot. She arched back and he guided her down to the sofa cushions.

"Let me taste you," he murmured. He knelt next to the sofa, pushing her skirt up over her thighs. He spread her folds, pressing his hot mouth against her clit, licking her and sending what felt like electrical charges through her belly.

"I'm going to come," she moaned.

"Not yet, hold on for me. We both know what it took for you to learn to obey me. Need another lesson?" He laughed, low and rough, the sound vibrating over her clit and making her shudder.

"You won't. Here?"

"I would. Where ever I please." He flicked his tongue and then sucked her clit. Each time she slipped closer and closer to falling over the edge. He slipped one long finger inside her pussy, finger-fucking her until she writhed under his hand.

Shawn rubbed his thumb expertly against her clit and she bit the back of her hand to keep from screaming out. "Shawn," she whispered.

"Remember, I claim you. If you come early, I'll only be too pleased to remind you why you'd better mind me." His seductive voice was steeped in the power of knowing she'd do what he told her to do. "Whose are you to possess? Whose mark do you carry?"

She began to shake, her muscles quivered uncontrollably. "Yours. Only yours."

"Do you want me to let you come?"

"Yes, Shawn. Please." No matter how hard she battled against her feelings, she was going down fast, falling like a brick with no possible way of stopping. He commanded her and she was almost powerless to hold back.

"You've been a good girl this week. Come so I can taste your sweet honey."

He plunged two fingers into her and rapidly brought her to the edge of release. She kept her gaze on him, aware he expected her to maintain every possible connection. He was hard underneath his pants and she didn't know why he held back from taking advantage of this opportunity. She came, her pussy clenching around his fingers, and her tissues were swollen and wet. He began to suck on her clit, making the wave of her orgasm build and grow even more powerful, and then she released again against his mouth.

"I want to feel you come all over my dick. Tonight," he said in a low growl. "I could lick you all damned day. You are coming back home with me tonight?"

"Yes. If you'd like."

He lifted up and walked toward his private bathroom. He returned with a warm washcloth and hand towel. "Let me," he said. He wiped her and then patted her dry. "Do you want company for your meeting?"

"How long have I got?"

"About fifteen minutes if Peter Ikashi is on time. Which I suspect he will be."

She'd never conducted a meeting on the cusp of climaxing. Standing up, she pulled down her skirt, wondering if her face was as red as it felt.

"You look beautiful. I wouldn't worry. Peter will just want to share his magnificent vision and get a round of high-fives for being a genius. He loves attention and will be too consumed with himself to notice anything else. If you had a mirror in your office, you could position him in front of it and he'd be pleased as punch."

Her hands fell away from smoothing her hair. Shawn came up next to her, his expression as feral as it was the night they'd first fucked. He owned her, and gazing into his fiercely seductive and powerful face, all she could do was wonder how long until this game was over and her heart shattered into a billion pieces.

• • •

Sitting in first class on the short flight to Vegas, she tried to concentrate on typing an acceptance speech. She'd put it off and only now, after Shawn insisted, did she consider the possibility that she might win. The American Design Award nomination had been a fluke. She'd come up with a design by chance, unlike the other nominees who had a consistent history of award-winning designs. She was the youngest artist ever selected, and Shawn's decision to close up shop and take all of his staff only made her more apprehensive about the expression she'd have to plaster on her face, clapping and accepting everyone's "better luck next year" wishes when she lost.

The plane began its descent and she saved her speech, gazing over at Shawn as he read the *New York Times*. He arched a brow, and folded the paper. "An acceptance speech is more than 'good evening' and 'thank you'. Shall I write the damned thing for you?"

"No. Of course not. I was merely considering my choice in words."

"The seasons will change at this rate before you've named the project and your client. It's not that difficult. Just view it as good coverage for your client and throw in some tidbits on how you came up with the design. I know you don't like drawing attention to yourself. Make it easy, then, and don't look at it as spotlighting your work. Think of it as opening a door into the design firm in which you, my dearest, are partner. On every level, I think you're awesome."

She reached out, caressing his arm that rested between them. "You're less than objective, but thank you. That makes more sense. I hate the idea of talking about myself. It was so much fun dealing with Serena on the project. She should really be recognized. Her products could sell themselves."

"I think not. But you two made an explosive team, insofar as clients and designers go. A certain type of synergy." He raised her hand to his lips, making her gasp. "No one can see us here," he whispered, and ran his tongue along her index finger, nibbling the end.

"Synergy." She repeated the term, floating in the erotic sensation of his mouth on her finger, and his evocative expression. That's what she felt when she was with him. What would she be like without him? The opposite of Teflon.

Then she knew, no matter how hard she'd tried to stay aloof, she'd fallen. Fallen so hard, the only thing she could do was try to keep a superficial distance when all she wanted was to feel him. On her skin, between her legs, and more importantly, swim through her thoughts without fear that, one day, she would be alone without him.

Shawn interlaced his fingers between hers, bringing her closer to him. It was impossible to keep him at arms' length. No one was around, and she wasn't even certain she cared any more if anyone knew. The staff at Matrix didn't care about gossip unless it had to do with the best technology or how to obtain cutting-edge info.

The only comment came from one of the fellow designers who unexpectedly came upon Shawn and her in the hallway. Shawn had caressed her face absentmindedly and she nearly jumped out of her skin upon seeing the designer. He had come up to them and said, "It's about bloody time you guys came out of the closet. Now, can we get on to the real issue at hand?" The man had proceeded to target an ad campaign that he was running.

"And you're certain about the luggage?" Coming out of the terminal, she was struck by a wave of dry heat bouncing off the blacktop, and the glare from the surfaces had her squinting. Shawn loosened his tie. "Yes. The driver had instructions. The staff is catching a ride from the hotel transport. You and I have a car waiting. Do you remember Santo?" He steered her over the sidewalk toward a private car.

"Santo, it's good to see you again," Diana said.

"Likewise. Ms. Hambre?" The driver moved forward, taking hold of their attaché cases. His half-lidded eyes were similar to Fin's, quicksilver laced over expansive black. Steady. Deadly.

"Thank you," she said, the hairs all over her body rising.

He nodded, a slight curve to his wine-colored lips. He pulled his lip upward, for less than a second, and she gasped softly, noting the capped canines behind his lips. Santo was no shifter. He was a most unusual *man*, with tanned and smooth olive skin; café latté came to mind.

"You've been outdoors, it seems. Vegas weather seems to agree with you," Shawn remarked.

"Surprising what can be purchased out here." Santo's eyes skimmed over her momentarily, then around the sidewalk. Diana got the impression he was openly on guard, even though she had not sensed any threats in their vicinity.

"Either way, you appear more in your element here than in the mountains of Colorado."

Shawn inquired if the baggage had been collected. "Yes, three pieces as you indicated. Here are the tags." The tickets were pinched between Santo's long, elegantly-tapered fingers. Santo spoke in a low European accent. Spanish or French. She couldn't decide.

"Then get us to the hotel. I hope you'll reconsider the insanity of staying out here without a break and return to Denver for a visit. I've something that needs your attention. We can discuss later." Shawn directed Santo back to the limo, and indicated that he'd get the door.

"Assuredly," the driver said. Silence swathed the man in an aura of ferocious loyalty. The word *relentlessness* came to Diana's mind. She'd never met a man—other than Shawn—around whom she was completely secure, yet somehow she knew Santo could physically maim her in countless ways if he chose. Turning, she noticed, below his severe military haircut, he sported a tattoo similar to Fin's on the back of his neck.

Shawn had followed her gaze and she arched a brow as if in question. He held her gaze, "Something wrong?"

"Fin, Tristen? And Santo? A club?" She shrugged her shoulders. "Features that all three men possess." The added similarity made her realize they were of the same clan. It was unusual that they'd all be working for Shawn, who wasn't part of their club.

"They all served in Afghanistan. He's actually European, but you know war heroes. They seem to congregate."

"Probably seen too much blood," she said.

"From what I know, they're blood brothers, of sorts. But then there was a falling out. When they're together, they are a force to be reckoned with. They party hard, but they're all heart. I trust them with everything I own."

"The graphic design is one of yours?"

"Yes."

"And the one on your body. How many other people wear your ink designs?"

"Let's not discuss it. I don't know. Is it important?"

"No. But now look who's eating humble pie. The tats are stunning."

Inside the car, the air conditioning alleviated the dry air that smelled of smoky brush fires, and kept her from openly panting. She was mid-cycle and her hormones were on a rollercoaster ride, unlike anything she'd experienced. Smooth sailing was what she'd expected after Shawn took care of her and continued to provide sexual release, not once but several times a day. Now, going on the third week, she was seeing signs of her leopardess wanting to be free.

Stress—whether it was work, hunger, and now she understood, even heat—made her want to shed her clothes and be free. She supposed good stress would also provoke this reaction. So much change, and she was scrambling to find a calm place. Home had become Shawn's mountaintop retreat or downtown apartment, or the firm, and she'd not had a moment to herself to just relax. She worked the knots of tension in her neck with her fingers.

"Let me," Shawn said. His warm fingertips miraculously damped the stress down to a workable level. They drove along the Vegas Strip, pulling into the MGM Grand.

"We're here." The car sat in the queue coming up to the hotel entrance. Vegas had an energy that keyed her up. Even Shawn looked like he was consumed by the place.

Excitedly she contemplated the hotel. "The Sky Loft has a tremendous view. I looked at the suites online. Wish all the staff could stay up there. What a party."

"No. I want some alone time with you. We've tickets for a couple of shows and the awards ceremony. The after-party follows at XS. A popular nightclub."

"Are we all going together? It's a private party at the Encore Hotel. Isn't it?"

"Yes. Every one of the staff and some clients in town are invited. So you'd better win. We're not staying there since I figured it would be overrun with the design industry. You said you wanted privacy." He smiled at her provocatively, hinting about his plans, none of which brought to mind drinking or schmoozing. His hand snaked around her hip, patting her bottom.

Santo opened the car door; fumes and a blast of dry, hot air rushed inside, and Shawn released her, stepping free of the car. He bent and held out his hand, waiting for her to rise. "If it were up to me, I'd shout from the roof top that you were mine."

"I don't think I'd mind," she murmured into his surprised face. "Really."

"Jesus, what was in your soda?" He pulled her to him as though testing the strength of her words. She came to him willingly, more than she'd ever imagined possible. Maybe there was something in the water in Las Vegas. Home of the drive-through wedding, complete with Elvis officials.

If he wanted to shout, well, she'd join him. Regardless of the relationship expiration date, she wanted to live fully in the moment with Shawn. No more hiding. She came to Vegas ready to lay it all out on the table. Chips or no chips. Black, red, green, white. The odds didn't matter; with Shawn, every second was a winning hand.

"Let's go get checked-in and then we need to talk. Seriously."

She smiled up at him, intertwining her fingers with his. He kissed the space over her knuckles, shaking his head. "Women," he muttered, pulling her along with him toward the hotel entrance.

...

He came to her as soon as the door of their suite was closed. "Tell me what changed your mind."

"I don't want to waste whatever time we've got. Nothing lasts forever and I'm tired of regrets. You were right. The people at Matrix have bigger concerns than my romantic life. They don't care. I didn't realize it, but there are several department staffers that are in bed together. No one talks nonsense because time is precious. Sex is only interesting when it sells a design scheme. Otherwise, stow it. You've a fascinating atmosphere built up at Matrix. No backstabbers."

"If no one talks about who is sleeping with whom, then how did you find out there were other couples?"

"People let down their guard when talking. The last week, I decided to do as you suggested and get to know the other designers over lunch and coffee. I found out I'm more 'approachable' to co-workers. You marketed me well to the Matrix design team. Branding par excellence, at least for me. I don't know about you. I'm climbing the charts."

"I think that's because you're a partner. Not because we're a unit."

"Maybe. But people talk *with* me. Not *to* me. I like the interchange. Prior to this, I felt like an outsider."

"Perhaps it's your training. Did you ever think that as an alpha you'd naturally have this essence or quality that others would pick up on? Humans haphazardly perceive the non-verbal. Shifters would know. Stick that feather in your cap as well. But I've got a more important question. Care to take in the view?"

"Oh, lets. I've eagerly wanted to take in our view from up here." He ushered her into the living room and continued toward the terrace. A *whoosh* of the French doors and they were standing outside, up so high the breeze caressed her face and skin, making her body automatically unwind as though massaged. "This is gorgeous. Up here you can see in every direction."

She held up her hand, shielding her eyes from the sunlight, and stopped. Shawn was down on his knee, holding her hand, and gazing up into her face. His amber eyes glinted in the light, making her swallow unsuccessfully around the lump wedged inside her throat.

He began, "It's not merely east or west, north or south, that I want you to see. Baby, look into my eyes and into my heart. I love you. You fill me completely. Diana, marry me. Mate with me and we'll be as one. You and me, sweetheart, forever." He opened his palm, holding out an aqua box tied at the top with a white bow.

Joy welled up inside her. A geyser ready to overflow. She flung her arms around his neck and he stood crushing her body against his.

"Shawn, I love you, too. Yes. Yes."

"Tell me what you think of this." He took hold of her hand and placed the box within her grasp.

She stared at the box, her fingers trembling. "I know it'll be perfect."

"Open it. I was going to wait, but then, given what you said downstairs…it felt right to ask and I didn't want to put you on the spot in the driveway of the hotel."

"Darling, it would have been just as special." She pulled at the ribbon, tears welling in her eyes. Lifting the top off, she gazed at the black velvet box inside.

He laughed. "Two boxes." He took the top of the box from her hands and she removed the smaller one inside.

"Do you mind?" She handed him the bottom of the aqua box. Her fingers continued to tremble, making opening the velvet box a heart-pounding endeavor. She held the box in front of her, staring down at a huge marquis-shaped diamond engagement ring.

"You'll wear it?" he asked.

"My goodness, you certainly know how to surprise me." Running her finger over the metal and stone to see if this was a dream, she nodded. Her finger met the hard surfaces nestled in a satiny material.

"It's five and a half carats. I thought the shape suited your nature. Like a cat-eye. If it's not what you want, we can exchange the ring for anything you'd like. Baby?"

"It's perfect, Shawn, just like our love. I wouldn't trade it for the world." She threw her arms around his shoulders, burying her face against his chest.

He kissed the top of her head, cradling her next to him for a beat. All of sudden he pulled her back, his intense eyes filled with emotion as well as his ever-present possessiveness. Shawn lifted the ring out of the box. The diamond glittered fire and brilliance; even with tears blurring her vision, the ring was dazzling. "Give me your finger, then. Let's see if this little monster fits." He removed the ring—really, it was the most gorgeous ring she'd ever seen—and he placed it on her finger.

"Perfect fit," she murmured, as Shawn pulled her into another fierce embrace.

"Damn right," he said, before he kissed her, making her toes curl and her breath leave her body.

This was the moment that said it all. No more pretense—she'd found the mate who would come for and claim her. She loved him with as much fierceness and ferocity as he'd displayed. Nothing would keep her from claiming him, either.

"The ring is magnificent." She held her hand out to the side, so they both could see how the ring was displayed on her finger.

"Tonight we'll celebrate. But now we've got a check-in for the ceremony. There's a staging event where they'll show the nominees where to sit and get to the stage."

"I missed that memo," she said, sighing, wishing to stay in the hotel room and relish this moment.

The knock on the door interrupted their interlude. "That would be Santo. I told him to give us a few minutes before coming upstairs."

"I want to change. Do I have time?"

"You look beautiful, but I won't argue. There's not a specific schedule. Only a block of time. So, yes, but make it quick."

Within twenty minutes she was showered and changed into a business suit, her hair swept back in a chignon, and she clasped a small portfolio. He whistled from the living room as she entered into the foyer.

"I'm ready if you are."

"I'm ready for you. I can't wait to get you back here and show you what engagement sex is all about."

"I can hardly wait. Anything you find alluring has to be mind-blowing."

"I guarantee it, where you're concerned."

Santo waited outside with the car and she noticed that Fin was seated in the front passenger seat. Shawn walked up to the car door and motioned for him to lower the window. Fin opened the door and got out. "Everyone's checked in and accounted for. They're on their own until tonight for dinner. Tristen went to the restaurant to make certain everything is a go as planned."

Diana gazed over at Shawn, wondering why so much planning was needed for a simple staff dinner and dancing. "Did you invite some business prospects or clients?"

"Actually, I think we're going to have some gate-crashers. I'd hate for anyone to be disappointed. That's the name of the game in Vegas. Plan a party, don't put people on a VIP list, and boy, will they show up." He muttered, "This is Las Vegas, after all."

"Sounds passive-aggressive."

"Sounds about right." Shawn sat next to her in a brooding silence, staring out the window. He held onto her hand, rubbing his finger over her ring. She tried to pull her hand away to smooth her hair but he held onto her fingers, squeezing her left hand so hard that the diamond bit into her finger. Santo delivered them to the side entrance at the Encore Hotel, where a sign was posted for the award nominees' entrance. The driver got out first and opened the backseat door for her.

"Let him feel useful," Shawn whispered.

She placed her palm against Santo's and almost flinched. His palm was ice-cold. In this heat, she wondered how that was possible until she peered upward and met his pitch colored eyes. She saw a mercurial flicker, as though a mask had been lifted for a millisecond and then dropped, and only her subconscious held the deeper meaning. He released his businesslike grasp on her hand. Professional and devoid of emotion. Jesus, what had the war done to him?

Moving toward the doorway with Shawn's fingers digging into the flesh above her hip, she glanced over her shoulder. A man with a clipboard stopped them. "Your name and company?"

She gave him the information, and in return she was handed a sheet of paper filled with the answers to FAQs. He instructed to enter at the door, proceed down the corridor, and stop at the check-in station to obtain her badge. They entered the building and Shawn's grip on her lessened as they walked in silence, following a group who preceded them.

Diana made eye contact with a woman standing behind the table at the end of the corridor. The woman's steely gaze swept over her from head to foot, then back upward. Diana reacted instinctively, going into offense mode. She couldn't pinpoint what it was about the woman, but something prickled her to the marrow.

Diana was not one to be jealous, even if the woman's tailored suit was remarkable in how it went beyond fitting her body to melding with every breath the she took. Whoever she was, her bravura style reflected an L.A. chic, and Diana imagined her clothing came from a closed-door showing on Rodeo Drive. The woman's drop-dead looks hit like a meteorite and were the type that stunned a person speechless.

Interesting, Diana thought as the woman continued to stare her down. It made no sense. The woman put it out there, owning it, flaunting it. The right clothes, the right hair, the right everything. Not an article out of place. She dripped style like a leaky faucet until the airspace around her was filled with her essence.

"Just a moment," the woman said to the group in front of Diana.

As if on cue, the she softly snapped her fingers, and the young woman next to her leaned over. She whispered into the woman's ear and then traded places with her.

The woman swung her gaze back, focusing on Shawn, and ignored Diana. The air didn't just crackle, the particles burst apart. A sonic wave couldn't have been more powerful. Diana prayed she didn't just hear what she thought she did. No, this had to be a mistake. She gazed down at the woman's identification badge. *Mia Velarte*.

"Only two?" Shawn's ex-fiancée spoke to him with an exaggerated, condescending tone that scratched the surface of Diana's composure, before taking hold in a vise grip. Mia sneered as though she'd just smelled cauliflower cooking nearby.

"So, you're here. I've been expecting you and your…team."

"Mia, we're here to check in. Why don't you address the nominee? I'm not here to receive an award, as you well know. This is Diana Hambre, from my team." Shawn pressed the small of her back, then moved to take hold of her hand. "Diana, this is Mia Velarte."

Mia laughed, looking between Shawn and her. "Ah, she's so young. Your protégé, I suspect." Mia swung her gaze back to Diana. "Well, Ms. Hambre. Here's your badge. Follow the red arrows on the floor. A greeter will meet you and take you through the motions. Any questions?" Mia held out the badge.

Diana's fingers were intertwined with Shawn's. He didn't release his grip, but lifted her arm as though presenting her hand. Naturally it was an odd movement, and Mia's gaze dropped. The arched brow and flinty look were rounded out by a vindictive smirk.

"Tiffany's. The recession reached Denver, I see. Did you send one of the boys to fetch it out of some showroom case? Darling, if you're going to settle, at least make certain he's house-trained before you let him into your bed. Otherwise, you'll be cleaning up his mess from the get-go."

A closed-fisted punch to her jaw would have been easier to take. "The badge?" Diana asked, notching up her chin.

Mia still held onto it, apparently having forgotten all about the badge.

For Diana, Mia's behavior was a sure sign she'd been disturbed by her. This was totally a mess. She sneaked a glance at Shawn. Obviously, Mia wasn't the only one playing. This was a show, and Shawn was simply gauging her reaction. The ring, the hand-holding, the staff trip. This was the ultimate Vegas show. Lights—camera—action.

She would have crumpled onto the floor if this had been a month ago. Her conscience tugged at her to be reasonable, unwilling to believe that Shawn's hatred for his ex-fiancée would involve her and her emotions.

The only rule Shawn played by was to win. She'd been a fool to let him into her world. A raging lunatic to believe a man who'd shown little interest in her until she'd been nominated for some stupid award was not angling for something. Mia handed over the badge, and this time Diana reached for it. This was one of those moments when her world threatened to come tumbling down, and it took every ounce of her strength to maintain her composure, gazing across the table at Shawn's old lover.

Thank God for Tristen and this training. The leopardess in her stirred near the surface, straining to break free, and she held back, controlling herself. She absorbed this woman's scent, and squinted. From Mia's wrists, a strangely familial aroma wafted upward. Not entirely Shawn; more of his family, or lineage. Barely discernible, but as Diana panted her Jacobson organ went to work, confirming it was not an olfactory mirage. Mia carried some part of his mark. Why hadn't she noticed while standing in the line?

A group of people crowded around them, and someone asked a question, reminding Mia that they had an appointment.

Mia straightened her paperwork on the table. "Yes. Well this has been glorious fun. Now, I've others to assist."

"All set? There's a sign over there for the auditorium entrance," Shawn said, leading her away from the table as she clipped the badge to her collar.

Christ, she hadn't even known this check-in had been scheduled, or that there were appointments for the rehearsal. And then it dawned on her. Shawn had offered to take care of all the details, and she'd let him. Right down to the smallest one. Her heart.

She started away from Mia, walking close to the wall, the warmth of Shawn's body easing past the bitter cold that had filled her, freezing her emotions. They turned down another hall where, up ahead, the main auditorium was a blitz of people, cameras, and noise. Shawn's fingers brushed heat over her hand. "Please don't touch me," she said, between clenched jaws, snatching her hand away after several people had walked by and nodded.

Shawn took hold of her by the arm and hauled her next to him. "That was the woman who stole from me. I won't let her take you as well."

"Stop playing games with me. I get what you did. I understand that she screwed up your life and messed with your head. But that's no reason to pass the poison," Diana whispered, then stopped talking as a young woman smiled and came up to them. Shawn finally let go of her even though the blaze from his eyes was hotter than a Santa Ana wind.

"Hello, I'm Tara. Ms. Hamble, please come with me. I'll show you where you'll be seated, and how to get to the stage easily and quickly. This ceremony is televised. So we want to make sure you know how to get on stage and then exit. It won't take long."

"Uh, excuse me, Tara. My name is Diana Hambre."

"Oh, I'm terribly sorry, Ms. Hambre." The young woman peered down at her papers, then she scrutinized Diana's badge. "The rooster has you listed incorrectly."

Diana looked down at her badge as well. Great. She'd failed to notice that she'd been walking around with the wrong name clipped to her collar.

"I'll have that corrected. I assure you by the awards ceremony. *Diana Hambre*. Right this way."

"Yes. I'll follow you. Excuse me just a moment."

She turned to Shawn and lowered her voice. "Maybe you'd like to stay here and play catch-up with Mia. Anger has a strange way of dissolving during face-to-face meetings. I don't want to go forward, not knowing where I stand."

"There's nothing—" Diana placed her finger against his lips. The texture of his mouth sent a tingle of shock racing up her spine.

She whispered to him. "There's everything on the line. Maybe not to you. But to me. Sort it out and don't drag me down. I'll be back. If you're here, fine. If not, I'm a big girl and have been on my own for too long not to know what to do. I can find my way back to the hotel."

She exhaled, gazing into his face, his eyes so fierce she should have melted on the spot. But she didn't. On shaky legs, she followed Tara, leaving him standing in the corridor.

Chapter 16

With his back to the wall in every way possible, he watched Diana walk away, and he wanted to slam his head against the stone surface next to him. After surveying the auditorium, he strode to the area behind the tables where the media were stationed, reluctant to wait in the corridor and chance another conversation with Mia.

From what his sources had relayed, he knew Mia had already planned on shamelessly showing up at their dinner tonight. Somehow she'd managed an underhanded wheedling of an invitation. Since he couldn't outright stop Mia from inviting herself, he set about putting enough security measures in place to keep Diana from spontaneously shifting and getting into trouble.

The sight of Mia in person was worse than he'd anticipated, but not for the reasons that Diana asserted. He'd gotten over Mia's crap and superficial charm, and had no plans on looking back or revisiting anything from his past that concerned Mia or Frazier. What had him by the balls was the thought that Diana would undoubtedly be cast in the middle of this showdown and, in her condition, she might snap.

Mia had emailed him as soon as he'd returned from his week with Diana, wanting to do a meet-and-greet. That ludicrous statement about the economy back at the table in front of Diana…He should have thrown back in her face that several of her creditors had called him to discuss Mia's dismal financial picture as if she still worked for him.

He had Quinn check Mia and Frazier out again and he'd found out answers to his questions. Up until then he'd not thought much about either of them over the last six years.

He hadn't wanted to start something with Diana there. Mia was on a manhunt and he knew when she had begun casting her net that she was looking for bigger fish than Frazier. Her partner had hit bottom in the design industry and hadn't had a good idea since he'd split from Matrix. Mia and Frazier burned the clients they'd stolen and now had a mere handful left, not enough for a firm to survive.

Mia was looking to jump ship and he ascertained she'd been scouting for information about him. Quinn said she'd made calls to the Den and had gotten hold of Sonya, pretending to be a design consultant working with Matrix. Sonya didn't buy it and had relayed that she'd recognized Mia's voice with that all-too-perceptive coyote hearing. His manager had informed Quinn that someone had given Mia some information when she alluded to Shawn leaving the Den with a Matrix designer. Once Sonya had made it clear she wasn't going to divulge anything, Mia became riled and went so far as to insinuate that Shawn's business was more hanky-panky than aboveboard with his staff.

Quinn had sworn he'd fucking kill Mia and that the leak didn't come from him. Hell, he had also sworn that he didn't even know that Shawn had *relations* with Diana. The way his friend phrased "sex" as relations made him realize that Quinn was being respectful, and he'd smiled ruefully.

No, the leak was one of the room attendants, possibly the one he and Diana had passed on the stairs. That night had been crazy. Mind-blowing sex, all right.

Hell, he'd never come down from that high and he never intended to, ever. Diana was his. He waited for her to return, only letting his gaze break when he texted Tristen to get his ass over here. Stress. Yeah, he'd say that this situation with Mia reeked of stress.

He stood in the shadows at the back of the room, tracking Diana's movements as she was escorted to the location of her seat, and then up across the stage. Her grace and ease were a masterful cover for the tumultuous undercurrents that were roiling through her at this very moment, while she smiled and listened to the young woman next to her. From his vantage point, he sipped the air currents for Diana's scent.

Diana turned slightly, apparently feeling his gaze. She lifted her head and stared at him, unblinking. Her slightly-parted mouth briefly displayed the tips of her canines, while the skin across her face tightened.

Had she been in leopardess form, her ears would have laid flat against her head while her tail whipped back and forth. Diana and he were now deeply marked by each other, and that came with a heightened sensory perception that easily interpreted non-verbal nuances--especially when their gazes clashed and her eyes shot daggers across the room at him.

Fuck, Mia and her games; he should have been better prepared.

At the end of the rehearsal Shawn walked back to the corridor, arriving before Diana who had to weave through a throng of people in front of the stage.

She appeared at the end of the hall, the color high on her cheekbones; her eyes gleamed green, then flashed red.

Christ, he could see that only her will to control shifting kept her from prowling down the hall toward one deserving target. He couldn't let her do that. This place was so full of security that they'd cart her away to some facility for uncontrollable shifters. No one in his inner circle had ever made the mistake of thinking a wild animal would be welcomed at an event. Shifter or not, in human form they were all vulnerable and, regardless of what sentiments a shifter had, the law was the law. This wasn't the time of Jesse James, and busting someone out of a lock-up facility didn't happen.

This required that he assert himself so that she could fall back upon instinct, if nothing else. The leopardess would respond to the leopard. "Come, kitten. The car waits outside." He took hold of her elbow, drawing her next to him firmly and securely. She flinched, nearly yanking her arm from his grasp.

He pulled her into an alcove and positioned his feet on either side of hers, his hands holding onto her squirming body. "Don't fight me. I promise if you let this situation get away from you, from your training, I will assist you to regain control. Twenty hand prints across your ass will be nothing." His voice had dropped down to a growl, into the range that piqued the feline within her.

From the slight flaring of her nostrils and dilation of her pupils, her leopardess brain was reacting, even though he could see the woman was very much not letting the issue go. So he changed course, and set out to get the woman's attention. Without warning he feathered his fingers across her jaw, over her cheeks, and then ran his fingers through her hair. His mouth came down upon hers, and he wasn't gentle or coaxing.

He kissed her fiercely, demonstrating that he wasn't playing or teasing. His mouth set to work on her, first getting her to simmer down long enough for her passion to override her rage. Hell, he'd be boiling mad if the shoe were on the other foot.

She pushed against him, using her palms on his chest, but he was having none of it. When his phone buzzed, he refused to stop kissing her. He met force with force, driving her back easily, up against the wall, and following with his body. He snarled across their lips, a heated conversation they both understood. Twisting his fingers within her hair, he yanked just once, then deepened his kiss, thrusting his tongue over and over again into her mouth. Finally, he released her lips when her body relaxed. The feel of her easing up had his hands coming out of her hair and running down over her clothing. He took her waist between his hands, exhaling, debating whether he should finish this in the car, or look for an empty office.

"Don't push your luck, or I swear I'll be only too happy to show you how committed I am to you. *Listen to me. I love you. Only you. No one else.* Now, let's get the hell out of here. I need to explain a few things."

He backed off of her slowly, taking in her reaction and watching for any sign that she was less than ready to walk out into the corridor. He didn't trust Mia, and looked both ways down the hall in case she reappeared. Now that she'd tasted blood figuratively, she more than likely would seek another bite. He'd seen this type of move in shifters. Mia wouldn't understand that an alpha such as Diana held back, but didn't waste time with sparring. Mia didn't have the good sense to take in her environment, or to comprehend that Diana was a force to be reckoned with when thwarted.

Mia had become a wannabe-human. From what he knew, she tried to meld with them, rarely shifted, and had even gone so far as to prevent any pregnancies or hormonal rifts. That didn't mean that shifters like Mia couldn't shift, but they'd be more akin to tame animals who no longer relied upon instinct, became docile, and wouldn't know an alpha leopardess from a housecat…until it was too late.

Diana straightened her clothing. "I'm fine, really. Don't worry that I'm going to make a spectacle of myself. I won't and certainly not here."

"Sweetheart, I'm not concerned about that. You're so far off base. Whatever you've got roaming around in your lovely head is all woefully wrong."

He had to get her out of there and set her straight. Of all the things he should have done, explaining this situation beforehand would have been a much better idea.

Stepping back into the hall, he led her to the intersection where the check-in table was stationed. No sign of Mia. Only the other young woman remained and he waited as Diana handed back her security badge. Outside, Santo leaned against the trunk until he noticed they'd exited the building. He was wearing a Bluetooth clipped to the collar of his black shirt, and Shawn wondered what was up now.

"Please, give me a few moments." He opened the car door, assisting Diana into the backseat, and then turned back to Santo. "Something's up?"

"You're upset?" Santo asked, his voice so low it was difficult to make out the words.

"I asked you a question first. But, no, I'm not upset."

"Tristen wasn't able to come. Is that a problem?"

"Tell me the reason why he didn't and I'll let you know."

"Tristen tried to phone you, but couldn't reach you, so he called me. A group of dancers showed at the venue for tonight."

"Dancers?"

"Strippers. Four of them. They told the manager that you had requested their services and were there to rehearse and change."

"And where are these dancers now?" Shawn gazed into the back of the car, checking to see if Diana had heard any of this.

"Gone. Tristen didn't think it prudent to leave the place unattended. Fin grabbed a taxi and is on his way there now."

"Good call. Take us back to the hotel."

Shawn unbuttoned and removed his jacket. After loosening his tie, he rolled up his sleeves, in preparation for whatever came his way. This was going to be a roller coaster ride. His entire focus was on enduring the next forty-eight hours and then getting the hell out of Vegas, He'd be damned if he ever came back here, even if it meant selling what area businesses he owned. He got into the backseat, tossing his jacket to the opposite side of Diana.

"We're going back to the hotel so we can bathe and then leave for dinner." He wound his arm over her shoulders, waiting to see if she'd go tense. When she sat relaxed under his arm, he lowered his hand, palming her ass. "You've got to get control of yourself. There's nothing going on here, outside of you and me."

"I don't understand why you didn't say something about her being in charge of this event. Was I even nominated for my design? Or is this just a reason to get you to come to Vegas?"

He'd wondered if Diana would come up with that assessment. He had to reassure her that Mia didn't have any power; just a big, vile mouth.

"No, it isn't. She's doing PR for the design committee and this is some type of *pro bono* work, I imagine. Or she's getting paid, which is worse. Either way, she and Frazier are financially in dire straits. They're struggling and scrounging for work. I knew she was here; same as I knew Frazier was. Didn't I already address the fact that they live and work in Vegas? This is a microscopic town for the design community and many things for that matter. Of course I expected to run into them. But if I'd imagined it was going to be catastrophic, I never would have brought you here. Or I wouldn't have come. Mia brews trouble. Don't let her words twist in your head. She wants to mess with your mind."

"I get her personality type. The timing is suspect."

"What timing?"

"Asking me to marry you. That seems rather convenient. Your showing up with a fiancée."

"I already explained that. I acted on the spur of the moment when you gave *us* the green light to come out of hiding. Not because I wanted to show up with a woman on my arm. Don't think so little of yourself, or me."

"I don't know…things have a way of creeping out of the darkness and, you're right, into the mind."

"Baby, I'll fuck you mindless as soon as we get upstairs. If that's what it takes." He pulled her over across his lap. "Diana, I love you. I'm here to support you."

• • •

Entering their hotel suite, he stripped her down, then picked her up and put her on the table in the dining area.

He pulled her legs apart so her thighs straddled alongside his hips. "Lean back," he said in a rough, hoarse voice. "God, I've wanted to do this since we departed this morning. And you've sorely tempted me. Brace yourself. Do you remember our first night, how you wanted me to take you up against the wall?" He leaned over Diana, the scent of her rising around him like a tide rushing over his senses.

"You wouldn't do it. You said it would exacerbate my heat."

"Yes. But there are times when you need to know who you belong to. Tonight is one of those times." He trailed his mouth along her jaw toward her neck, nipping and sucking pressure points that made her flinch. Her breasts were tight against his palms. God, he wanted her more than ever. Soon, he would forego condoms and empty himself deep within her body. Her whole body would be his to do with as he pleased. And he planned on bringing her plenty of pleasure.

Shawn pulled a condom from his pocket, which had become a practice of late. Tearing open the foil packet, he gazed down at Diana's pussy, and groaned as he rolled the condom down his length. Entranced, he watched her rub her clit and writhe. "Oh baby, I love seeing you touch yourself. Right now, I've got to fuck you."

The head of his cock pressed against her opening, and he stared down at her glistening and pink skin abutting his crown. He swiped his dick across her pussy and then returned to her entrance, pushing forward. She was tight, and he had to force his way into her. She might act relaxed, but her body and her pussy said otherwise.

"Keep touching yourself." He pushed, driving his cock inside her body. "That's it. Help yourself to relax, kitten. Let your fingers work to make you feel good," he said in a voice pulled taut.

He held onto her fingers, guiding her to play with her clit. Slowly, she opened up to him. Thrusting forward, she felt like heaven; a velvet-lined nirvana. "Oh baby, you're so tight and so wet."

He pressed into her, stopping to gauge if she could take more. "Shawn, please, babe, I need you."

Now, with her moan, she was on fire and he eased himself forward, forcing himself to go slowly, nudging the rest of the way inside her. He pulled on her legs and she nearly came up off the table. A groan lodged in his throat. He'd not last more than a couple of strokes at this rate. There wasn't anything left to do here but fuck her like she'd wanted the first time they'd made love.

Christ. That's what they'd done that first night. And many nights after. But tonight wasn't about making love; it was about control and branding Diana. It was about making certain she understood they were together and soon would be bonded. No more doing whatever the hell crossed her pretty little mind. No way. He'd not let her wild instincts get away from her. He'd promised he would train her and he'd neglected this part for too long. Down, dirty, hard, and fast.

"This is exactly what you need. Isn't it?" He fucked her, riding Diana hard, moving into and out of her in a sex-sprint, pounding a rhythm into her body. With every slam of his hips, she moaned. He was riding her in a relentless, forceful rhythm that had her gasping with every breath.

"Just like that. Shawn, you feel incredible," she whispered, her eyelids fluttering. Diana looked overwhelmed as if caught on a tide of ecstasy that he delivered. This was their bliss.

His balls tightened in the familiar way that sent a tingling slither up his spine. "Baby, I'm going to come. Are you near?"

"Close. Very close." She pressed back onto the table, thrumming her finger in a pattern around her clit, then she opened her mouth and his name spilled from her lips. "Shawn, that's it. Oh, God…"

"Baby, come all around me. You feel fucking fantastic."

His back arched, and the spray of semen leaving his body made him shudder. At the same time he clutched her waist, slamming into her, delivering his cock as far as he could go. Her pussy clenched around him, holding him tight, and he continued to pound into her. Another jet of semen left him, and his mind blanked.

Forget the gym. This had been an aerobic workout. Sweat droplets ran down his face and splattered on the table. Her skin had the faint speckling pattern and glowed golden. Leopardess eyes stared back at him for several moments, until she blinked. He picked her up and took her to the sofa, her legs still straddled around his waist. For a long moment he held onto her, not bothering to say a word. They sat there, silent and suffused in pleasure. She pressed her cheek against his shoulder, sighing softly.

"I love you," he growled, wanting to forget the dinner and make love to her all night. He wanted to see his cum running out of her, down her pussy, after he'd finally mated with her. Then she'd be his, without question.

"God, I can't wait until I can fill you so full of my semen that it will run down your legs. Possess you and release inside you."

"Are you certain your bonds with Mia are truly severed?" She stared at him with unblinking, human eyes.

"Absolutely. No question as to that part of my life being over. Thank God."

He and Mia had had sex, but nothing like this. With Diana, there was a deep, unwavering hunger that until now, he'd never understood or even known existed. With other women and shifters, sex was an orchestrated event. Controlled. A physical release.

With Mia it had been destined for failure. He could see how far off the mark he'd been in selecting a mate without this connection. What the hell had he been thinking? Mia was anything but a true leopardess. Back then, Mia been adamant in her refusal to shift. She abhorred being part leopard. Everything had to be structured, purposeful, and he'd only witnessed her shift a couple of times. She wasn't anything like Diana.

"Kitten, that *woman* isn't proud of her heritage. I love how you own your leopardess nature. It's one of the reasons why I love you. All of you."

She stiffened, the tension hiking in her body. "Sometimes, when I'm unable to control that side of me, it feels anything other than attractive. Especially when you're not only head of Matrix, but working on a council that expects shifters to restrain themselves. I just wish I wasn't always on edge…feeling as though any second I was about to shift without warning. I know I've changed, but I still feel out of control."

"You're utterly intoxicating to me."

How could she not know her charm? An alpha leopardess such as Diana was a rare specimen of utter beauty from nose to tail. Her power, grace, and stamina combined into a relentless effervescence and had gotten under his skin with one taste. No healer would bring him back if something happened between Diana and him. She may feel the pressure of being in a relationship at this second, with his ex breathing down her neck. But this was temporary, and he'd make damned certain this situation was never repeated.

Exhaling the oxygen from his lungs, he contemplated his own state as he caressed Diana's silky skin, and was assured more than ever that he'd burn, incinerate, if she left him. There'd be nothing left to save.

Chapter 17

Seeing Shawn's ex-girlfriend or ex-fiancée or ex-whatever hadn't been the worst; not by a long shot. It was the expression on his face that had nearly broken her heart in two. Wasn't that what she had feared all along? Pasteurized milk would have lasted longer than this relationship.

The novel weight of the beautiful ring on her finger kept stabbing her memory, so cutting that she wanted to remove it and give it back to Shawn. The irony of having started out with a band of metal and now, again, caught tightly by another band, imprisoned by her own desire, wasn't lost on her. No matter what Shawn said, the fact that she continued to feel less than in control of herself had her reeling.

She rotated her engagement ring around her finger as her stomach continued to clench. If only she could be the perfect mate for someone such as Shawn. He was so in control of himself with his iron will. He deserved a stately mate, a woman to be by his side in the world of business and politics who wouldn't go over the edge at the snap of a twig…or appearance of an old lover.

She gazed at her reflection in the mirror, wishing she'd listened to her own argument that Shawn was temporary. He was too caught by his own lust to see her clearly, as he admitted. He wasn't thinking straight. How long it would last, she didn't know. Her options were to stay or return to Denver; to break it off or… what? Leave Matrix, move, and do what she'd done before, which amounted to the primal reaction of running and hiding.

She struggled to keep the tears at bay, taking a slow breath. Her heart whispered hope. If this were a choice, why couldn't she choose another option? She wasn't the same leopardess as when she left home. Not the same as when Cole had died. Not even the same shifter as a month ago. To leave Shawn and never experience the pleasure of him…Her claws threatened to spring free of her fingertips.

That option didn't dampen her desire, though, or diminish what the leopardess inside her craved. A silent roar reverberated inside her mind, aching for the chance to seize this opportunity. Ever since she'd stayed her ground with the bear, the idea of backing down and walking away tasted bitter. Too bitter to swallow. Not when it was Shawn's well-being at stake.

Diana's mind and heart raced, recalling Mia's scent and demeanor. The woman gave good face, but that was it. At first, the scent of Shawn on her skin tore at Diana, prickling a sense of jealousy. Well, if Cole was here and they'd somehow broken up, her scent would be on him, as his would be on her. Shawn never mentioned if she still carried a tinge of another male's mark. Her mate's death would have changed her own scent when she licked his broken body. Perhaps that's why it was her instinct to bathe him, clean his fur, and why she'd felt an insane need driving her to find another mate so soon. Nature's way wasn't always kind or generous; the fittest survived. It was the only law of the jungle— concrete or vegetative. Right now, that's what this matter boiled down to: who was most fit.

She inhaled, gazing into the mirror, and refrained from acting on the desire to gauge her surroundings. Another deep breath and her heartbeat didn't seem as wild.

Was she willing to stand and fight for what was hers, or give in to a woman who, by her very nature, would destroy whatever she touched? The flaming heat and ensuing color rising along her cheekbones, her neck, and over her chest would betray her.

No signs of blotchy patches on her skin. Not yet, at least. Peering at her reflection, she contemplated the rate at which her skin mottled; a sure sign rosettes were on the way. If she gave in to unrestrained temptation.

Tonight, arriving in a slinky cocktail dress required that she pull her instincts back into the realm of cool observation. Had she a tail, it would snap every now and again, demonstrating a lay-in-wait attitude. Now wasn't the time to be careless. High atop a Las Vegas hotel situated in a Sky Loft or down on the Strip, were no different than traversing mountainous terrain near Denver. She'd been taught well by Shawn and Tristen. Last week, she'd practiced new skills in letting prey come to her. Not the other way around. Tonight, she'd be shrewd for Shawn's sake.

Exiting the bathroom, she found him sitting on the bed. He stood as she entered, dressed in a dark suit, bringing out the color of his eyes. His shirt was unbuttoned at the throat and his cuffs twinkled with a hint of platinum links. A gift she'd had made for him as a small token for what he'd endowed her with over the last few weeks.

"Come here and let me look at you," he said. "You're too gorgeous for words."

"You clean up well yourself," she said, lifting her chin and staring into his striking eyes.

He took her by the shoulders, drawing her to him. He rubbed his cheek against the side of her face, firmly pressing and stimulating her glands, and marking her almost primitively. In turn, she pressed her cheek to his face, and stroked his skin. The sensation was exquisite, a release that bordered on a mini-orgasm, and bathed her bloodstream with a rush of hormones. Instead of intoxicating excitement, this ritual sated her, prepared her, and if they continued, both of them would be pushing the need to mate.

"This feels so good. Shawn, not much more."

"If you only knew what you did to me. I love you. You are mine. It's only a matter of setting the date, baby. I'm ready right now."

The words she ached to tell him swelled in her chest. She fought bringing up the subject of just what type of shifter he'd be better suited to find. After nibbling on the corner of her mouth, she decided at least one of them should strive to be transparent.

"Are you? Or are you uncertain and need to find your footing? You always told me to play my edge. How certain are you that Mia or someone just as sophisticated isn't an edge that will keep coming back to haunt you? My God, you're so generous to everyone and I don't want to be a place where you get stuck."

He kissed her temple, whispering, "Oh, I'm stuck on you in all the right ways." Shawn pulled back and met her gaze. "Mia means nothing to me. There's no way to compare what I feel for you to a mistake. And I don't know what you mean by *sophisticated*. You are that and more. Put that idea outside your circle of concerns. She and Frazier may be up to something, but nothing that need concern us. What we need to do is to get going." He smacked her bottom, squeezing her ass cheek in his hand.

Of course his sentiment was perfect, as were his words. It was his nature to be munificent. He was selling himself to her and she wished with all her heart that he realized, before it was too late, just what he was doing. She wanted to believe him because he sounded so certain; but what one believed was subject to change, and that lesson she'd also learned.

God help Mia if she tried something. Diana vowed to herself that this time she wasn't about to run away or turn the other cheek. She squeezed Shawn, wanting him to know he might consider her his to claim, and that was true. Her chest tightened. He was the perfect mate. The leopardess in her rioted to submit to him, let him claim her as he desired. Something inside her unclenched, and her heart burst apart, filling her with a dizzying love. Just as the first time he'd said it had rocked her world, the realization that she was desperately in love with him bubbled inside her. If that were the case, then, he was hers. Even if this ended tomorrow, at this moment, rightfully in all ways, he was hers, and she wasn't about to let some fur-biting tramp with a closet of expensive clothes hurt her mate.

"I'm more than ready," she said.

•••

The car pulled up to the restaurant and Shawn clasped her hand. "Let's have a good time. We'll celebrate you and me, baby."

She smiled back at him, caught in his enthusiasm. "I brought my dancing shoes."

His eyes slid lazily down her legs, and he inhaled. "Baby, those shoes say many things. Dancing isn't what comes to mind."

She held back from laughing. Slingbacks with six-inch-heels weren't exactly Ginger Rogers's knockoffs, or the reason behind prompting her selection. These little gems were worn to excite him, and his reaction sent a jolt of satisfaction into her core.

Alpha leopardess or not, the woman inside her rejoiced in scoring one for the home team. The dress was something she'd accepted from him. A slit going mid thigh-high required just the right accessories. Baring her body was one thing she did for him in private; dressing up to titillate was new ground for her. She found Shawn alluring and empowering in the way he continued to touch her, stroke her, and growl promises of what he planned on doing when they returned. Oh yeah, she was pleased with his reaction.

They were escorted inside and while surveying the room, she noticed the presence of the Matrix staff as well as countless unknown faces. She observed Shawn's ease in dealing with the restaurant staff. Not unlike how he operated at every moment:

distinguished, and so sure of himself. He stepped away from her to speak with Tristen.

Out of the shadows, Mia came sauntering over. Diana casually glanced to the maître d's desk where Shawn had been standing and he was gone. Every hair on her body bristled. She shifted her gaze back to Mia, lifted her chin, and held the woman's mocking glare. The conversation from the other room receded, but she was aware that all eyes were on them, and she tried to maintain an air of placid coolness as her insides tightened.

"My, my, look what we have here. The honored guest, and you're all alone. Good thing I just arrived to keep you company. Dearest Diana, lurking in doorways isn't always a good sign. Didn't your family teach you any manners?"

The tips of Diana's fingers and toes flexed to the point of pain. Her muscles contracted and she pulled in a steady column of air to calm her mind. *Remember, she's here to undo you. Keep steady.*

"The woman from the rehearsal? Are you working here as well?" Diana's question struck home, the direct hit revealed in the widening of Mia's eyes.

This sparring was very much a dance, and exactly the type she was prepared to engage in with this woman. Mia's eyes dropped, as though she were assessing Diana for the first time. Diana refrained from stepping forward and coming toe-to-toe with Mia. Tempting as Mia was as prey, she held back, unmoving.

"Don't try those middle-school tricks on me. I'm a professional and I'll eat you up in one bite. Not a threat. A promise. I don't care if you think Shawn's interested in you. He's not. Do you know how many times he's come to Vegas with a different woman on his arm? Ask him. I see him every year. That's right. Oh, he didn't disclose that small detail? Did he tell you we traded emails about this event? I know that you know who I am. Shawn's a man who doesn't just walk away. You know that's the truth. Do you think he'd let his cousin just take what was his and then play nice? I left

Shawn because he wanted too much. His nature is to consume, overpower, overshadow, and I've got my own dreams. He wants me. I've had to teach him that I can stand on my own two legs. Not four. I'm not some animal he can mount and bite and own." She smiled a wicked grin, her gaze lowering and focusing on Diana's neck.

Diana refused to react, keeping herself from reaching up and touching the places where Shawn had indeed marked her. Puncture marks, fresh and healed, ran up and down her body, but especially along her neck and shoulder. It was pointless to try and hide what he'd done. With her hair partially covering her neck, she wasn't concerned about anyone's reaction. It was what it was—his marks, and now she wore his ring. She hadn't gone to an underground club and had her ass publically spanked while some stud banger man-handled her.

Mia scoffed, "I don't wear any shifter's mark. I'm Shawn's ultimate climb. His Mount Kilimanjaro. You're a well-worn trail. Exercise. Nothing more."

Shawn came around the corner; it had only been a minute that he'd been gone, but the poison darts thrown had landed. Her training allowed her to remain in place, but her mind wasn't so easily appeased. Every word Mia uttered succinctly countered what Shawn had told her. Two sides of a coin, and she was in the middle.

Mia's amused smiled widened in self-satisfaction. Shawn's gaze snapped together with hers. She stared back, unable to smile.

A crowd entered behind Shawn, more Matrix staff and a client. Max Keton, one of Matrix's bigger accounts. Felicity, Matrix's retail design department's head, had entered the area and brightly announced, "Shawn, look who I found at the blackjack table."

Shawn released Diana from his gaze to attend to his client. "Max, good to see you."

"I'm the official party crasher." The man held out his hand to Shawn.

Clasping Max's hand, Shawn shook it vigorously. "Nonsense. The more, the merrier. Besides, you know the ground rules: any party in Vegas is an open invitation."

Max laughed, slapping Shawn's back. "I'm learning." Felicity pulled Max away, entering the main dining area, and the other people in their entourage from the outer area followed.

Shawn crossed in back of Max, coming at Diana with a force that made her step back. The door opened again, and the man who entered had to be the tallest man Diana had ever seen. Basketball proportions. Shawn's lack of affect in his reaction to the man's arrival shouted that this was not someone who was welcome here.

Mia held out her arms. "Frazier, dearest. Finally."

"Apologies." Frazier grimaced as he took his place alongside Mia. "I settled the arrangements for later."

Mia flashed Frazier a brilliant smile and curled her fingers around his arm. "I'm pleased, then."

Diana's vertebrae reacted as though snapped in place, bringing her to full attention. Mia commanded Frazier in the same way that Shawn liked to get her attention. A simple, direct command. Maybe they weren't opposite sides of a coin, but one and the same. Two heads that butted. Mia was right, Shawn didn't let things go. She'd been a fool to think he'd casually let this type of problem dissolve.

The inhalation from Frazier was audible. "Shawn, it's been too long. I hear congratulations are in order." He held out a bottle of expensive champagne. "I'm glad to hear things are going well for you." The man seemed genuine. There was an awkward pause.

"I'm Diana." She stepped forward, employing all the feline grace she could muster in denying Mia the chance to own the evening. "Frazier, it's so nice of you to join us. Thank you for the champagne." Shawn's fingers pressed into the skin at the back of Diana's hip. He patted the curve of her waist.

"Frazier, you're the last person I'd bet would show up here." Shawn stared at his cousin's extended hand, shaking his head. "Don't push your luck." He reached out and briefly shook Frazier's hand. It wouldn't do for Shawn to do much more, or less, considering they were in front of the doorway, in full view of a room full of staff and clients. Mia had played her hand well. Diana wasn't about to be the one in this foursome to act foolish. No, she'd pick her time and place, and then she'd take care of Mia. The woman met her gaze with the same smirk she'd worn earlier, and the silent challenge grated upon Diana's nerves worse than a slap to her face.

Shawn's jaw muscles bunched, moving rhythmically. He spoke in a voice that crept into the space, his tone low and smooth.

"You both are here. Make no mistake, I'll have you hauled out of here by your posterior ends if you so much as blink in the wrong direction. You—" His eyes flicked over to Mia, then flashed back to his cousin, as he squarely faced Frazier, "Keep her under control. You brought her here, you should take responsibility for her. Otherwise, I'll throw you both out of here. With pleasure."

Shawn took hold of Diana and walked away from them. She didn't have a chance to do more than keep up with his steps, not that she wanted to trade barbs with Mia or Frazier. "What will they do?" she asked.

"Suck up to someone. Tristen and Fin are positioned to escort them from the premises on my word. I'd rather see what they're up to than lay back and wait."

She stopped walking. "I thought that's what you taught me. Why so much *do as I say, not as I do?* I'm confused, and you're not making this any easier."

"Some rules are broken to level the playing field. With those two, playing fair is how people get blindsided. Best to keep one's enemies in the same room than allow them the opportunity to come at one from behind. You just need to be aware that anything that comes out of Mia's face is a blatant attempt to sabotage you, me, and us. Be *very* aware of that, and don't let her twist your thoughts."

She leaned closer to him. "One question. Do you come to Vegas each year?" She couldn't ask him if he'd seen Mia on those occasions.

"Yes. I've clients here. You know that. If it weren't for this kerfuffle, we'd have come here annually for business. I also have other annual stops. Nothing unethical, just business. What the hell did Mia say?"

"Only that you visited the city every year...and you traded emails before we arrived."

"It's true. We did. I told her to step back. I refused her offer. She's looking for financing, and we've already discussed this. You see, you're letting her get to you. Just stop, Diana, and ask yourself, why would I want anything to do with the woman my cousin is sleeping with? I couldn't possibly care less about her. I never felt what I feel with you. She was a business partner and I thought, why not do something that would please my parents and free me from having to think about family obligations? Nothing more. We've been over this."

"I don't know what to think. You both have good stories."

Perfect stories. It was as though they both knew what to say, had prepared their arguments, and delivered each side perfectly. Her heart told her one thing while her mind considered other issues. She was at war within herself. Again.

"I don't want to argue with you. Not tonight. Not ever. Baby, put aside her stupidity and let's enjoy this evening."

Diana gazed around the room, spotting Mia shaking hands with some of Shawn's clients. She'd be damned if she'd give Mia the satisfaction of ruining their evening.

"I'm here to enjoy our evening together." She laced her fingers with his.

They'd dined seated with Matrix clients and now danced, Shawn holding her closely, hardly moving to the music, and she nestled in his arms. This was the first time they'd appeared in public as a couple, and just as she expected, not an eye was batted except by Mia. The little conversation she overheard didn't ruffle her feathers. Mia must have been adept at reading body language, and Shawn's staff was loyal to a fault.

At least they were better at brushing off whatever Mia had prepared. From across the room, Frazier and Mia sat alone at a table, having scared off the other people who originally had been seated there. It was getting late, and several people had come and said goodbye. They wouldn't stay much longer, and Shawn waited until their clients had departed before suggesting that they dance one last dance before exiting.

All she had to do was get past tomorrow night and she'd be home free. With Shawn's arms around her, everything he said made sense.

"Are you ready to split?"

"Yes. My feet are ready to be free of these shoes."

"I've been invited for a game of poker. Private. Men only. I'll drop you at the hotel."

It was only eleven-thirty and this was Vegas. What was she going to do, demand that he babysit her? She longed to get into bed, and the prospect of an early night didn't seem at all bad. "Truth to tell, I'm tired. I'll work on my speech. How long do these games go on?"

"A couple of hours. Nothing too serious. But this is what's done in Vegas—schmooze over cards." He swung her around, pivoting on the dance floor before he dipped her back, almost touching her head to the floor. "Tell me you'll wait up for me, baby."

He brought her upright, slowly cupping her head, looking her straight in the eye, and making her reconsider an early night. "Of course I'll wait up," she murmured as her voice shook.

"That's my girl. I'll be back early."

"I'm not envious. Cigars, cards, and plenty of schmooze. Have at it."

He patted her rear end, making her gasp in surprise. They left after saying their last goodbyes to the few remaining staff. She sat under Shawn's arm, cuddling against the warmth of his body in the backseat of the car, and she toyed with the words that spun around her mind, aching to tell Shawn how much she loved everything about him.

"I enjoyed tonight. So much," she said as the car pulled up in front of the hotel.

"Santo, give me a moment. I'll be back shortly."

Shawn escorted her upstairs, kissing her heatedly at the doorway to the loft, and rubbing his knuckles across her cheek and jaw. "You're beautiful. I love you. While you're thinking of work, think of a date. I want to marry you soon."

"I love a pushy man." Her heartbeat thundered as she fought to keep a placid expression plastered on her face.

"Just wait and see how pushy I can be."

She closed the door, her body responding to him down to her racing pulse and coiling belly. Mating for life with a man that made her head reel; she was ready, and wondered what type of wedding he'd want. With so many clients, it would be an enormous event with a guest list of five or six hundred people, at least. And what a mix. Matrix, the Downtown Den, his other businesses and the council. No, the guest list would easily top a thousand. Those events were never easy to do, or to survive.

Removing her shoes, she wondered if a small chapel wedding was even possible. A small, intimate wedding sounded divine.

She was about to shed her dress when a slow, laborious knock sounded at the door. She smiled and called out, "Did you forget your key?"

The prospect of one more kiss from Shawn had her moving to meet him at the door.

"Come here and let me show you what I've got planned for later." Swinging open the door, she stared at the faces of Mia and Frazier. A blinding chill overcame her senses. She tried to slam the door in their smug faces, but Frazier was too quick. He stuck his foot in the jamb and his massive body laid into the door, moving it as though she were nothing more than static cling lint. He pushed in, and Mia followed in his wake.

"Yes, you were saying something about your plans?" Mia slinked by Diana, going into the living room. She walked down the hall, stopping in front of the bedroom. "All alone?"

"What do you want?" Diana asked, already imagining nothing good. "Shawn will be back in a couple of minutes."

"That's not what we heard. We know you're alone and will be for hours. Shawn's on his way to a poker game of sorts. One which we've arranged as a special treat. Now that Shawn has plans for the Vegas justice council, we thought it an apropos welcome. How rich! An eye for an eye."

"That's not what the council is about," Diana retorted.

"But wait, that isn't what Shawn espouses. Or is it? Where you're concerned, he seems to forget that he can't simply issue threats. Like all other shifters, if he has a problem, it must go through the council. Not have his lackeys go around and tell our clients to stop doing business with us."

"You're the ones who have lost your own accounts. You're blaming him for your own issues."

"Not exactly. Ever since he arrived in town, we've seen a record number of our accounts close. That's not coincidence, it's Shawn acting as though he were above the law. And now this seems fitting; since he seems to believe he can do as he wants, then we can act freely as well. I also don't think the actual game will last long. Not to worry, though. We've got special times planned for you as well. And your lover won't have to miss a thing. We plan on webcamming this event for a whole lot of viewers' pleasures."

The feeling of blood draining from her face kept her desperately attuned to them. "What do you want?" Diana repeated her question, buying time.

"Why, you, silly. And we mean to have you…in every way possible. By the time Frazier's done with you…not even a dog will come near you." Mia patted Frazier's meaty arm.

Diana noticed the case Frazier had been carrying as he swung it up onto the table and the latches clicked open. He glanced over to her, then nodded his head to Mia. "Get her ready." His stony voice came out in a bark. "Prepare her the way I like."

Mia beamed. "He's becoming impatient. Note to self, Diana… uh, he's failed at anger management."

"You're twisted. Sick. Do you think you'll get away with this?"

Mia came at her, taking hold of her dress, her face contorted. "Shut your slut mouth or I'll shut it for you."

"Threaten me. Go on. I'd like to see you try something yourself instead of hiding behind…your henchman," Diana said.

Even with her small stature, Mia was able to grab Diana and pull her roughly. Whispering into her face, Mia spoke slowly. "Truth. You won't know. A little preview on the events: after we finish up with you here, we plan on taking both you and Shawn out into the desert. And this won't be a pleasure trip, *dearest Diana*. There will be nothing left after the buzzards finish with you. Now, get undressed, you stupid fool. I can't even imagine how Shawn got involved with someone like you. He is so out of your league."

Diana studied Mia's movement, her breath and heart rate. The physical exertion taxed Mia, and she wanted to see just how much of a toll it took on her reserves. Resisting, Diana pulled back, forcing Mia to hunker down with her grasp upon Diana's arm.

Mia spat, her anger starting to leak through. "Fucking bitch. We can do this nice, or not. I'd rather you do it not nice. Personally, I'm aching for a fight. Of course, I'd be just a sideliner. My money is on Frazier. He likes it rough."

Diana stared open-mouthed at Mia for an instant before assessing her options. Mia shoved her up against the table, across from Frazier. Mia blocked the hallway, and the only way out of the hotel room was off the balcony. But this was the rooftop. A magnificent view. And no way down unless she jumped.

Frazier began methodically removing and arranging handcuffs, ropes, and an assortment of clamps and chains in a row along the top of the table.

"May I, love?" Mia fingered a mask, dangling the leather, then put it down and picked up a red rubber ball with elastic cords. She snapped her fingers at Diana. "Let's go. Time is running out."

She'd never seen the thing that Mia held. Unable to keep silent, she shook loose of Mia's arm and said, "Keep that vile mouth of yours shut. The lies you spread are notorious. But no more."

"Keep talking. This type of verbal foreplay gets my baby rock hard." Mia turned back to Frazier. "Did you bring the spreaderbar? Oh, the things I've planned for this one."

The anger that had been on a slow simmer roared to life within Diana. Instead of dropping her dress, the gown tightened around Diana's body. It had been designed and altered to fit her as a woman, and her shifting form began to widen. Her bones elongated so rapidly that the pain seared her joints. In a split second, her size six, womanly human form no longer stood in the room.

Diana morphed into a lithe, powerful leopardess. The shift occurred spontaneously, rapidly, and her emotions rioted, inciting the need to attack. From controlling herself while contained in human appearance, her leopardess form blazed to life, already stalking Frazier from behind as Mia backed away.

"I can't believe you still shift like a heathen. What the hell? Who in this day and age still fucking shifts like that?" Mia actually rolled her eyes, as if she didn't grasp the issue for a moment.

Frazier's face scrunched up before he swore. He picked up a handgun and aimed it at Diana. "Shit," he yelled.

Diana smelled their fear. Words were distractions she didn't heed. Instinct prompted her to powerfully leap, knocking Frazier down, and rip into his body with her claws extending and curling.

In one moment she'd gone from a petite woman to a leopardess weighing a hundred pounds more than Frazier, the man whose neck she held between her jaws. She snarled while holding him caught, her canines piercing his skin, his trachea flexing under the pressure of her jaws.

The door opened and Shawn burst in, followed by Tristen and Santo.

"Diana, let him go!" Shawn approached her while Santo took hold of Mia.

From the scratches on Frazier's body, the air swirled with the scents of blood, rage, and revenge. Diana's snarls became the sound of silk being ripped, but then with each step closer by Shawn, her snarl changed to a contact growl resembling a rapidly-moving saw cutting across wood.

Releasing Frazier wasn't in the cards from her vantage point. The view of the toys of torture spread around his body on the table frustrated her.

Shawn reached out, touched her flank and stroked her, murmuring soothing words. Primitive volition demanded she attend to her alpha's command.

Diana vacillated, unable to release Frazier, and so she picked him up in an ironclad bite. Again Shawn's voice and touch gained entrance into her rage, and she reacted by tossing Frazier to the marble tile, the sound of his skull striking against the floor echoing hollowly throughout the room.

Regardless of Shawn tempering her anger, her gaze shot directly to Mia. Diana crouched down, and it was apparent she'd not let the other troublemaker go. That one meant harm to Shawn. All the leopardess knew was to seek protection for her chosen mate.

Roaring powerfully, the louder-than-normal growl was meant to warn those present she was incapable of listening to reason. Diana bounded from the table, and stalked over to where Santo held on to Mia. He walked backward, dragging Mia away to relative safety.

Tristen approached Diana, holding out his palms. "Diana, no. Don't follow your instincts! Draw from your training."

The words flittered around Diana's brain, as though she had a choice to acknowledge or disregard them. She skittered close to Mia, swiping out a paw to claw the woman, eliciting a shrill scream from her. There was a purpose to this toying with one's prey, one she'd learned from Shawn during her training.

Tristen and Shawn tried to draw her attention. She didn't care as she snarled a warning for them to get back. She leapt back up onto the table, causing it to tip and crash as she jumped into the hallway.

Santo pushed Mia back, unable to make her stay quiet. "Stop her, fucking stop that crazy bitch!" Mia shrieked, over and over.

Diana roared, coming up to where Santo and Mia had stopped, cornering them against the loft door. Blood trickled down her fur; she didn't know if it was hers or Frazier's, and she didn't care. She only inhaled the scent, fighting her primal urge to attack and destroy when her prey was so near. Mia's form and tone taunted the leopardess within Diana. Her prey's blood would give her peace.

The instinct grew stronger, and she couldn't put aside her anger and rage, her humiliation and desire for revenge. The leopardess recognized that to let a hazardous beast free meant they'd meet again, and the law of nature didn't think that was the best route. The alpha DNA in her ruled that predators killed by instinct, knowing a better day to destroy an enemy may not come. Seize opportunity when it was presented and save the tears. That's why animals didn't cry. It was a luxury they couldn't afford.

Diana roared again, demanding that her target be let loose. But it didn't matter, really. If the man continued to stand in her way, she'd do what needed to be done. That was what her nature told her she must do, to protect herself and her mate. She sniffed the edge of Mia's skirt and a blood-curdling scream erupted from Mia's throat.

Diana ears pricked, understanding that this was the type of terror that goaded an animal to run. The predator appreciated this type of fear in others and she paced the hall, waiting as she'd been taught.

"Diana, no. Don't do it. You'll lose. In the end, you won't be free," Tristen pleaded, edging closer to her. "You must listen. Her death will mean nothing if you're taken away from Shawn."

The words spilled over her, and she batted her tail at him and what he was trying to preach. The air tormented her focus. She snarled, then issued a low roar. A moment later she sniffed, opening her mouth to bathe in her alpha's scent.

Shawn appeared in leopard form, coming down the hall. Mia fainted, going limp in Santo's arms without warning, and he didn't have a chance to stop her from slipping to the floor. The movement caught Diana's attention; she jolted instinctively toward Mia and took hold of her by the hair. Her claws flexed and then curled. She faced Santo, with not more than a few feet between their faces. Diana blinked at him, a low snarl fell from her mouth, and she pulled Mia's body across the space along the floor. Santo released the woman.

Shawn's roar echoed loud and forceful, and he was on her, knocking her body gently but with his alpha intent. He came off her and circled in front of her. He stepped over Mia, and gazed into Diana's eyes. They touched noses, and he proceeded to rub his cheek across her face, bathing her in hormones and his scent, calming her nerves, and giving her space to decide her next move. Shawn switched sides, stroking his face against hers, licking her muzzle, and butting his head against her forehead.

All of sudden, holding onto Mia didn't seem important. Following Shawn held her rapt attention, so she paused, absorbing that her immediate instinct to acquiesce to him overwhelmed her being. Their natures allowed for one leader, and she wasn't about to buck him. In her world, there was zero need to challenge him into a skirmish. She hissed, releasing her hold on Mia.

Coming to Shawn, she rubbed herself down the length of the leopard shifter who had come to claim her. She settled down on the cold marble floor at his feet. He panted over her, roaring several times. Moving carefully, Tristen collected Frazier while Santo picked up Mia. They exited the room, giving Shawn and Diana privacy to shift back to human form.

They stared at one another. Diana could feel her body changing, her muscles rippling from pent-up energy. Shawn in both leopard and human forms was the most beautiful creature she'd ever seen. She wanted a life with him, bearing his children, and caring for him as her mate. She huffed out a breath of air, signaling her submission.

In less than a second, Shawn shifted and then picked her up and gently tossed her on top of the bed. "Turn around for me," he said.

Shawn mounted her from behind, their bodies completely shifted back into human form. He penetrated her in a rush of heat. The bite into her flesh spiraled into exquisite pleasure. She moaned and arched back, giving him a better angle in which to drive himself home inside her body.

He released his hold on her skin, groaning into her ear hoarsely. "God, I've wanted this since the first time I saw you," he breathed.

"Shawn, I'm almost there. This feels magical."

Her mate's strokes sped up; his thrusts went deeper than they'd ever gone. Her climax was there on the next thrust, and then they both exploded.

Shawn let go a loud yell, "Diana, you're mine." His body shuddered with the force of his orgasm. The feel of his hot jet of cum filled her. The nerves of her body tingled and she moaned under him. Shawn wrapped his arms around her hips as continued to he slam his cock further inside her, claiming and forging a true mating bond with her. She gave into him, completely as a leopardess to her mate. The golden haze surrounded them, the sensation of being one with another overwhelmed her. Diana cried his name in a euphoric wave of ecstasy, "Shawn, I love you." They both lay sprawled on top of the bed, gasping, with their legs and arms intertwined for long moments. Her heartbeat pumped wildly and she purred loudly, rubbing her hips against Shawn's body. Her mate. Forever. Even though she desired to lie next to him in leopard form, this was more than perfect.

"I hope you're not disappointed in me," she whispered, caressing his forearm. "I've never been that upset. I won't say I'm sorry for what happened to them. I can't."

"I'm amazed at you. Jesus, I thought you were going to crush his skull." Shawn turned her in his arms, concern flagging his face.

Tears rimmed her eyes. "I wanted to. I had no choice. I listened to you. Your voice filled my head much like a calming balm. The effect was extraordinary."

Shawn pulled her up into his arms. He kissed away her concern, taking his time until her body relaxed. Brushing her hair back from her face, he murmured. "You did better than I would have, given their fucking tricks."

"They didn't touch me. Not yet." She recalled the items on the table. "Did they think they'd get away with attacking us?"

"I don't know. Tristen checked out the game and sent word to turn around. They knocked out Fin. Slammed a pipe against his head. Tristen will take them to the police station. This is a federal crime. No matter what they didn't do, they're still going to prison for a long time. I'm sorry, I should not have left you alone. Not with them in this town."

She closed her eyes. "I'm not sorry. Now they won't bother us again. It worked out. Just as you taught me. Patience, planning, and confidence. To wait for the prey to come to me."

"I never thought in a million years the prey would take this form. I can't believe you were able to refrain from tearing them apart. This news will spread like wild fire in the underground clubs."

"Is that a bad thing?"

"My God, no. To refrain from taking an eye for an eye. You've shown shifters that revenge is not the route to take. You're really the first shifter to show such restraint, considering what you've been through. Baby. I love you so much."

With their gazes tightly locked, she said the words she longed to share with him. "Shawn, I love you so much. I never could have done that without you showing me the way."

Chapter 18

Standing inside a plane circling Las Vegas, Shawn and she held hands. He'd agreed to a small, intimate wedding, and so she acted. If they returned to Denver, they'd be obliged to a large, formal affair. She'd always wanted to skydive and this was one way to get Shawn to herself.

The ex-military paratrooper-turned-chaplain pronounced them husband and wife, and then said, "You may now kiss the bride."

Shawn enfolded her body within his arms while his warm mouth devoured hers, heating her whole body in a blaze of love and lust, curling her toes just as he'd done the first time they'd kissed.

Fin thrust a glass of champagne into their hands. "Say 'cheese.' Look this way." Angling the camera, Fin snapped the wedding pictures. "These will go viral, I bet."

"Tweet and Facebook them. What the hell?" Shawn chuckled, turning his attention back to Diana, and her breath caught at the gleam in his eyes. "Cheers, baby. I love you, Mrs. Barclay." He pulled her into another hug, lifting her up and letting her slide slowly down his body.

"I love you," she whispered, suddenly shy in front of so many men whose expressions had softened for once, making them seem young and boyish. It was a welcome change from the tense pack of shifters who normally surrounded Shawn and her.

Tristen cinched up Shawn's parachute for the second time while Fin did another check on Diana's. "Everything's kosher," Fin finally said.

"Shawn's chute checks out. Good to go." Tristen punched Shawn's arm. "Nothing to this. Count to twenty and pull the line.

Then you'll bounce and float. *Booyah!* We'll be right next to you, of course. But still, it's a mad rush."

Fin and Tristen high-fived each other, a rare show of any emotion between the pair of wolf shifters. Santo came forward with a camera for a second picture. The paratrooper preacher, another wolf shifter who'd didn't mind the jump, cleared his throat, "Just sign this certificate and it's official." He clicked a pen and held it out to Shawn.

"Sorry to interrupt. Man, we're circling around the drop point. You guys have to be ready," Tristen said, glancing down at his wristwatch, then stood back to speak into the microphone in his helmet. "Charlie-Alpha-One. They'll be ready."

"Wait a minute," Shawn said, positioning the clipboard against a seat for Diana to sign the marriage license.

Diana tilted her head, now encased in a drop helmet. "Not reconsidering, I hope."

"No," he softly laughed. "I wanted to tell you…how much I love you. You know I'd fly to the moon. I'm more than amused you took me at my word. Touché, kitten."

"You've been there for me and helped me find out who I was meant to be. How can I ever—"

He scooped her up and kissed her before she could finish. "We both are brilliant for each other. Soon we'll be accelerating toward the ground at one hundred twenty miles an hour, but hey, it's all going to be an amazing journey as long as we're together." He pulled her against him, tracing her lips with his thumb. "Baby, I'll come for you. Any time. Any place. I'll always come for you, Diana. You're mine. Forever to keep."

"I know, babe. I've known that from the first time we met. I love you just as much." She held onto his hands, looking up into his eyes, and wrapping herself in the intense ferocity of his love. "You're mine. Forever and ever."

About the Author

Susan Arden writes sweet and spicy love stories within the genres of Western, paranormal, fantasy, and contemporary romance. Heat level is steamy. You can keep in touch with her online at Twitter *@romancebysusan* or on her blog: *http://susanarden.blogspot.com*.

More from This Author
(From *Tempted by Trouble*)

"Hey, we're here," Carolina poked her cousin. She parked the car near the side entrance to the chapel. "You'd better get on the move. My mom is pointing to her watch. Crap, she's undeniably on the war path."

Sam's delicate brows drew together above her sunglasses. "My head is splitting. What time is it?"

"Just past eleven."

"We're late," Sam grimaced. "Yep, *Tia* looks upset."

Carolina waved. "By a few minutes. Besides, you look fabulous."

"You mean for someone who spent the entire night drinking?"

"Don't blame me. You were the one who wanted to remember your last night as a single woman. I simply complied with a smashing bachelorette party." Carolina drew in a breath. "Sam, you're really lucky."

Her cousin nodded. "I can't believe after four years, I'm about to see my dream become my life." Sam sniffed and twisted her engagement ring.

"No, don't you start crying," Carolina ordered.

Sam smiled, her chin trembling, and her azure eyes filled with tears.

"Here," Caroline whispered, holding out a tissue while her own eyes became misty.

Sam pulled down the visor and dabbed at the corner of her eye.

Carolina's mom opened the car door. "Ay, *chicas*. Are you both crazy? *Vamos.* Really Carolina, of all the days to revolt."

"This wasn't a revolution. We had to celebrate Sam's last night of freedom," Carolina said. "*Mami*, we made it on time."

"Barely," her mom glared. "Cynthia, say goodbye to my wayward daughter. We need to get you dressed. You both always push limits. Well, we'll see how you do now that you're about to be separated. *Venga*." Her mom turned toward the young man tapping her on the shoulder.

Carolina rolled her eyes to the sky. It was true. The two cousins had been inseparable until now, and with Sam getting married, they'd be separated for the first time in twenty-six years.

Cynthia—*Sam*—and she had grown up in Miami, only months apart in age. They had attended St. Teresa's Academy from kindergarten thru high school. Both of them had lost a parent. Both of them had suffered heartbreak from a jackass.

The only difference was, Sam's jackass turned out to be Prince Charming once they reconnected. Today was Sam's wedding to Rob Graham, former jackass, and evidence that happy endings do come true. At least for Sam.

Carolina's future, however, looked very different.

"I'm so happy for you and Rob," Carolina said. In an hour, her cousin would be walking down the aisle toward wedded bliss. In two days, Carolina would be on a plane headed to Annona, Texas. No, that wasn't exactly true…to Clarkesville. Annona, a town too tiny for geographical reference on a map, was too small to have an airport.

"Thanks," Sam blinked her false eyelashes rapidly. "This is great. I'll be a crying mess before the wedding. Rob will take one look and shout, *yeah right*."

"Never. Not him. He's madly in love with you. Shoo; I'm going to park the car. I'll be right in."

"You better rescue me before they turn me into an iced cupcake." Sam titled her head toward their aunts and cousins waiting on the sidewalk.

"Get ready to have this entire event captured. The photographer just set up. Remember to smile."

"Give me a hug. You're my best friend. Always." They wrapped arms around each other. Sam drew back and picked up her purse, murmuring, "No looking back now."

"Hold that," the photographer called. "Okay, take a couple of steps and then let's get one with the family coming to meet you."

"Good luck," Carolina said, before she took a wide loop around the church parking lot in search of a parking place.

Then she saw Jeff's Jaguar drive into the parking lot, and she pulled her car up next to his. His timing was impeccable. That fact she could never take away from him. She'd invited him to the wedding only because they'd spent time with Sam and Rob. It was a polite gesture, even though all she wanted to do was formally end the relationship long over. He'd texted her and said he'd meet her at the church. She hadn't expected he meant almost two hours before the wedding.

She didn't bother to get out of the car and neither did he. She rolled down her window. "You're early," she said.

"I'm on the run. Just got a call and I'm flying out. I wanted to touch base since you said you might have a job, something you needed help on."

"It doesn't start until next week. I'm fine." *Christ, he could smell money a mile away.*

"Doll, don't start with an edge to your voice."

"Jeff, let's just get things clear. I already told you that us as a couple was over. For business, okay. Fine. I don't need your excuses. You could have called."

"Carolina, don't talk like that. One misstep and you act like we're married. Sweetheart, what do you expect when you're so uptight?"

Not screwing any and everything that walks doesn't make me frigid. Her knuckles went white from gripping the steering wheel. "I'm late."

"No kiss. Just goodbye."

Good riddance was more like it. "Just bye."

"Carolina, I know you'll be in touch. That, I'm certain of. Take care, precious." He drove off. At least she'd be free of that piece of baggage when she left next week.

She spotted a shaded parking space and headed toward the corner, away from the church entrance. She needed a couple of minutes to get her head on straight. She was still half-hung over after spending all night partying and drinking her way around South Florida in the company of thirty screaming women in two limos. They had stopped for an early morning breakfast at Chartreuse, an after-hours club catering to late-night stragglers who wanted breakfast before going home and crashing.

Only she hadn't gone home. Instead, Carolina showered, dressed, and escorted her cousin to her hair and nail appointment, and then took her to have her makeup done before bringing her to the church. Definitely, she could have a moment alone while Sam was getting dressed by an entourage of aunts and tipsy cousins. She wouldn't be missed if she grabbed a catnap. The wedding march wouldn't start for another hour and a half.

Alone, she set her alarm and plugged in her iPod before she pushed her seat backward until she was fully reclining. With the windows up and the air conditioning on, she closed her eyes. Forty-five minutes later she woke up, stretched, and yawned. *Talk about the benefits of power napping.*

She sat upright and peered into the mirror on the visor. Not too shabby; if she could get some eye drops, she just might pass for a bridesmaid. The parking lot was filling up with cars. There was even another car parked next door, all the way over here. Then she glanced inside the car and gasped. She turned away from the man and woman inside the other car.

From the bouncing motion of the woman's head, Carolina was quite certain she knew what was going on. In her Audi SUV, she sat slightly above the other car and gazed back at the man holding onto the woman's head with both of his hands. She could see the woman wore a blue dress, and he had on dark trousers.

Carolina glanced away again, heat searing her neck, and played with the ring on her thumb. The wedding was scheduled to begin in thirty minutes, and she needed to change into her bridesmaid's dress.

Shoot, she didn't know what to do. If she opened her car door, she'd find herself smack in direct sight of them, not exactly a sexy ménage with herself as the uninvited guest. The irony of this voyeurism pretty much represented her entire sexual experience. She was an outsider.

And now seated here, secretly watching her neighbors further inflated her bubble of loneliness. Why didn't she feel what other women described? *The Earth move*. Nope. Not a quake or shimmy. Not once. The woman next door squirmed on top of the black leather seat. Carolina banged her head back against the headrest. The minuscule amount of heat and attraction she'd experienced rarely amounted to all consuming blaze, never took a leap into ecstasy. Forget bliss. Not an iota of delight. Unlike the other woman in the car next door who just screamed an expletive. God, what it must be like to be on fire. So consumed and willing to do things on the spur of desire.

Would she ever meet a man who made her give in without caring if it was in his bed—or parking lot? Just thinking about such an encounter made her go hot all over. Lately, she felt her days where marked. Boring. Vanilla. Glancing back at the man made her long for raspberry fudge ripple. With whip crème. And her on top.

If she remained inside her car much longer, her mother would to throttle her. Weddings did strange things to people. She nibbled on the inside of her cheek and nervously glanced back at the couple, wondering if they were just about done.

"Oh, Christ," she said aloud. The man's hand was between the woman's legs. Carolina couldn't see his face. The things he was doing to his "date" made the space between her own legs tighten and grow warm. She watched him move his hand upward, fondle the woman's breasts, and then move his hand down between her legs again. All the while, the woman worked her head over his lap.

Carolina told herself to look away, but she was mesmerized by the man's hands and the way he made the woman squirm and writhe. There were too many layers to the woman's dress to see much flesh. From what she could tell, the man seemed to be an expert in foreplay and wasn't the type to lose steam after five minutes of sex which, unfortunately, made this situation extremely tricky. She could just back out her car, without looking over and then she'd be free.

Carolina threw the car into reverse and pulled out of the space. She turned the car around and drove forward, only slamming on the breaks after a scraping crunch sounded on the right front side of her car.

"Oh for the love of…Damn it." Some get away. She had actually hit the other car.

She closed her eyes and counted to five. When she opened her eyes, the occupants were not outside the car. Instead, there was movement inside the compartment so at least they weren't still going to town on each other. She hoped by this time they were decent. Carolina opened her door, slowly walked around the hood of her car to inspect the damage.

"Thank God…only a bumper-to-bumper contact," she said to herself.

"Look like much damage?" a deep male voice asked.

Carolina's flippant response choked in her throat.

The man from the inside the car continued to come closer. She gazed up into the face of a man whose smoldering dark eyes and quirked lips galvanized her conviction of what she observed scant minutes ago. From the bulge still evident in his dark trousers, she could tell he undoubtedly knew what to do in bed. His liquid brown eyes flickered over her face, settling upon her mouth in such a way as to cause her to smile without her consent. He tunneled fingers through thick black hair. The second their eyes snapped together, her stomach clenched.

"I think the bumper scratches are minor. Otherwise, my car is fine." She had to concentrate just to say each word since her composure was off on hiatus.

"It's nothing to get your panties hitched up on, little lady. I can think of so many other things to get excited about." His voice was constructed by the devil himself. Nothing short of warm and soothing and enthralling in how he shaped letters into sounds that begged to be captured. It was as if she listened to a message meant only for her ears, a whispered evocation. Carolina's skin beaded. She stymied a shiver that unfurled inside her body. Must be the remnants of alcohol in her foggy brain, she thought.

"I'm not the one who's excited. I merely pointed out the damage is minor." she retorted. She'd be damned if she would make this easy on the guy who couldn't keep his pants zipped in the middle of the day.

"Just glad there's no harm done from where I stand," he replied, not even bothering to inspect the condition of his car. "Are you here for the wedding?"

"Yes, and it's about to start." She couldn't help notice his sensuous lips. Again.

"Then we'd better get a move on. Bride or groom?" he asked while his eyes languidly traced a path down her body.

"Bride," she said, and moved behind her car, using it as a shield from his perusal.

"Makes sense. I don't recognize you. I'm Matt." He shot a thumb back to his chest. "Groom's side."

His bowtie was undone, the ends lifting in the breeze. His white tux shirt was partly open, revealing an expanse of tanned skin. Carolina let her gaze follow a pair of long legs housed in dark dress pants that didn't hide his muscular build and then she frowned. Cowboy boots stuck out from the bottom of his trousers. Black polished ostrich boots that were spread apart in a wide stance.

"Oh, I see what you mean."

Rob's family was coming from all over the nation, unlike the bride's familial hub, which was housed in South Florida. Living in another state would explain this man's sexy rolling syllables.

"No reason we can't get acquainted, is there sugar?"

She stopped gawking and tore her gaze from Matt's face and body convinced he was just another smooth talker. "I'm late and should already be inside getting ready. Well, I'm glad this worked out for you," she shot him her best *I-don't-think-so* glare.

"Come again?"

She arched a brow. "Seems you've covered all your bases today." Carolina faced him, wanting to take his puffed-up, self-assured persona down a notch. "I was parked next to you and had to move my car. I didn't want to interrupt your little…party." She expected a smidgen of shame. Matt's unrepentant expression told her otherwise.

"Darlin', you could have joined us instead of watching. Someone with a mouth as pretty as yours, hell, I might have left my own party and gone AWOL." His voice and dark good looks stoked her banked sensual embers, igniting a cavernous erotic craving Carolina kept on a back burner turned way below simmer.

Carolina's hell-raiser tendencies surged to the forefront. This type of man bored holes in her resolution to avoid men who promised to deliver heaven. She reined in her control even though a slight shiver rippled up her spine.

She smirked. "No thanks. I had my share of partying this week. I'll catch you and your date inside."

"Suit yourself. There's a lot two people can do in five minutes. 'Course, I mean *the right two people.*"

His smoky gaze made her hair hurt. She faltered, as prey did before deciding to hunker down or break cover, but her resolve surged upward. "I don't think you could keep up, cowboy," she replied, her voice dropping into a zone of husky desire. Inwardly, she groaned; that was a dare she hadn't meant to fling back at him.

Damn it.

This walking piece of sex in a suit, in the blink of an eye, tore all the veils and walls away she had built to keep her wayward urges from reappearing. He was the exact type of man women found irresistible. He was also a hazard to her because, deep inside, she wanted nothing more than to taste, crash, and combust from passion. Carolina's cravings were never gone, only kept at bay. She, for one, didn't need to follow another jackass into a promised liaison that didn't deliver, or another man accusing her of being frigid, unfeeling and uncaring. Jeff had taught her about lust and lurid decisions until she was burned and broken. An alarm bell tolled in her head, warning her to be wary in the vicinity of sweet-talking men with one thing on their minds. "Nice meeting you, Matt. But it's bye-bye."

He paused, lips quirked all but promising a comeback. "Sugar, give me a chance. I'll show you the way to heaven's gate, and you won't need a Bible for the verses that you spill from your…lips."

His inference struck her harder than if she'd stuck two wet fingers in an electrical outlet. She didn't respond to his invitation. He looked like the type of man that took his time. At all costs, one to avoid.

"No, thank you. I appreciate the offer, but I'm good."

"No argument there." He touched his head and bent forward with a small bow. "Until we meet again. What's your name?"

"My name?"

"I'm not asking for your Social Security number. Just your name?"

She stared at him. "Carolina," she breathed out.

"Carolina, maybe someday I'll be so lucky to get to know you better." He winked and walked around the car toward his passenger side.

"Whatever." She rolled her eyes, fuming.

Matt had caught her unprepared. She wanted to argue with him on one hand and realized, she also longed to feel his lips crush against her mouth in a savage kiss.

Oh hell… She held and framed her wayward thoughts, including some raunchy images of him holding her head above his lap and guiding her mouth over him. For a second, she delighted in her private fantasy of hot public sex. Definitely way too much alcohol was in those Jell-O shots last night. Carolina pressed fingertips to her brow as she opened up her car door. Matt opened his passenger's door. Two shapely legs extended, bent, and touched the blacktop. She felt a twang right beneath her breastbone watching the man hold out his hand and receive his date's fingers.

Judas Priest. She slipped back into the driver's seat, floored the gas before she acquiesced and begged him to join her and see what they could do in five minutes.

At least there was one consolation. He wasn't in the wedding party. Last night she didn't remember seeing him at the church rehearsal or dinner. Chances were, they'd not see each other more than in passing at the reception amongst the hundred people expected.

No, this would be goodbye to a fantasy come to life. She was safe. Just one day spent in the midst of a family wedding, and then she'd return to her vanilla existence for a couple of days before she started her new job in god-knows-where Texas.

The chapel dressing area inside was overrun by women in sage green dresses and one exceptionally dressed woman in an ivory wedding dress. "Sam, you're too perfect," Carolina whispered.

"Where have you been?" Sam threw up her hands.

"I caught up on my beauty sleep." Carolina's cheeks warmed unmercifully, giving her thoughts away.

Sam pulled her into the private dressing room. "Come on. Your dress is over here." Sam shut the door and turned back. "Tell me. I know something's up."

Carolina stepped out of her sundress and sandals. "It's nothing."

"Bull," Sam returned. "You're as red as a tomato."

"This is your day. You're projecting. It must be nerves."

"Don't use your medical mumbo jumbo on me. Spill the beans," Sam walked over toward her. "If you don't, I'll go get your mother to help you dress."

Carolina unzipped the silky green gown on the hanger. She smiled and shook her head. "It was this guy," she started out as a heat wave billowed over her whole body. "Oh, this is silly."

"What guy? Rob has so many good-looking relatives. Who'd you meet?"

"No, Sam. I didn't meet anyone. Not like that."

"So you did meet a man. Outside?"

"Yes. It's so screwed up. It's wickedly messed up."

"You're not giving me much to go on…" Loud knocking broke their conversation.

"Sam, is Carolina in there with you?" Sonya, Carolina's mother was on the other side of the door.

Carolina's eyes beseeched her not to open the door. Sam nodded silently. "Yes, Tia. Give me a minute. Please."

Sonya sighed in exasperation. "A minute. It's time. Your father is in the receiving room waiting for you."

"Talk fast." Sam came over and arranged the gown on Carolina's shoulders.

Carolina twisted her fingers. "Oh, Sam. It's crazy. I woke up and there he was in his car."

"What's so wicked about that?"

"He had his zipper down."

"Excuse me. Was he tucking in his shirt?"

"No," Carolina sucked in her breath. "He was getting a blow job."

Sam shrieked incoherently, tugging up the zipper of Carolina's dress. She let go of her cousin so quickly, Carolina stumbled forward. They came together facing one another. "You mean there was a woman in the car with him?" Sam asked.

"Yes. She was over him so I couldn't see the whole thing. I tried to leave. I never imagined I'd hit his car."

Sam grabbed her cousin's hands. "Are you all right?" Sam's eyes widened, searching her cousin's face.

"Not a scratch. The bumpers did a face-off with not so much as a dent," she exhaled. "But, there was definitely…there was something about the man."

While Carolina spoke, a swarm of confused butterflies took flight inside her stomach. Even after leaving Matt, she couldn't stop herself from thinking about his animal magnetism. It was primal, wordless, and took hold, deep inside her, drawing out a sizzling ache she never imagined actually existed within her body so near to the surface. He was the first man who had sparked something dark and hungry inside her that even now continued to flame.

Maybe that's why she had held on to her past lover so hard. Believing if *it* could happen with anyone, her chance of discovering an orgasm would be at the hands of Jeff Welch. Sexy, elegant, and an experienced lover. Top vet in his field. She believed if she gave into his every demand, eventually she'd learn to respond, let down her walls, and give in. *It* didn't.

That part of her—the unfulfilled part—nearly pushed her over the edge with Jeff, the man she dated on and off for two years. He'd left her a vacuum; depleted and empty. It had taken her a year, maybe longer, to wake each morning without questioning herself about being cold, unable to experience what every red-blooded woman felt. An orgasm. In wanting to overcome her hesitance to let go, she gave into every one of his suggestions without letting him into her world, and in the end he'd used her. Nearly up.

Sam's narrowed her eyes. "Carolina, what are you saying? You know you can't make rash judgments about any man. What you feel is what you bring to the table. If you think he's a savior, it's because that's what you're looking for. We both have learned a lesson."

"What do you mean? You're about to marry a man you fell in love with on your first date. That's the absolute opposite of your advice."

"Wrong. The first time I met Rob, I thought he was a player, a user, and someone who would hurt me. I wasn't ready to accept him. I saw a monster instead of my soul mate. So, it's exactly the same thing. Just be careful that it's not some secret hidden judgment that you'll try and make come true. The Pygmalion effect is not something I thought up, Carolina. You're still attached to Jeff."

"Correction. *Was*. I finally said goodbye. So there. Today is a day of new beginnings; I thought how appropriate it was to finally let him go. I was hoping you'd share in my joy."

"Hallelujah. But that relationship was toast a long time ago. All I'm saying is keep your eyes open. Listen to yourself. A man who's having sex in his car. And you're attracted. That's wacko coming from you. Sounds like a rebel and we all know you've got a soft spot for a bad boy. It's your libido sparking, nothing else."

"I'm not just desperate. But I hear what you're saying. Let's not talk about this anymore. I'm not going to become OCD over the man. Give me a couple of minutes to get my face back on. A mascara moment. You're so beautiful, Sam. Rob will fall over when he sees you."

"Let's hope not. I've waited four years to get him up the aisle. Don't worry, Carolina. Your Prince Charming is on his way. Just keep the faith."

Sam opened the door, and Carolina's mom, Sonya, burst through the doors with several other family members. Carolina applied several coats of mascara while the women chatted in *Spanglish*. Isabella, Sam's daughter came over to the table.

"Hey, baby doll, you look so pretty," Carolina said. "Give me a *besito*."

The little girl puckered her lips and kissed Carolina's cheek. "'Lina, c'mon."

Carolina joined with the other women surrounding her cousin. A bottle of champagne was going around. Someone pushed a glass into her hand. They all toasted the bride. Carolina came over to Sam, setting down her champagne flute.

"Here, let me straighten your train." Carolina gently shook the material and settled the gauzy silk over the carpet. "*Mami*, where's Sam's bouquet?"

"Right here," Sonya said.

Sam's father, Randall Cainwright III, stood at the door. They all walked forward, a cloud of perfume, voices, and laughter. Sonya met Randall's gaze and lifted her chin. The rivalry between her mom and her uncle had gone on forever and exacerbated when Sam's mother passed away. Today, a truce was in place. Yes, today was a day of newfound starts.

"You look beautiful," Randall murmured to his daughter. "A vision. Sam, you remind me of your mother, dear." He looked over to Sonya. "You've done a marvelous job, Sonya. Thank you. Isabella would be so happy," he said gruffly.

"Yes, I think so." Sonya blinked and kissed Sam on the cheek. "*Bella*. Cynthia, you're no longer a girl with large eyes. Yes, so much like my sister. You're ready, *Mija*."

Sam squeezed Carolina's hand. She turned, and they looked at each other. No longer little girls waiting on the threshold of their dreams. Today would be the first day of the rest of their lives, changing both of them forever. Sam would cleave to a man and Carolina would learn to ground herself. Or else.

"Well, Dad, I'm ready," Sam said.

He came forward, took hold of her arm, and awkwardly kissed his daughter on the forehead. "Me too," he replied.

The music changed to the "Canon in D," the song for the bridal party to begin their procession into the church.

"God bless you and Rob," Carolina whispered and hugged her cousin. "I better go take my place."

In the mood for more Crimson Romance?
Check out *Blitzkrieg Love*
by Livia Olteano
at *CrimsonRomance.com*.

www.ingramcontent.com/pod-product-compliance
Lightning Source LLC
Chambersburg PA
CBHW010635100726
47900CB00011B/2838